MEN IN MY SITUATION

Per Petterson

Men in My Situation

A Novel

Translated
from the norwegian by

Ingvild Burkey

GRAYWOLF PRESS

First published with the title *Menn i min situasjon* in Norway by Forlaget Oktober AS in 2018. First published in English by Harvill Secker/Penguin Random House UK in 2021.

This publication is made possible, in part, by the voters of Minnesota through a Minnesota State Arts Board Operating Support grant, thanks to a legislative appropriation from the arts and cultural heritage fund. Significant support has also been provided by Target Foundation, the McKnight Foundation, the Lannan Foundation, the Amazon Literary Partnership, and other generous contributions from foundations, corporations, and individuals. To these organizations and individuals we offer our heartfelt thanks.

This translation was published with the financial assistance of NORLA, Norwegian Literature Abroad.

Published by Graywolf Press
250 Third Avenue North, Suite 600
Minneapolis, Minnesota 55401

www.graywolfpress.org

Published in the United States of America

ISBN 978-1-64445-075-8

2 4 6 8 9 7 5 3 1
First Graywolf Printing, 2022

Library of Congress Control Number: 2021940561

Cover design: Kyle G. Hunter

Cover photo: plainpicture / Jan Håkan Dahlström

For Geir B.

PART ONE

CHAPTER ONE

It was Sunday, September 1992, a little before seven. I had been out the night before, the last hour in a bar that was once a pharmacy on Tollbugata, but I hadn't left with anyone. That was almost unusual at the time, during that year, for more often than not I would head into Oslo city centre and against my own nature go to bars and cafés and walk through the doors into the smoke-filled loud premises I suddenly felt so at home in, and still against my own nature would take a close look around and think, where shall I spend the night. When I left the café or pub or bar a few hours later, I was rarely alone. When those months lay behind me, I had been to more bedrooms, in more houses, in more parts of the city than I would have thought possible for a man like me. But it stopped of its own accord, I'd wanted to be like a fire, but there were more ashes in my fire now than there were flames.

So when the phone rang that morning, I was lying in my own bed. I had no wish to answer it, I felt dead tired. I had been drinking, yes, but not much, and definitely not after eleven, and had taken the Tåsen bus up from the city and got off at the junction where today there is a round-about and walked on past Sagene church towards Bjølsen in the light drizzle. When I entered my apartment, I felt perfectly fine and was certain that by now I was no longer under the influence.

What made me so tired were the dreams I was having. It's not easy to explain already here, on page two, what it was about them that made me feel so exhausted, I will have to come back to that. I had planned to stay in bed at least an hour longer and then get up and put the kettle on for coffee and sit down at the desk, and if possible write for a couple of hours even though it was Sunday. But the phone would not stop ringing, so I swung my legs out of bed and walked quickly to the living room to pick it up, and that I did because it felt unlawful just to let it ring. I have always had, and still have, the notion that answering the phone is mandatory and if I ignore it, I might be taken to court.

It was Turid's voice. It had been a year since she left and took the girls with her and moved to a terraced house at Skjetten. She was crying, and as far as I could make out, she had her hand close to her mouth to muffle the sound, and so I said, Turid, what's wrong, but she wouldn't answer that. Are you at home, I said, but she wasn't. But Turid, where are you then, I said, but she didn't know. Don't you know where you are, I said, and she kept crying and said, no. She didn't know where she was.

Damn, I thought. If she's crying like that and is not at home, then where are the girls. There were three of them, after all. They were certainly not staying with me, and her mother was in Singapore. My mother was dead, and my father was dead, and my brothers were on the whole dead. Do you want me to come and get you, I said, for I assumed she didn't have her car where she was, and she kept crying and said yes, that's why I'm calling, I have no one else, and I thought, if you have no one else, then you don't have much. But that was not what I said, I said, but then I have to know where you are. What does it look like where you are standing. There's a train station here, she sobbed, the building is yellow, but there's no train. Well, I said, it might be a bit early, it's Sunday, you know, and then she said, no, that's not what I mean, what I mean is there are no tracks for the train to run on.

I thought for a moment, where could it be, there weren't many places to choose from within a reasonable distance, it had to be Bjørkelangen, I couldn't think of anywhere else. Jesus, it was fifty kilometres, or more, maybe sixty, why was she there, without a car, without anyone, at this time of day. But I couldn't ask her that, it had nothing to do with me, I could mind my own business, which more or less I did. All the rest was over and done with anyway. I didn't even miss it, I thought, after such a long year, but when I had finished that thought, I couldn't say for certain that it was true.

I know where you are, I said, I'm leaving in five minutes. Thank you, she said, and I said, of course it will take me some time to get there. I am aware of that, she said, and

I thought, how can she be aware of that, she doesn't even know where she is.

A red telephone booth, an abandoned yellow-painted station building she could probably see from the booth. If I was right, it shouldn't be too difficult. It could of course be some other abandoned railway station many miles in a totally different direction, but none came to mind.

I took a quick shower, pulled my short James Dean jacket on, and with half a bread roll in my hand I hurried down the steps, out to the parking place right by the bus stop in front of the yellow brick building I lived in on Advo-kat Dehlis plass at Bjølsen, and got into my thirteen-year-old station wagon, a champagne-coloured Mazda 929.

I got there in forty-five minutes. That was fast. Faster would have meant prison.

At the junction by the petrol station on the way into Bjørkelangen I turned left and drove all the way down past the Felleskjøpet grain cooperative whose yellow logo had been painted directly onto the sky-high cylinder-shaped silos, an ear of grain in the middle, and on either side of it the letters F and K painted green. Then I turned right on Stasjonsveien at the next junction, where the little hotel with the café was; all the windows dark now, not a lamp lit, so I supposed it had been closed since the last time I was here, it was hardly unthinkable, for how could it pay to run a hotel, at Bjørkelangen.

*

A bit further down the road stood the red telephone booth, as expected, not far from the old station building. I drove down there and parked in front of the station, and there was a bus stop too, the last one on the route by the looks of it, but Turid I could not see.

There was no bus at the bus stop, it was completely still, and my car was one of three parked by the station. The other two were a sedan and a station wagon, both Volvos, both blue, both had seen better days. At Bjørkelangen everyone probably knew which car belonged to whom, and so the Mazda stood out in its somewhat rusty champagne-coloured state of decay with plates no one had seen around here, and perhaps one resident said to another, who the hell does that car belong to, when he saw it through the window of one of the houses nearby. The thought of it made me restless. What counted now was to get in fast and get out just as fast, and of course she wasn't sitting out here in the limelight in front of the station building, so I walked around to what strictly speaking was the front or at least had been when the shiny rails ran into the station here, all the way from Sørumsand in the west and came out again going east, this time with the train on top of them, and the conductor on the footboard, he leaned out with his green flag flapping, and with the whistle in his mouth he blew: off and away! And he blew again, he was proud of that whistle and the sound that it made, who wouldn't be.

But the rails had been narrow gauge and had lost the battle for the future a generation ago and more, but still, only two decades back the train ran unsuspecting out here to Bjørkelangen, turning south towards Skullerud, to the lake and the steamboat that could carry you down through the sluices from the deep inland all the way to the outer Oslofjord and on from there to anywhere in the world, to Spain, to America, if that's where you wanted to go, and it wasn't really far to Sørumsand nor to Skullerud and the dialect pretty much the same, and the rails had been torn up a long time ago and carted off as scrap metal and new ones were never laid.

She was sitting on the grass with her forehead on her knees on the slope down to the little river I knew was called Lierelva. I knew everything about these places spread out across a wide area of eastern Norway. I had driven through them and past them countless times, alone in the daytime and night-time too, sometimes with the girls in the back seat, all three of them, or just one, in that case Vigdis, who was the eldest. I had driven and driven again until I was tired of it, I was incredibly tired of it right now. Of the roads. Of the cars, of Mazda and Ford, of Opel, of any brand at all, of manuals and automatics, of petrol-powered cars and cars that were diesel powered, of quiet-running cars and cars that spewed coal-black smoke out over the tarmac in a miserable tail from their exhaust pipes. I hadn't worked out how much carbon dioxide I emitted on these trips. It was probably a criminal amount, and honestly, it bothered me, I thought about it often, I lay awake at night counting litres of fuel, counting cubic metres in my sleep, but what could I do, should I take pills, how damaging was the pharmaceutical industry, certainly very damaging, though I didn't know with what substance or how; toxic runoff into the ground, crap in the air, or just narcotically destructive in general.

What I could have done was to keep a journal during that period. It would have been enough for a book of several hundred pages, it might have been interesting, I thought, geographically, topographically, biographically not least, I was restless and had been for a long time, and it was hard then to keep away from the car. This last year I had used it as dope. What else was I to do in the evenings. It was Oslo city centre or the Mazda, and as often as I went to bars, I went out and sat behind the wheel.

I could see from her shoulders that she was still crying, and I thought, how can she keep it up for so long. It was hard to understand. But then I didn't know what had happened and did not intend to ask, it was her life, not ours.

After a pointless, failed attempt at a fireman's lift I managed to get her into the passenger seat. It wasn't easy, her legs were like rubber, apparently having no joints, and at first I thought that she was drunk, and she probably had been, maybe very drunk, but she wasn't drunk now, she said, I'm sorry Arvid several times, and I said, just relax Turid, we're doing fine, though we would've been doing even better if she hadn't relaxed quite so much. I had never seen her in a state like this, not once in all our long life together, and now I was forced to put my arms around her, but her body didn't feel like I knew it from before, it was confusing, I had expected at least a mild form of recognition in my palms or something like recognition, but now her body felt private, and at the same time more distinct, yes, that was it, like a body not moving away but a body coming towards me, but that was not how the land lay, her body was not coming towards me at all, and then I had to place my hands so they didn't settle where they once had settled, just a year had gone by since the last time, but right now I couldn't remember whether I still held her in my arms then, I was certain I didn't, I was too afraid, walled up in my own self, anything could happen if I held her in my arms.

I parked by the terraced house right after hers to make it easy to take the shortest route across the lawn to the flat she lived in, at the very end of the row, and in that way avoid being seen by her closest undoubtedly nosy neighbours. I assumed it was a consideration. Would you like me to come in with you, I said, and immediately thought, I shouldn't have said that, I really didn't want to. Would you, she said. If you like, I said, and she said, oh, that would be so nice of you, almost gushing with gratitude, and that made me embarrassed, it felt humiliating, I got mad, she had said on the phone that she had no one but me, but I didn't want to be her shining knight, her saviour, and get nothing in return but gratitude. What use was gratitude to me. And when the year before we'd stood face to face for the last time in the flat we shared on Advokat

Dehlis plass at Bjølsen, she smiled and said almost wistfully, I was so certain we would grow old together, and her friends who were not my friends, but several years younger, as Turid herself was, were standing outside on the pavement by the heavily loaded van, a Volkswagen Caravelle, I remember it clearly, it was garishly yellow, and it was sunny out there where her friends were, and it struck me that their clothes were particularly colourful, almost hippie-like, I would never have worn clothes like that, and I said, then you have to give me what comes before, what comes after now, but before old age, what's in the middle, but she wouldn't give me that, she said, she couldn't, and I said, okay then, goddammit.

But it was true that the last year we lived together the days and the nights had slid into each other so slowly that in the end they stopped altogether and everything was on hold, and more and more often in the evenings I couldn't bring myself to lie down in the bed where she had already been lying for an hour or more. We'd become like magnets with identical poles turned towards each other, plus to plus, minus to minus, I could thrust myself towards her and instantly be knocked out of the bedroom as I passed the threshold and fly backwards into the living room as if from a heavy blow to my chest and slide across the floor and hit the wall on the opposite side, and this happened again and again, so instead I remained sitting on the sofa playing the records she could easily hear through the wall and know which ones they were. It was the music from when we were new together and I still didn't know who she was, who hid inside her body, nor she who in mine, who I was, and the only thing we wanted was to find that out, for I was flying back then, I was carving myself out of the person I had been, I was in love, that was why, those were the records I played. But eventually I gave up the records too, and well after midnight I would go down the stairwell with the nearly hundred-year-old, many of them cracked, star-patterned Moroccan tiles I'd always liked so much on every landing and then out through the gateway from the backyard with the old stable that was now a garage for the neighbour with the longest seniority who every Sunday could be seen standing on a stool in the cobbled courtyard in his absurdly spotless boiler suit polishing his ancient Volvo Duett he hadn't driven one metre as far as I knew, and below the gateway ceiling it was pitch dark on my way out to the Mazda which was parked in the marked-out space in front of the tenement, close to the bus stop. And I got into the passenger seat and tipped it back as far as it would go, and half sitting, half lying I settled there with my warm coat pulled tight around me, hoping for sleep after the day bestowed upon me, until the first buses came down the hill from the plain on top where the big bus depot stood in the semi-darkness and the sports fields and the margarine factory in the same dark. And the buses came, almost invisible and silent they pulled into the bus stop and swung their doors open with a sound that later was easy for me to remember, a discreet and intimate sound so close up, a soft and well-oiled exhalation from the doors, because the buses were new, probably, and after that the sleepy steps of the people travelling; two steps up and one step inside to the driver at the very front and their muted voices and every word between them turned down low as if they were embers of yesterday's fire, and all of them sounds that were rarely heard by anyone other than someone like me. I could see them all in my mind's eye, their cars parked in places like this, along roads and streets, by bus stops, in garages and driveways, with men in my situation, half lying, half sitting in their seats with their coats and cars pulled tight around them, trying to doze off for a few hours alone and finally being gathered up in the dark of night by soft hands and soundless winches, hauled together in long rows, one after the other, bumper to bumper, button to button, headlight to tail light, in a fellowship ranked by the man's age and the brand of the car, as if waiting for the last rites, for oblivion, sleeping in a foetal position, their unshaven cheeks against the cold backs of their hands, barely breathing in the cold darkness.

Not once did it strike me that she could have come down the stairs, out into the dark in her nightdress and boots and opened the door to the front seat and asked me to come back in, come back up, up to the warm bed, said, but Arvid, you can't sit here, it's so cold, why don't you come up where it's warm. That would have changed everything. But not until I realised that it had never crossed my mind that she could have come down, nor could remember having wished for it a single time, did it dawn on me that all was lost.

Now I walked behind her across the lawn to the terraced house, and my shoes sank into the soft grass, and so did hers, for the ground was still damp from the night and the rain, and from behind I could see that her right stocking had run from well up under her skirt to down over her thigh towards the back of her knee where her skin was exposed, dull and white in a broad stripe with the shimmering fabric on either side, and I thought, when did she start wearing stockings like that. Not in my time, that's for certain, and before me there was nothing, there was nothing before you she had said early one morning the first spring we were together, and I remember how I blushed with pride like a child. But now I couldn't keep myself from staring at the skin on the back of her thigh through the ladder in her stocking, and I felt a sudden thump in my stomach, and a pillar of red rising to my close-cropped hair, but she couldn't see that, she couldn't see me or my gaze, but walked unsuspecting and dejected across the grass towards the house, and the feeling was one that was hard to remember from a year ago or more or whether it had been there back at the beginning. That sudden thump. But I knew that it hadn't, this was something else, and I suppose I might have been ashamed of that feeling, seeing her as I saw her now before me, the bent back, her desolate palms.

*

We made it into the hallway, I shut the door behind us, and she leaned against the wall and closed her eyes, and something confusing met me there in the hall, for even though it was the woman I had been married to for so many years who lived in this flat, and my three daughters, my own children, who also lived here, the atmosphere, the air, the smell, everything I could feel, could touch and see was completely alien to me. I didn't recognise a thing, which was not so strange, since in fact I had never been inside her flat but had refused to cross the threshold and always stayed outside on the flagstones in the sun or rain, waiting, or waiting in the car in the parking space until I could see the girls coming around the corner with their bags carrying extra clothes and perhaps their school things, but still I had expected something that was not yet a thing of the past; a last remainder of what was me, which all four of them each in their own way had brought with them from Bjølsen, a small but still noticeable absence, a bottle not quite filled up again, but there was nothing there. I was as if erased.

I had to help her get her shoes off, she couldn't manage on her own, she bent down, and then she just fell over, and I pulled the little chest of drawers from below the mirror and helped her up from the floor and said, now sit here Turid, and she did what I told her, and so I went down on my knees to undo the laces of her shoes, an iconic sight, I would imagine, but still a posture I had never been seen in, kneeling before her, even though we had been together for fifteen years.

Now she leaned forward with one hand on my shoulder, and then the hand slid slowly off past my neck, and her head followed, and her hair tickled my ear on its way down. Finally her forehead lay heavily against my shoulder on one side, and her right hand hung loosely down my back on the other; an embrace, if you like, it could hardly be called anything else. These were awkward circumstances. She didn't move, and her cheek lay close to mine, and her warm breath seeped under my jacket, down over the skin on my back. I could feel it clearly. She wasn't crying any more, each breath in the right place after the one before, and it was excruciating, I couldn't move anything except my fingers around her laces, and I thought, has she fallen asleep there on my shoulder, she was so quiet all of a sudden, did you fall asleep Turid, I said. No, I'm not asleep, she said almost in my ear, can I just sit like this for a little while, and I said, that's fine, you can sit like that for a little while, if you want to. It wasn't fine at all, but what the hell could I say.

When her shoes were off, I managed to support her across the threshold and into the living room, and I wondered if it wouldn't be the right thing to help her into bed, which was where she belonged just now, but I couldn't cope with seeing her bed, or, I wouldn't mind seeing it, the strangeness of it, the painfully attractive newness of it, the surge in my stomach I knew would come, but I couldn't, although everything inside me yearned to, I had to get out of this, I had to get away.

*

We crossed the floor and I carefully loosened my grip and lowered her slowly in front of the sofa so she could sit down, but then she just kept sliding all the way to the floor until she was kneeling with her neck bent and her palms heavy on the carpet and started crying again, and then she pulled herself together and crawled the few metres over and sat with her back slumped against the wall between the kitchen door and a cabinet that used to stand in the hallway at Bjølsen. She had painted it an insistent blue, to remove all memories, no doubt, and I could barely recognise it.

I could have sat down on the sofa, it would have been easy and perhaps the normal thing to do, but I didn't sit down, I said, Turid, where are the girls. What, she said. Where are the girls, I said. Oh, the girls, they're with a friend. She mentioned a name. I didn't like that at all. Why were they with her. Why are they there, I said, and she said, she was the only one who said yes. But did they want to go there, I said. Not so much, Turid said. She let her forehead sink to her knees. Turid, I said, do you want me to fetch them for you. I felt I had to ask, I was worried. Would you, she said, and I said, sure, I can do that. Thank you, that would be so nice of you, she said. Maybe you could wait until this afternoon. Okay, I said, then I'll wait. I really didn't want to wait, but it was still early in the morning. Turid, I said, is there anything I can do for you before I go. She turned her face so I could see it, it was wet with tears, and she said, do you have to go, and I said that I did. But I wish you would stay, she said, and

I said, that's understandable, but it wouldn't be the right thing for me to stay. I wish you would, she said, there are things I want to talk to you about, I have no one else, she said for the second time that day, and I felt the sudden yearning for her, not for the woman she had been when we were together, but for the one she was now, and I knew only too well it was because I was the stronger and she the weaker; her defenceless body, her broken will, and I said, goddammit Turid, don't come to me with your life. And I meant it, I didn't want any of it.

I caught a glimpse of the incredulous look in her eyes before I turned and walked straight out of the living room and out through the hallway where the chest of drawers from below the mirror stood blocking the way, and I pushed it roughly to the side, but then I might as well move it back where it belonged, and so I did, making sure it was perfectly centred, and out on the steps I shut the door behind me with a bang. I walked across the lawn and got into the car, and my heart was thumping and I sat there for a good while breathing heavily until it turned quiet and I was able to drive off.

PART TWO

CHAPTER TWO

I cannot remember exactly the first time I took the bus down to Oslo city centre to walk the streets of an evening, go to bars, visit pubs and cafés, but it must have been shortly after Turid marched out, the same month, most likely, and therefore one long year after the ship burned with my loved ones in it, as they put it on the news, his loved ones perished onboard a burning ship, in a cabin, in a corridor, they vanished at sea, they fell out of this life not far from a duty-free shop.

What I remember is sitting in my usual seat at the very back of the bus, on the way down from Bjølsen, Sagene, wearing my best clothes, which was my reefer jacket, the same old, but with new brass buttons I had bought from a helpful lady with needle and thread at the Button House behind the Parliament building, and every button shiny bright with an anchor stamped on it. I wore a yellow neckerchief with the knot at the back and outmoded, undramatically flared trousers to accentuate the sailor style. I was freshly showered, my hair freshly washed, I was making up for what was lost, whatever lost there was, I was thirty-eight years old, everything was blown, I had nothing left.

*

It was already autumn, or something like autumn, it was hard to say. In any case it was chilly. At the bus stop right below my flat I pulled the jacket collar up against the wind from the north, but there was no wind from the north, it was quiet everywhere, it just felt like the right thing to do that day, and it certainly looked better.

When I got off the bus at the end of Storgata the sky was black above the city, but the shop windows were full of light and the lamps shone along the streets, and in the streets two shimmering pairs of tram rails ran like liquid silver between the cobbles, in the asphalt, and the neon signs hung sated with yellow over the doors of the book shop, the shoe shop, with red and blue in the humid sticky Oslo air, each drop tinted in the drizzle and the colours inverted on the moist pavements, and in the replete, almost plump space between the buildings the air felt extra cold against my cheeks as I came walking in the warm reefer jacket, past Strøget, past the Opera Passage, with pockets full of my own hands, and just there, as I turned and looked in through the big not very beautiful building, it dawned on me that I had never done this alone before, that I had always travelled downtown with Turid to meet other young adults we knew, communists and poets, trade unionists, welders and lathe operators from Akers Mechanical and Myra Workshop, to drink beer and talk politics and books at Cordial, Dovrehallen, Lompa, places like that, even after we had children. But then it slowly ebbed out. Turid turned away and found new friends, who did not become my friends, and in the last year I had gone down to Gamla on rare occasions to have dinner with Audun, my brother in arms from Veitvet, and even more rarely to meet one or two of the few other friends I had who were only mine, or had been before Turid and I became a couple. But for the most part it didn't go well. I was too restless, I couldn't sit still and always ended up apologising and getting out before the session had ended, and at times it was taken badly.

Anyhow, I wouldn't want to be with any of them now, certainly not with Turid, nor with friends, not even Audun, and that gave me a feeling of recklessness. Being alone in an apartment was one thing, in my own flat with everything that was mine, the books, the pictures on the walls, the Buddha on my desk, or inside a bus or on the Underground with my father's satchel and an old Pax edition of the more than thousand-year-old Chinese poet Du Fu's poems in my lap, or perhaps Bertolt Brecht's *Tales from the Calendar*, and if so, an early Lanterne edition; another thing was to step out into the world where roofs flung up and walls burst open to the flooding city. It was risky, but honestly, if everything went awry I could easily find a taxi and be back home within fifteen, twenty minutes before panic took hold. It would have been worse in San Francisco, in Berlin or London. That taxi did not exist.

But Oslo was my own town, and I thought it would be okay.

*

First I stopped by Cordial, at the top of Storgata, right across from Hornaas Musikk where the shiny, silent and to me almost occult guitars lined the windows. But inside the pub there were far too many people I knew, I remembered them well, they worked for public transport, for the railway, and had been friends of mine before and had hung out in this pub for a decade or more, you could hear it from their laughter and the noise, how their voices had grown coarser since I saw them last. Many were also members of The Clan, Vålerenga's fan club which as such was all right, Vålerenga was my team too and always had been, I was born in that part of town, baptised there, my father played on the second team in the years before the war and had later been a member of the Old Geezers' Club, as they called it, at Vålerenga church, and had been friends with the old heroes, Tippen Johansen, the Braggart, you name them, and those among them who were still alive came to the big funeral with their walking sticks and shiny bald heads. Your father was damned good, they said, and he could sing, he hit the right note every time, he hit the ball too, they said and laughed and coughed, and it is true he had a good voice, but I didn't know what to tell them, that sorry to say I hadn't appreciated my father, I hadn't known who he was, nor that he was one of them, the Old Geezers, among the legends, the pride of the nation, I hadn't been listening, and outside on the chapel steps I only said, thank you all for coming, and they lifted their caps just a little, for it was cold that day, and wet.

*

But at Cordial I stopped just inside and turned around at once and walked out again before anyone had time to shout, well hello there Knut Hamsun, get yourself over here.

Nothing that I had written pointed towards Hamsun, not as I saw it. But that's what they used to shout. Well hello there Knut Hamsun.

Out on the pavement I walked back again, down towards Dovrehallen on the opposite side of Storgata, right before Gresvig Sport, where I had a pint of beer in the gallery. I didn't speak to anyone, I didn't know anyone in there, it was a bit strange, actually. Not that I minded, on the contrary, but I sat down in the wrong place before ordering, the neighbouring tables were empty and it would have felt awkward to stand up and without good cause move to a chair right next to the few others present, although two of them were women and one of them sat alone at her table. I didn't have it in me. So, no more beers then. I should have brought a book up my sleeve, a French New Novel, Claude Simon, preferably, say, *The Flanders Road*, which I liked a lot, or something to do with philosophy, Camus's journals, that kind of thing, then I would've had something to anchor me if necessary, and any one of those books would have been exclusionary enough to make it clear to all and sundry that I wanted to be by myself. Which in fact I didn't.

All this I should have thought out beforehand, but I hadn't. So I paid and went down the steps and back out on Storgata.

*

I stood on the pavement, at a loss for what to do. To the right lay the shopping centre Gunerius and Teddy's Soft Bar around the corner on Brugata; to the left Storgata continued until it met Kirkeristen where you had to take the road down to Jernbanetorget or up to Glasmagasinet department store at Stortorget. But what would I do there. It didn't feel safe.

I lit a cigarette, an unfiltered Blue Master, that was my party brand. I liked the shortish cigarette and the blue horse's head inside the white disc printed on the soft pack, I always had, even back when I still hadn't started smoking, which would be before I turned fifteen. I remembered all the times my father and I took the Grorud bus from Veitvet to Carl Berners plass and walked across the junction towards Tromsøgata where we caught the 21 bus which was still a trolleybus then, right behind Ringen cinema, next to the pastry shop where my mother nearly fifteen years later would give me a crucial slap in the face. Starting from there the bus went up along Dælenenggata to Sannergata and the whole way in a big arc around the centre of Oslo, and finally we got off at Bislett stadium right by the entrance to watch Vålerenga play their matches and lose most of them that season. From the bus, driving between the tenements towards Bislett, you could see an advertisement for Blue Master Virginia cigarettes painted right onto a building with the horse's head enormous, and it filled the entire end wall four storeys up and filled my body with a surging sensation I think only a young boy in short trousers can feel, a vibration, an expansion of the lungs, of all things, sending my imagination straight out into the great blue yonder, out on the plains, up into the snow eternal.

I liked to smoke. Even though now, as I write this, I have given up for good reasons, I can clearly remember the best cigarettes. They immediately made me calmer when the restlessness came over me, and I have missed them later in life, countless times.

On Storgata that evening, in the first year after Turid's farewell, I chose the road to the right as the safest bet; it was the part of town my father belonged in and Storgata had been his main street, and shortly afterwards I walked through the door to Teddy's, and the premises was packed with people and there was dense grey cigarette smoke all the way up to the ceiling and barely standing room at the bar where I asked for a double Ballantine's, and then doubles weren't allowed, so instead I got two singles with ice and lifted them one in each hand from the counter and took two narrow steps backwards while I poured one into the other and set the empty glass on the edge of a table and stood there with the full one held close to my chest in the crush. I looked around. There were some men in there that I knew of but didn't know, and I didn't know any of the women. A couple of them looked as if they might have come here alone, but I felt no attraction, no pull towards them, and in any case the place was too crowded, it would have been a slog to get close enough, and I thought, okay, that's it, then.

I downed the glass and felt the whisky warm my chest. It was a welcome feeling and very pleasant, so I decided to stay a little longer. I ordered another Ballantine's, only now just a single on the rocks, and drank it slowly while I waited for something maybe to happen.

By the wall a small stage had been rigged up, where someone clearly was about to play, there was barely room for a red chair on the podium and a low microphone and a stand with a guitar plugged into a PA system with only one speaker. That must be why Teddy's was so full in the middle of the week, because someone was going to play, maybe a local grandee, but that wasn't why I had come, to listen to someone play. I drank up and set the glass on the counter and thought, I guess it's time to go, and then someone slapped my shoulder. It could have been anyone in the throng, I was probably blocking the path to the toilet, but it wasn't anyone, it was Randi. We had been members of Red Youth together in the seventies and had worked at the same factory, although each in our unit, and for a while we had been close, even after she quit and I stayed on, but I hadn't seen her for a long time and was certain she had moved to another part of the country. Hello Arvid, she said. Hello Randi, I said. Are you alone, she said. I looked at her. Yes, I said, I guess I am. You're not divorced, are you, she said with a laugh, it was apparently an amusing thought to her, I'm just kidding, she said and laughed again, but I did not, and so she stopped. Are you, she said, really, in that case I am sorry, I was just joking. You can joke if you like, I said, it's not your fault, I would have been every bit as divorced if you hadn't joked about it. But you were always together, she said, you did everything together. Did we, I said. Yes, she said, didn't you. No, I said, I don't remember that. But, Randi said, I remember how I stood at the window watching you walk past, down the road from Dehlis plass towards Bentsebrua bridge to take the 20 bus, you always looked so nice holding hands, no one else I knew held hands in the street, Randi said. Did we, I said, yes, Randi said, don't you remember. No, I said, I can't remember that. But I did remember the Sunday we walked down from the roundabout towards the bridge, we were taking the bus and the Underground up into the Grorud valley to have dinner with her parents, but we weren't holding hands, we were quarrelling, and more than that. It was a trifle that suddenly blew out of control, I didn't understand why and wanted it to stop, I wanted to get away from it, but I didn't know how, we were like two bicycle wheels stuck in a tram rail, and it felt ominous, because she was unafraid whereas I wasn't, and a trapdoor beneath my feet might open any second. In despair I closed my fists and raised them, and it must have looked threatening to her, for she said, are you going to hit me, are you going to hit me, and then suddenly she hit me in the stomach, quite hard actually, but I wasn't going to hit her, why would I hit her. I didn't know what to do, no one had hit me since

27

primary school, and then I always hit back, I had learned it from my father, always hit back, he would say, or else they lose respect, but I couldn't do that and didn't want to, and we had crossed a border, and I knew no one on the other side. Should I go home, it would be understandable, if not heroic. Instead I remained, but I didn't do anything, I didn't say anything, and she with her taut face turned away and I with my chest up against the cast-iron railing and beneath me the rushing river after the rain coming down from the Lilleborg factory, through the rapids and on down past the Myra workshop, towards the city and the fjord. I had no idea what to say, I didn't know which words to use that weren't catastrophic, irrevocable, practically life-destroying, and it may have been over already then. Vigdis wasn't even born.

But you moved out of town, Randi said, all of a sudden, I missed you both, you the most, she said, I thought you were fun amid all the nonsense, and I liked that, everything was so damn serious in those years. We laughed a lot, you and I, didn't we. It was true, I thought. I laughed a lot more with Randi than I did with Turid. Once we kissed, a long and totally unexpected kiss, and afterwards she laughed and said, so, now we've done that too. Isn't it nice. Yes, I said, it's nice, and I meant it, although neither of us wanted to take it any further. That was nice too. We did come back, though, I said. That's true, she said, but how long is it since you got divorced. Turid moved out a couple of weeks ago, I said, or maybe three weeks. I don't remember exactly. You don't remember when your wife moved out, she said, even though it was only two or three weeks ago. No, I said, not exactly, but it was a few weeks ago, I'm pretty sure it was a Thursday. I see, Randi said, and then she said, I know about the ship that burned, the whole country knows, what happened there, with your family, all one hundred and fifty-eight, wasn't it, she said, it was one hundred and fifty-nine, I said, we mustn't forget the last one, he died in the hospital, and there was an unborn baby too. Yes, of course, she said, anyway it was terrible, but I didn't know you were divorced, two things like that, she said, one thing almost on top of the other, Jesus, poor you. It wasn't really one thing on top of the other, I said, and she said, maybe it feels that way. And that was true. You don't have to feel sorry for me, I said. Don't I, she said. No, you don't. Okay, then, she said, and then she said suddenly, so now you're out trying to pick up ladies, to fill the void. That was pretty bold, I thought, all things considered, but I was charmed by it, and she smiled, she still looked good, in her own peculiar way. Yes, I said. Wow, Randi said, are you. Yes, I said. She went silent then, for quite some time, and I was sure she was thinking, am I the one who's supposed to fill that void, and still she didn't say anything, and finally I could see she was telling herself, no, I'm not the one. And I agreed, and I said so. I agree, I said. First she smiled, and then she laughed. Oh, is that how it is, is it, she said, and then she said, yes, I guess so. But I like you. I like you too, I said. I always did. I know, she said and looked me a little extra in the eyes, that's what it seemed like to me, but she turned around and shouted, hey, Tore, come over here for a second. A man at the back of the room looked over at us where we stood at the bar. He was tall, much taller than me and easy to spot, but I had never seen him before. He made his way slowly through the crowd and was still tall when he reached us, and Randi said, Tore, this is Arvid Jansen, a friend of mine from the olden days, we were in Red Youth together, bloody hell, what a slog that was. She laughed, almost crudely, and I had always liked that laugh, I thought it was exciting. I gave him my hand, hello Tore, I said, and he shook it, pretty feebly to tell you the truth, but he didn't say anything, instead he stood there scrutinising me, from the flares in my trousers to the yellow neckerchief and down again, and he said in a low, almost uninterested tone of voice, ship ahoy, and then he said, ship ahoy and shiver my timbers. Now we looked straight at each other, irony oozing out of his eyes as if from a tube, he was maybe a little drunk, and I guess I was too, after a pint and a double Ballantine's and then a single. I turned to Randi, are you two together, I said. Yes, she said, Tore is my husband, we've been married for nearly a year. So then I guess that wasn't what she'd been thinking after all, that she might be the one to fill my void, I'd felt so certain, but anyway I said, that was a hell of a let-down. And I turned again to leave, I said, bye Randi, see you around some time, and on my way towards the door someone gave me a hard shove in the back, and I fell forward, but not all the way down on the floor, it was too crowded, and I hit someone's pint and got beer in my hair, and of course, when I turned around it was Tore, he was even taller now, he said, Captain Blackbeard, you stay away from my wife, is that understood. I pulled my hand through my frothy hair and came to think of a neighbour I'd had as a child, two doors away in our terraced house, his name was Clausen, he washed his hair with beer once a week, Bavarian beer, it's the B vitamins, he used to say, I can't do without it, you should try it Arvid, you won't be able to do without it, I promise, but out loud I said, Randi is not my type, and at the same time got back on my feet. Oh yeah, Tore said, why not. She's married, I said, to you, it's a matter of taste, it would never have worked. This time I hit the floor, for everyone took a narrow step back and gave me the landing space I needed, you wouldn't have thought it possible, and someone even opened the door for me and said, good luck Knut Hamsun, wherever it is you're going, and now I recognised several faces, open, kind faces, they had been a part of my life, my life's story, but clearly they were not any longer, and I heard Randi shout, hey Arvid, take care of yourself, and fool that I am, I shouted, thanks, same to you, on the way out.

CHAPTER THREE

It was a cold autumn, the first after Turid. I felt cold all the time. I wrote almost nothing. I could wake up at night and not remember that her side of the bed was empty, a certain number of kilos permanently lifted from the mattress and her smell fainter with the passing days, and with the nights, weeks, and in the end completely dissolved and gone. Half asleep I would still expect to hear her steady breathing, and even believe I was hearing it too, for she always slept well once she had fallen asleep, which unlike me she usually did right away, regardless of what was going on in our lives. In the same way I expected to hear the small sounds she unwittingly made when she turned over under the duvet, and then would remember down in my sleep that she no longer turned towards me, but turned away, and as far as she was concerned I might as well go back down to the car and lie there in the cold, it didn't matter to her where I was, and then I had no wish to wake up, and I struggled against it. But it didn't work, of course, and after a brief moment with my eyes open I realised how the land lay. I lay there alone.

And there was the fact that she hadn't taken her duvet with her when she moved out. Maybe out of consideration for me, because it would look unsymmetrical in a painful way if the duvet on her side of the bed was gone, and thereby make the whole bed tip over towards the opposite side under the weight of the only remaining duvet, which was mine, and dump me on the floor in front of the window which used to be open most nights, in the winter too, when we still shared this bed, or because she had suddenly got it into her head that her duvet had gathered so many unwanted imprints and impressions over the years that she preferred to buy a new one.

I didn't know what to do with that duvet. At first I left it where it was without changing the cover to soften the transition, but after only a month it felt sad and wrong and plain embarrassing. So I pulled off the pillowcase and the duvet cover, and washing nothing I crammed the smooth sun-patterned material into a plastic bag from the Co-op and tied the handles and threw the bag into the dustbin down in the yard on my way out of the building. Then I rolled the duvet up tight and stuffed it onto the shelf at the top of the wardrobe, where six months later I accidentally found a white cotton top with lace around the neck and waistline and could remember well how her skin looked after summer when she wore it. Underneath the top there was a letter she had written but not finished and therefore hadn't given me or sent me, and it wasn't hard to understand why when I saw the date she had neatly inscribed at the top of the sheet. It had been written nearly a year and a half before she finally moved out with the girls, and exactly one week before the ship burned.

She had probably meant to finish it, but then suddenly it was impossible. In all decency she could not take away from me the very last thing I had, moving out with the girls when all of a sudden I had so few people around me. She was too late, death beat her to it.

So she endured for one more long year, out of necessity, not by choice, but finally it was over, and the letter began like this: 'Dear Arvid. I woke up one morning and didn't love you any more. Don't be sad, it's not your fault.' It was hardly a bombshell, but still I felt dizzy and had to lean against the wardrobe for support. A whole year, I thought, without love, that's a long time. For all I knew it may have been even longer. But when I stood there, letter in hand, I could clearly remember lying close on top of her, chest to chest, not heavily, but still I covered her entirely and held her arms out to both sides, her fingers folded in mine, and I said, what do you feel now. She was silent, she took a deep breath, she said, I feel I am loved. You *are* loved, I said. It really wasn't that long ago, not years, anyway, but I never acted on it, not firmly enough, I can't possibly have understood what I was saying, not in its fullest sense, but a door had been opened, and I closed it without knowing. Or perhaps I did know and closed it anyway, because it would have been asking too much of me to keep it open.

I didn't know what to do with the letter either, it didn't feel right to get rid of it, as if the Keeper of Public Records at any moment might bang on the door and shout, no, no, no, for God's sake, it must be preserved, because it was an important historical document. And I guess it was. So I put it back and threw away the cotton top and thought, why is she writing that it was all her fault. It couldn't possibly be true.

The emptiness, the bare space behind my back, felt even worse. I should have known. I always woke up right after midnight feeling ice-cold in the most inaccessible parts of my body, on the back up towards the shoulder blades, uppermost between my wings (oh, fly me away), even though I had closed the window permanently and turned the heater to 3. But in the long run the close air, the sleepless nights, the headaches and the working days down the drain became so exhausting that I thought I'd see my doctor who admittedly was a sly old fox and a trickster and ask him to give me some pills I knew he kept in a bottle discreetly in the back room, which he himself might take in the middle of the day and suddenly feel his spirits lift. I had seen it a few times when I was there with a pneumonia that wouldn't clear up, I felt flat, squeezed, I could hardly get air into my lungs, and this made him sincerely concerned and empathetic, but he said, could you wait a moment, and would then disappear behind the door and remain there for a while, and his gaze was clearer and more sparkling when he came back out than when he went in. For me it was the other way round, I could fall asleep from those pills and in fact had done so, which was the point, but this time I couldn't bring myself to go there.

I was afraid of becoming addicted, to drugs, to pills, for the paradoxical reason that it was precisely now that I needed them the most. But I would have been greedy once I got started, I was sure of it, so I let it drop and decided the cigarettes and the car would have to do.

Every morning I got up and tried to write some more on my big novel about the factory. That's what it was going to be about, all the years I'd spent there, the bus to work in the darkness, the bus back home again to Turid, in the same darkness, my work mates in the vast hall, the congealed colours in the dust and the light from the tall windows, in the rumble during day shift, in the rumble during night shift, and the morning after how overtired wide awake we were with a liquid like champagne fizzing through our veins, it would be about suicide and rage, and the laughter, how crazy we were, how loose-tongued towards the end of a shift, these were the important things, but it was difficult to concentrate, I couldn't do it, and finally it ground to a halt. I didn't even try. But I had nothing else, had nothing published in magazines or newspapers, nothing I could send to my editor of what I found in the desk drawer. There was nothing in my desk drawer. What could there have been. The grant I was living on I spread out thinly, I had to have enough for petrol and for the girls when they came.

I had left the bedroom and gone into the living room to smoke a cigarette and wait for sleep. It was a little past one. I was alone in the apartment. I was so tired it was difficult to hold on to my thoughts. But I couldn't sleep. The bed was still a difficult place. I lay down on the sofa. That didn't work either. I got up and went to the window and stood there smoking, looking out over the square in front of me and the roundabout and the few lights and the Mazda I hadn't slept in since Turid left, there was no reason to any more, but finally I thought, what the heck, I'm so tired, I'll do whatever I have to. I stubbed out the cigarette and went into the hallway to the wardrobe in the corner and found a frayed old Icelandic sweater that had belonged to my father. I should have thrown it away a long time ago, but he wouldn't have liked that, and I had so little left that had been his. I hadn't cared about it and it never crossed my mind that maybe I should have kept some of it, it didn't seem to matter. Later I have come to regret it. But I had this sweater. It was at least thirty years old, maybe forty, and if it was, it was older than me. I couldn't remember him ever not having it.

I pulled on my reefer jacket over the Icelandic sweater, and went down the stairs in the pitch-black cold and out through the gateway to the parking space and got into the car and soon fell asleep in the same position I had slept in so many times before.

I dreamed that I died. I often did, but unlike before I could still remember the dream the whole of the next day, and for months later, years later, if not every detail then at least the essentials, that I died, and the way I died. I couldn't remember what led up to it, in the dream, it didn't feel like I had done anything very wrong, had committed a crime or a misdemeanour and if so been sentenced to death, or had been in an accident or had become incurably ill, but I was in a funnel, or not a funnel, but more like inside a flower, a tulip, a very large tulip which was narrow at the top, and it wasn't really a tulip, I didn't know what it was, but I was already in it up to my waist, and then to my chest, and the thing that wasn't a tulip squeezed my body, not very hard, only so hard, so tight, that I couldn't get up again, and I knew that once I was all the way down, I would be dead. I felt very sad, and a little afraid, but I didn't panic, I didn't try to kick and push, there was really no point, this is where it would end. My left arm lay tightly along my side, against my hip, but the right one I had at some point managed to raise into the air, and she was holding my hand tightly, she was the only one who mattered. She was on her knees now and let her hand follow me down as far as possible from a floor up there in a room with white walls I could no longer see, I could only see the ceiling, where clouds drifted slowly by for the last time, and her hand felt safe and warm, it was her firm hand, and as long as she held mine, I could die without panicking. In the dream I looked up into the familiar face, and that made me calmer, and I saw how sad she was, but also how focused on the task she had taken on, as she always was when something was at stake and just had to be done, and not like me, who was flighty in most things. And what she had to accomplish now was to hold me tight as long as she could, so I wouldn't leave this life in panic and despair. I didn't despair, I was just very sad, and a little expectant too, I must admit, in the face of what was about to happen. And I kept sinking until I could feel the gentle tightening of petals around my chin, if petals they were, and then I drew a deep breath, as if I was about to dive, for this was it, and it was not unpleasant, as one might imagine, it had a softness of its own, its own kindness, and she still held my hand, it was the last thing I felt, and then I died and scarcely had time to take in death's vast valley of shadows made up of absolutely nothing before I rose rapidly and shot through the watery surface of life with a gasp so loud it woke me in the Mazda in the parking space by the roundabout close to Bjølsen school, where Grete Waitz, the long-distance runner, was a teacher in the seventies, I remembered her well, in the schoolyard with her shiny whistle, and my first thought was, who was the woman holding my hand. Her face was suddenly gone. It could not have been Turid, that I would have taken with me out of the dream, and the hand in the dream was not like Turid's hand, which was narrow and nowhere near as resolute, and with my eyes still closed I searched my memory to try and bring back the woman who had held my hand so firmly and followed me down into the tulip of death as far as possible before she had to let go. I narrowed my memory to a penetrating ray of light as from a torch large enough to hold a face, but nothing more, to be able to think the woman up out of the dream, out into the glare of the street light high above the windscreen of the Mazda where I was half sitting, half lying in the seat, and in that way see who she was and maybe find her.

But it didn't work, she was familiar to me, but I didn't know who she was.

The clock on the dashboard showed four a.m. The street and the square were silent and everything else just as silent, the doors that didn't open, the closed windows, the dark gateways, the street lamps with their light turned inwards and the air was dead calm, soft as water. At the top of the hill, by the plain, the buses were still resting in the huge garage, heavy, motionless in the slick darkness beneath the rafters, the fuel smooth and shiny in the tanks, the blind windowpanes, the abandoned drivers' seats, the naked cold gear sticks. Not a soul in sight. I felt cold, there was a tremor in both my legs and in one hand, but not in the other, which she had held.

I straightened up the seat and got out of my car and locked it and practically dragged myself up the three tall flights of stairs and lay down in bed, and now it was more than warm enough, and I fell asleep at once.

CHAPTER FOUR

I was often reminded of that dream, how clear it was, how definite, and when I was, it never occurred to me that it was a pity or in any way sad, or unfortunate, that the firm hand in the dream was not Turid's hand. Turid didn't exist in the dream's territory, she was not born there, nor created there. But in real life, in my waking state, it was different. There she had filled every room, filled morning and evening, filled east and west, there she overflowed, and there her spring slowly emptied, there she dried up and vanished, off to the colourful, and I often thought of that too, what did the colourful have that I didn't. Other than colour. It only dawned on me slowly, although it was simple. They had Turid. I didn't have Turid. The colourful had Turid, and they'd had her for a long time. They drew her in. I could see it in my mind's eye, a huge candy-striped straw, a smiling Turid moving at speed through the straw towards all the colourful lips sucking her in, in a sort of diving pose, Supergirl, with her cape gaily flapping.

One time we were going to an island far out in Bunnefjorden. Maybe Malmøya. We were still married. It was before the ship burned, but not long before. Things had been difficult for a long time, and I was afraid. It was Saturday. Someone was looking after the girls. Maybe my mother. She wasn't dead yet. Or one of my brothers. The first of them was already gone, soon one more would be lost.

We walked in pairs the whole way along the seaside, along the quays past the site where the Opera would open its tall glass doors nearly twenty years later, where the small ferry *Holger Danske* now lay moored, looking so absurdly little and frail that I thought, how did we survive all those years.

I cannot remember whom I walked next to, or if we said anything to each other, and in that case what. Turid walked three couples ahead of me. He was tall, he had long hair in a ponytail and a yellow jacket and couldn't shut up, he raised his hands as he looked down at Turid and rattled on. After a while as if moving in a queue we came past the Tollpost Globe building, which was where my mother was now working and not long after this night would spend her very last days two notches up from the wash buckets. Behind her were the factories, all those evenings at all those schools, the gym rooms, the chaotic ship's cabins, the parquet floors, the hotel corridors reeking of cigarette smoke, the toilets with the popstars' needles and cascades of vomit, she hurled the wash rag at the wall and didn't look back once, and from the window where her desk stood, there was a view of the fjord, and Tollpost Globe's neon green tally glowing faintly on the wall facing the road.

*

It was dusk now, a peppery grey darkness surrounding us, but from Sjursøya the lamps of the cement silos lit us yellow and red, and from the harbour across the fjord the light came in a broad sweep, as it did from the streets of the city and the Royal Palace, and high on the hillside behind the city there were lights tracing the thin falling silhouette of the ski jump, and all of it spread out on the water like a multicoloured rug unrolled from a pier some-where between Vippetangen and Aker Brygge, not a Persian rug, but an Impressionist rug woven from shim-mering threads somewhere in the Andes, or more likely in one of the hanging houses way up in Nepal, whipping prayer flags, white flakes in the air, rushing down from the high Himalayas where the snow leopard last was seen. I was not sober. We were drinking more in those days, though no one had touched the bottles yet, except me, who had done so at home before I left, and uninvited, without warning had turned up on the sea side of the Central station, at the foot of the ruthlessly tall and oppres-sive sculpture just as they were getting ready to march off, and they were all younger than me, all of them colourful, only I was dark, not tall and dark, but rather short and dark, and my jacket was the dark jacket from my grandfather who had died not long before, the Danish cabinetmaker, everything being so dark in Denmark, dark and somehow backwardly sad to look at, the jackets were, the bicycles, the cars, but not the beaches, of course, nor the skies or the light over the heaths in the evening or the lighthouse's mild cuffs on the ear. He had a hunchback from toiling in the fields when he was a young boy in the countryside, his spine bent by the yoke, his father was a brute, and the jacket still kept the shape of his back, but I thought it looked fine. It made me taller, was what I thought, I don't know why, as of course it didn't, quite the opposite, but that was before I'd acquired anything close to good taste.

It must have been Malmøya. We crossed a narrow bridge from the mainland to Ormøya, the first island, and then a second bridge over to Malmøya, the outermost island, a short bridge, then a long one, a small island, then a big one. I didn't like Malmøya. The author Johan Borgen had lived there, someone said, but I was certain it was Sjursøya, before the cement silos and the asphalt. But all the same, it didn't make it any better, the houses were too big, there were villas in Swiss chalet style there, a good number of them, private beaches, old money, I thought. In fact I had no idea, I'd never been there before, but it was what I thought, because of the houses. And I thought, what am I doing here. That was simple. Turid was there. Where else would I be, should I have stayed at home, having the thoughts I knew I would have, the hand that slowly opened, letting me go.

But it was I who I was supposed to have stayed at home with the girls. Turid was going to Malmøya with the colourful. Not me. She had become one of them, you could see it in her wardrobe on every hanger, but I had asked my mother, it must have been her, could you look after them until tomorrow, and she must have said yes, she always did, unless she was travelling to Denmark, *going home*, as she said, and she wanted to more and more, but not that Saturday. The girls got the double bed, all three of them under the duvet, shoulder to shoulder and well contented. A bed was made up for me in the basement so I could be back before the girls woke up, and my father slept on the sofa without protest, and my mother lay in the room which had once been mine, in my bed. I don't mind, she said. Which I doubted. The mattress was too hard on her body, her weight, on her natural shape. She had survived a difficult year, but she was worn out after the operations and radiation, but as soon as I was out on the flagstones with my rucksack, I stopped thinking about it.

We were heading for one of the Swiss chalets. It was in Norse-inspired Jugendstil and painted grey, the ornaments beneath the gables all white and Viking-like, the windows pointy behind the veranda. It caught me unawares. Which of the colourful lived here, I thought, are none of them working class, are they all bourgeois, are only Turid and I working class; it had never struck me, I didn't know the first thing about them, I hardly knew their names, it was like in the Party, where most of us had code names. And I had never seen any of them before, how was that possible in a town the size of Oslo, in that generation, I don't even think any of them had children, though Turid had three; they floated free, they flew high, and yet, one day they were there, a part of her life, a big part, but not of mine. It was as if she was leaving home for the first time and I was her parent, standing in the draught from the wide-open door.

But the house finally gave me the opportunity to see one of them from the inside, and despise it, observe the height of the ceiling, three metres at least, and despise it, the multi-paned windows with their red and blue glass in the corners, and then the staircase to the third floor, polished teak and carvings, large paintings at the bend of the stairs, I'd even seen one of them in a book, I gave the house a close inspection and despised it. I had no choice.

There were two motorcycles standing on the paved driveway in front of the house, one black, the other blue, with helmets red and white placed nonchalantly on their petrol tanks. I had heard about them, they belonged to two of the girls in the flock, it was very unusual, and one would have thought, then, that they would be dressed in black leather or some other material, protecting their narrow-shouldered bodies from the asphalt and the terrain if the whole show ended in the ditch, but they were not, you couldn't tell the motorcyclists from the rest of the colourful, nor see the trace of a helmet in anyone's hair, so then you could be talking to any one of them and not know if the person in front of you was a motorcyclist.

Not that I said much to anyone. Mostly I stood right among them, in the middle of the floor under the high ceiling with a glass in my hand or a bottle, and they talked past me, around me, and if accidentally I happened to stand between two of them, who felt they had something pressingly important and colourful to say to each other, they walked around me, they rounded me the way you would round a buoy, they smiled, they gesticulated, but not to me. I wasn't used to it, I was used to more attention.

I turned around several times, to see where Turid was. I saw her, and I saw her not. When I did see her, she never turned in my direction, but acted instead like I wasn't there, but that *she* was there, without me, in a way that was natural to her, because she felt at home and could move about freely. I couldn't believe it. If her back was turned, it wasn't easy to tell her from the others, not with those clothes on, and it shocked me when I suddenly realised that we were not *we* here.

I went out to the veranda. It was almost dark. Behind me the door stood open a crack. I could glimpse the fjord between the trees, its surface still, and behind the gravel paths, behind the ample but faded garden, lay several large villas, I saw the lamps glowing behind the curtains and heard faint music, as if they were giving a ball in there, a muted Jane Austen-type ball, that's how big the houses were, and I saw the annoying imitation cowshed lanterns they all had over their front doors, and this made the darkness on the veranda even darker. Straight ahead of me I saw nothing, it was still cool, and the lamp above my head had not yet been lit. Maybe the bulb had burned out. I took the pack of Blue Masters from my pocket. I was glad I still smoked, I wouldn't have given it up for anything in the world. Why should I.

On the veranda there was no one but me, and in a way it was sad, but a relief too. The cigarette gave me a reason to stand there, even though they were all smoking inside. I was drunk, but no drunker than when I'd come. I closed my eyes and drew the smoke slowly into my lungs. This could actually have been quite okay, I thought. For some reason or other.

I opened my eyes. I didn't think any more, I just smoked, and I smoked the cigarette down, unhurried, almost Buddhistic in its slowness, and crushed it between the flagstones as best I could with the tip of my shoe.

I turned around and saw the narrow strip of light seeping tall as a man from the crack of the door. I stood there. I thought, I'm leaving. I still had two Pilsners inside and the rucksack they came in, but it couldn't be helped, I couldn't go back in.

And then the door suddenly swung open, and a woman came stumbling out with the light from inside flowing all Christian-like around her, and she shut the door and was short-haired like a boy, and she laughed, she was a motorcyclist, I saw it straight away, that's why it didn't show on her hair, because she wore it short. She too was drunk, she was drunker than me, so there you are, she said, quite loudly. If it's me you mean, I said, well yes, I am. I could feel my voice trembling. Are you leaving, she said. I guess so, I said. Don't leave yet, she said, and I said, why wouldn't I. Come here, she said, but I did not. Obviously I should not have clung to Turid and come out here to this island, it was a blunder, but I wasn't anyone's poodle either, and then the short-haired walked the four steps up to me and took my face, my head, between her hands the way a boy would do with a girl, one hand against my cheek, the other behind my ear, and drew me lightly towards her and kissed me, and it felt surprisingly good and in fact it was a relief not having to take the lead, not having to make advances at the risk of being rejected, which in any case I would never have dared to, and I kissed her back and couldn't remember a kiss that was better, she tasted good, she was eager, but not foolish, and we had to come up for air, and then she said, can we do it again just one more time, and we kissed again, for quite a while. And then it was over. We took one step away from each other, both out of breath, so what now, I thought, but apparently that was it, I waited, but I couldn't see anything coming. And then she laughed and patted her cheek and patted my cheek in the same way, with the same hand, and said, you're a sweet boy, Arvid Jansen, and turned away, opened the door and went back in under the lights and in the same instant became colourful again, her clothes unfolding like wings, her short hair glowing, and she shut the door so hard that not even the good old crack of light seeped out. And at first I wanted to follow her, which was not unreasonable after a kiss that good, but she hadn't come outside to fetch me in, I was sure of that, she was bourgeoise, she had the self-confidence of a bourgeoise, and what was I to her, I was someone you could kiss and then just leave, so I couldn't follow her. Not because Turid was inside and might be offended if I came in with the kisser, or more likely be indifferent, but because out here, alone, on this porch, I was somebody. In there I was nobody, other than a buoy you could sail around. So I couldn't go inside. And now I took against her, and maybe it was nothing more than a bet they had made, which the woman with the motorcycle hair had won, or maybe lost, and I felt used, but still, it weighed heavily on me to have to go the long way home alone, because there suddenly was something for me to leave behind.

I pulled the soft blue pack from my pocket and put a new cigarette in my mouth and lit it with a match in my cupped hand, and then I smoked again, and it may have been a sound I heard, a very small sound, and I turned around, and at the end of the veranda, by the wall, there was a divan, and on the divan someone was lying. I hadn't seen her earlier, most likely because of the dark clothes she was wearing. They merged with the shadows in the corner, and she had been quiet and perhaps asleep most of the time, she must have been, since I hadn't noticed her, but now I saw the whites of her eyes, and she was leaning on her elbow studying me. Hi, she said. She said the little word slowly, with a slant, an ironic distance, with only two letters at her disposal she pulled it off, it was quite something. And I didn't like it. Hi, I said, but now she said nothing, and I went over and sat on the edge of the divan, up against her knee, something I would never have done anywhere else than on Malmøya. She had a blanket around her shoulders and hips. Are you alone, I said, and she said, yes, and I said, so am I. No, you're not, she said, you're Turid's husband, the one who writes books. Three books, I said, not very remarkable. Oh sure, three unremarkable books, she said, for Christ's sake, I have read them, haven't I, but you are not here alone. Perhaps not, I said, but you don't understand what I mean. Oh yes I do, she said. And what could I say to that. I pulled a cigarette halfway out of the pack and offered it to her, and she took it, and I lit a match and leaned forward, and then we smoked together, me sitting at her knee, she half reclining. Are you sad, I said after a while. Yes, she said. Me too, I said, and she said, that's not difficult to see. But it was quite the kiss, though, she said. It was, I said. Did it taste good, she said, and I said, it did, and I thought, maybe she wants me to kiss her too, and if she does, should I. But it was the short-haired who had kissed me, not the other way round. You're not one of the colourful, I said, which was obvious, since she lay here next to me, up against my hip, in her dark trousers and black sweater. Who, she said. Those inside, I said. I haven't noticed, she said, and I said, what, and she said, that they're colourful. You haven't. No, I haven't, she said, I know several of them, they're friends of mine. What colours would that be. They seem perfectly ordinary to me. That was not true, I thought, the clothes, the fluttering movements, everything I didn't like, it was clear for all to see, and this woman here was not one of them, just as I was not one of them. Maybe she wants to rib me, I thought, that's it, she wants to rub it in and pretend not to know, and I was getting sore. If they're your friends, then why are you out here alone feeling sad, why aren't they looking after you. But then she went all quiet again, and I thought, now she will feel even sadder. Do you want another one, I said and got out the Blue Masters, it was all I had to offer, there were only two cigarettes left, we could have smoked those together. No thanks, she said. And I too had had enough.

It was very dark now, and difficult to see where her clothes ended and the darkness began, do you want me to kiss you, I said, and the whites of her eyes vanished, and then they were back, and she said, don't you think it's a little too close to your last kiss. You probably still taste of her. She laughed briefly, but not happily, and I thought that she was probably right about that, it would be like kissing two women at the same time, which I guess I wouldn't have minded, but I had no trouble understanding that she did. Not for a moment did I think of Turid. That she existed. Until afterwards. It was odd. I'm sorry, I said, I'm sure you're right, I'm being too forward, I don't usually do that. On the contrary, I thought. But is it really that important, she said, to kiss me. I don't know, I said, maybe it is, maybe not to you, but to me. This conversation was absolutely meaningless, I didn't know why I said what I said, it wasn't important to me at all, and what in the world do I need this for, I thought, what in the world, but she raised her head, and I kissed her, and it was completely different, she was out of practice, that must be why she was lying out here on the divan all alone, and I regretted it at once, I would rather have kept the first kiss, let my mouth remember the first, but now it was too late. Did I taste of her, I asked. You did, she said, it was a bit weird, to tell you the truth, after all she is one of my closest friends, and when she said that I suddenly felt very tired, resigned, I didn't want any of this, I didn't want to hear about it, didn't want to be a part of it, and everything turns into dust and comes to nothing, I thought, it all comes to nothing this way, and then I thought, come on, it's not that bad. But it was, and I didn't know what to do with myself, if there was a place for me, if there was anything I could hold on to, and it all comes to nothing, I thought, and everything turns into dust, everything vanishes, and the self in me can't hold anything fast, and everything's untied, one thing after the other flung out with a sickening *swish* and is loose and never comes back, as in Yeats's poem, where the falcon cannot hear the falconer calling, but instead sails over the next stony crag and is gone some-where between the peaks of Mongolia, or to the west of Ireland, near the Blasket Islands with their roofless houses and the tumbledown stone fences I once had seen through the rain from the tall cliffs at the coast.

*

For a moment I felt very dizzy. I reached out in the darkness to steady myself, and my right hand struck a window-sill, the left knocked a flowerpot over. Can I lie down here for a little while, I said. I don't think there's room enough, she said. There has to be, I said and put my knees up on the divan and leaned forward and squeezed in between her and the wall, and there was enough space, but only just, and I was afraid she might fall off and hit the floor, so I put my arm around her. Don't go, I said. And closed my eyes and was gone.

I dreamed about my mother and father, it was late August in the dream, they were in the Danish house north of the town, by the sea, and were standing each by their own open door, the one that led from the kitchen onto the willow hedge, and the door to the terrace with a view of the meadow where the cows and their calves were grazing all summer long when I was a child, but now there were hares in the thicket, and pheasants, and roe deer, and right over them a buzzard hovering low and weightlessly patient, and further on beyond the meadow the horses were running along the big oak trees against the horizon, and the trees blocked out the light when they grew tall out there where the sun set in summer, to the west right on the opposite coast, that's how narrow the land was up here in the north. You could hear the rain outside, as on a cassette, a slight distortion of the sound, an audible treble, porous, and a constant, mild and yet compact hush over the lawn and the willows and the tall poplars bordering the neighbouring house behind the hedge and the sound of thunder through the rain like rumbling cannons in the distance, but not menacing, as in a war. And inside it was silent, you could hear the difference, inside, outside, and the rain falling behind the silence so rain and thunder and silence filled the dream at the same time, and the one did not touch the other, but each had their own space, and then the two of them, my mother and my father, each by their open door facing the rain, and the silhouette of each of them seen from the inside against the wet grey daylight outside, and they looked like themselves, but not like in photographs in the drawer at home. She said, we'll cycle in when it passes. Then there was silence again, and he said, it will soon be over. The sentences were far apart, and she said, yes, it will soon be over, and then she said, I made the beds up and closed the windows, and after a while he said, that's good, they shouldn't be open when we have left, it has to be tidy when we leave, and they were so gentle towards each other, so unconstrained, I couldn't remember having heard them speak like that before, no impatience, no heaviness, merely a gossamer gentleness, I could have wept with relief. And then the rain died down, and steam rose from the ground in the low white muted light over the meadow, and out of the mist a bright silvery sun came sliding like a Danish five-kroner coin over the willow trees and made everything even whiter, intense and blinding, and still they stood there, motionless each in their own doorway, their silhouettes close to translucent and nearly dissolved, and they didn't speak any longer, and then they were all gone, but the doors still stood open, empty, you could see steam rising to its full height and hear thunder in the distance, but not menacing as in a war. And slowly everything became quieter still, the summer house too dissolved, and it was colder without it, only the blackbird could be heard from its regular tree, its throat so clear it seemed freshly laundered, and it was with me still when Turid shook my arm. I didn't realise at first that it was her, since she was not in the dream, and I was not out of it yet, it will be over soon, I thought, what is it that will be over.

Arvid, Turid said loudly, okay, then, we'll leave. It didn't sound like she wanted to. I raised my head and looked around and rubbed my eyes and could feel how my face was wet. From an open window came a golden flow, and it was the sound of music and eager voices, so the party in there was far from over, but Turid said, Arvid, come on. We can go home now. It's all right. I still had my arm around the woman in black so she wouldn't fall overboard, and maybe she was sleeping, or she was lying there with her eyes closed. She had spread the dark blanket over both of us, or someone else had, and I slowly loosened my hold, my wrist aching, and she really was only a few inches from falling off the divan, but I held her back and drew her carefully onto safe ground while I struggled to get up. She couldn't possibly be asleep, the way I was carrying on, she let herself be tugged this way and that, but she didn't open her eyes, she didn't want to be the third party. It wasn't so hard to understand.

*

We came walking from Ormøya out onto the mainland. A light rain was just beginning. It was no longer Saturday, it was night and there was little traffic, but a solitary taxi with its light on came sailing past us right out of nowhere, I could hear the gentle sound of tyres on the wet asphalt, and the taxi suddenly indicated to pull over on the pavement in front of us and stopped before we had time to hail it, but we got in, and I said, Veitvet, and the taxi driver pulled out again, he knew where it was. Is that where the girls are, Turid said, at your mother's. Yes, I said. That's where we're going. There's a bed made up in the basement. No, that's where *you* are going, Turid said. I'm going to Bjølsen, I don't want to go to Veitvet. What's there for me. Your children are there, I said. Today is your day with them, Turid said, I had the night off. We'll go to Bjølsen first, then you go to Veitvet, and I thought, this is not going to be cheap. I looked at the back of the driver's head, how many couples must he have driven home from parties, in how many different states. Then I leaned back in the seat, I was so tired. All right then, I said, we'll do it that way.

We turned into Hausmanns gate from Storgata, by the blocks of bedsits. We were silent in the back seat. Why didn't you go with her, Turid said suddenly. Who, I said. Merete, Turid said. You mean her with the motorcycle hair, I said, why would I do that. I thought maybe you wanted to, Turid said. No, I didn't want to, I lied. She wanted to, Turid said. I don't think so, I said. You could have gone anywhere you wanted, Turid said, you could have gone upstairs. I didn't understand, I felt weightless, numb, why would she say something like that. I didn't know what to answer. Never mind then, Turid said, please yourself, and her voice sounded sleepy and suddenly distant. Did you wish I'd go upstairs with her, I said, that I'd go with her. Turid shrugged in the half-light. I wouldn't have minded, she said.

I don't remember anything else that we said in the taxi heading up Uelands gate and past Sagene church and Sagene Lunsjbar, if we said anything at all, what was there for her to say, or for me. She couldn't say that I should have stayed at home, and I couldn't say that she should have been *we* with me, when the whole point for her was the opposite, but when I let her go, out of the car on Advokat Dehlis plass, I remember thinking, if only I could stop giving a damn and be done with it. But I did give a damn. I didn't want to be done with it.

CHAPTER FIVE

It was as if she wanted to give me away. As if she didn't care who I was with, as if she didn't care where, didn't care when. As long as I was not with her.

For a long time it was I who went to bed early. She would be home late, and a time would pass, but she didn't come to bed, instead she would sit down on the floor of the living room, and sometimes I could hear her come from the hallway in the faint light and practically fall to the floor and maybe she'd been drinking, and she didn't take off her jacket or shoes, but straight away began to pull records from the shelf, with music that was not my music, nor was it our music, it was her music, music that had entered the house over the past few years via people other than me, maybe the man with the ponytail and yellow jacket, it was the music of the colourful, and she wept softly while she sang the songs they always listened to together, her voice close and intimate over Morrissey's voice, *to die by your side is such a heavenly way to die*, and so on in that way and obviously she didn't mean *my* side. I hated that music. She took possession of that music. She robbed me of that music. Gradually all other music seemed irrelevant and almost annoying, all of the sixties, the seventies gone with the wind, fluttering about, except maybe the Mozart records, which were eighteenth century and not nineteen sixties or seventies, but I couldn't play Mozart when she was at home. What use was Mozart to her, the piano concertos, number nineteen, number twenty, number twenty-one, the finest. Absolutely none.

The girls were asleep in their room, and still she played *if a ten-ton truck kills the both of us* and so on and so forth and not that low either. One time I heard the door to the living room open, one of the girls must have been standing in the doorway, it was Tine, she was six years old and didn't know English, but she knew her mother, she said, are you sad, Mummy, and Turid said, just a little bit, sweetie, but I'm going to bed soon, and then I'll feel better. That's good, level-headed Tine said, then I can go back to sleep can't I. Yes, you can, Turid said.

But she didn't, she didn't come to bed, there was nothing to draw her into my anguished silence, for all the darkness that was in me pressed against the walls from the inside and filled the room to bursting point and there was no space for anyone but me and it would have pushed her out the minute she tried to cross the threshold. So she kept to the living room, and there she played *the boy with the thorn in his side, behind the hatred there lies a murderous desire for love*, as if he wasn't me, the boy with the thorn in his side with his wild longing for love, it was *I* who had a festering thorn in my side, it was *I* who had a barb in the flesh, and yes, I could mime that it didn't hurt, it was my great talent, and it didn't make things better when I suddenly realised that was why she was playing that song, she was playing it for *me*, because she knew that the boy with the thorn in his side was *me*, that's what she wanted to tell me, but that she couldn't come into the dark room and pull the sharp thorn out of my body, out of my side, so instead she sent signals, the semaphore of music, the semaphore of the soul, you'll have to go elsewhere, Arvid Jansen, and she raised her arms, she lowered her arms, she held her arms out to the side the way the Beatles did on their album *HELP!*, with movements so plainly visible that even I could see them right through the closed door, I have to save myself, the arms said, I have to give you away.

PART THREE

CHAPTER SIX

It was still early in the day, it was not yet ten. I was driving from Skjetten over Gjelleråsen to Sinsen junction and on over Sandaker, past the yeast factory by the river. Turid had been collected and delivered and had left a very distinct sensation, an almost exhausting heaviness in my body, my thighs heavy, my shoulders heavy, my hands heavy on the wheel.

Now I swung up to the right by Bentsebrua bridge and parked in my usual place in front of the yellow brick building on Dehlis plass and walked in through the gateway to the cobbled courtyard with the old stable at the far end. There my neighbour with the greatest seniority was standing on his stool, balancing on the cobblestones at an alarming angle, washing his ancient, already thoroughly polished Volvo Duett, a station wagon, soon to be a vintage car, and the coal-grey lacquer shone and the weather had lightened up, there was sun now between the clouds and it felt warmer, there was a wind all of a sudden, almost cheerfully chasing around the courtyard, and I felt I had to say hello, so I said, Hi Jondal, what a Sunday it is. His name was Jondal, but he didn't come from Jondal, he was from Hamar, he had lived there when he was little, he grew up there, his father ran a kiosk not far from the railway station. He had met Rolf Jacobsen many times as a boy, when the poet came to buy tobacco for his pipe, but he hadn't read any of Jacobsen's poems, I have never been tempted to, Jondal said once when I asked him, and I remember it struck me as a bit odd. I would have read them. As in fact I had. By now he had been my neighbour for years, and I couldn't recall a single conversation between us that I would have called sensible, or interesting, at least not to me. He straightened up in his spotless boiler suit with the dripping, frothy sponge in his hand and said, yes, it is, isn't it Jansen, isn't the weather delightful, and I said I have never seen better. He was a Christian. Christians often said that things were delightful, I had noticed, 'delightful is the Earth', 'I know a delightful garden where roses bloom', et cetera, but it wasn't a word I would have used, it was stretching it I thought.

When Turid moved out, Jondal's wife came over a few days after and knocked on my door rather late at night and said, my condolences Arvid, and I said, but Mrs Jondal, no one here is dead, not this time, except me, maybe, a little dead, but it was a lousy joke, the both of us knew, and to be honest I was in a state of bottomless despair, it was the worst time, by far, I felt quite naked, quite cold. Oh, that's what I meant, she said, this sad thing now with Turid, on top of the terrible thing that happened last year, and she blushed and said, not that anyone has died, not now, those were the wrong words, I'm sorry, condolences was the wrong word, but I have baked a cake. She raised the cake to chin level, so I could see it properly. It was a chocolate cake sprinkled with shredded coconut, it looked really good, and she liked me, that much I had gathered, a lot better than she liked Turid, and I liked her a lot better than I liked Jondal. He was a good deal older than her, he had to be. He was away that day, he was in Hamar with his father and was going to stay there for a week. His father had to go into a nursing home, he couldn't remember his own name, everyone around him changed personality, it frightened him, and Jondal hadn't driven there, of course, but had taken the train instead, and so the Volvo was out in the cold for a whole week, and I had a feeling that Mrs Jondal was planning to seduce me. I wouldn't have minded, in fact it would have been good to have someone to put my arms around that night and the nights to come, it would have felt good with her, Mrs Jondal, it would have felt good to breathe slowly into the back of her neck. I was certain she was warm, she looked warm, and I would have welcomed that warmth without a second thought, but it wasn't proper for me to take the initiative, and then she didn't either, maybe her courage failed her, or maybe I was all at sea, maybe the chocolate cake was just a cake. It might well have been. But I was a little disappointed.

And now she stood in the kitchen window in the flat right across from mine and looked down into the courtyard at Jondal and the Volvo and me, and him standing on the stool with the bucket in his hand and the swollen sponge and the Volvo all glazed and glistening and I, on the cobblestones, with a wind whistling around my ears and the long drive to Bjørkelangen in my body, and to add to it, the long drive back again via Skjetten, which was not a big detour but had become one just the same. I looked up at her and almost imperceptibly raised my hand to greet her, and she did the same, in the same way, as if it was something more than a greeting, a code between us that we might have had, but we didn't. Mind the lacquer, I said to Jondal, so it doesn't get too thin, and he laughed and said, it won't get too thin, what we have here, you see, is a Volvo, and I said that it certainly was. I'm taking it for a long drive today, he said, all the way to Hamar, it will go like a dream, he said. It will be a delightful trip. Jesus, I thought, is he actually going to drive the car. Is it your father, I said, and he said, yes, he's not doing so well. Well, have a good trip, then, I said, and let's hope the car makes it all the way there. You can be sure of that, Arvid Jansen, Jondal said, this is a Volvo we have in front of us here, and I said I had gathered that much by now. And then I walked across the cobblestones towards the door and up the stairs where every crack in the tiles was an old acquaintance.

Inside the apartment it was cold. The bedroom window still stood wide open onto the parking space and the bus stop. I had started to sleep with the window open again, even though autumn was well under way, but had forgotten to close it in the rush this morning, and a cold draught was coming all the way into the hallway, and in the living room it was even worse, the curtains billowed and the art calendar let the months flutter by, and it was just so damn cold. I walked quickly towards the bedroom to shut the window and pulled it hard into place in the crooked frame and turned around and saw the chaotic bed, the sheet half on the floor, the duvet aslant, and I made the bed up the way I once had learned to, with military precision, and came back into the living room, and it was still cold. I had a paraffin stove in the living room in the corner near the stairwell, but I knew that the ten-litre tank on the wall was empty, as were the two plastic jerrycans holding five litres each that stood in the hallway at the ready as they had been for the past three weeks, for I should have stopped by Tollefsen's paint shop on the ground floor and filled the cans there, so I had something to help me face winter, when winter came, but I hadn't, I hadn't thought of it, the weather had been too mild. It was the same every year. It was almost like a joke. I had a small electric heater in the kitchen and a small one in the bedroom, that was all, and it was Sunday and the paint shop was closed. I went out into the hallway and put on an extra jacket, pulled the reefer jacket on over the James Dean jacket and sat down on the sofa and rolled a cigarette and looked around the room while I smoked, my pictures, a repro-duction of Munch's *The Day After*, or really just a poster that had been with me all the way back from my boyhood bedroom and in every place I had lived since, the Chinese characters for *no* that I had copied from the cover of Sven Lindquist's *The Myth of Wu Tao-tzu* in a silver frame over my desk, and on the desk the silver Buddha with an incense bowl in his lap which I had secretly taken from my mother's belongings after she died and the rest of them died. It had always fascinated me, ever since I was little, and now it was mine. And then all the records, and all the bookshelves, and all the years with all the books, my only real friends besides Audun, and behind every spine there was an open door onto a life that was not my life, but perhaps might have been, and in a way already was because I had moored them all to a buoy in my heart, every single one of them, yes, all the way throughout the years from high school and here I had kept them with me, and who would I have been without them, who would I have been without de Beauvoir, without Sandemose, Cora Sandel, Hamsun, who would I have been without Jan Myrdal, Hemingway and Jayne Anne Phillips, without Jean Rhys and Melville, Isaac Babel, Strindberg. All of them and more. Yes, who would I have been. I didn't know. I would have been someone else, someone I would rather have been, perhaps I would have traded it all for a little more love. No. Yes. I was thirty-eight years old, Turid was four years younger, we had been together since I was nineteen, which meant our relationship was illegal, but her mother had pushed us into it and practically told me, please, be my guest, now you can take over, I won't tell anybody. Nor did she, and I had received no less from Turid than I had given back to her. But it hadn't been enough. *The love you take is equal to the love you make*, the Beatles sang as the last line in the last song they ever recorded. Or maybe it wasn't the very last one, the debate still rages. In any event it was a sweeping finale. More mature than *she loves you yeah yeah yeah*. But then it was quite a decade that lay behind them.

I stubbed out the cigarette and got up from the sofa with my two jackets on and walked over to the window and looked down on the parking space where it stood, the champagne-coloured Mazda I had bought off a man from Morocco for fifteen thousand kroner behind the shopping centre at Stovner. He had stood in the shadow of the loading ramp and slowly counted every five-hundred note I had given him, and it felt like we were gangsters, a police car would soon come around the corner of the shopping centre and they would catch us red-handed at something that most likely wasn't illegal at all, but it was a bargain, even though the man who sold me the car wanted to squeeze the most out of not very much. When I took it for a trial drive, it ran out of petrol after a single spin around the shopping centre, and then a friend of his drove up in another Mazda with a five-litre jerrycan in the boot and poured it into the tank, but not all five. When we had shaken hands and sealed the deal and I was on my way home, the temperature gauge began to rise ominously already at Økern, and when I got out to check the oil, it was almost empty. I had to walk two kilometres to the nearest petrol station and buy a couple of litres, I didn't dare not to, the engine could have seized up at any moment.

A bus came down Bergensgata and pulled into the bus stop on its way into town and stopped quietly in front of the building, and then came the familiar sigh from its doors, and through the gateway right below me Mrs Jondal came rushing out and just barely made it to the bus, as if she was running away from her husband, because she'd had enough, it was over, she wanted another life with another man, a man like me, preferably, but Jondal made a good husband, he was kind, which I was not, not so you noticed, I didn't feel kind.

I looked at her back in her coat as she climbed aboard the bus, and I had a tenderness for her I am certain I wouldn't have felt if she'd really made a pass at me a year ago, or I a pass at her.

But who knows.

I went back and sat down on the sofa and rolled a new cigarette, I was restless, I've already said that, but I stubbed it out after only a few puffs and lay down and tried to think of nothing, nothing except where I was lying at that very moment, and who I was, right in the middle of time, nothing ahead and nothing behind, only this *me* in this room, a thin pencil line, the way a grey-bearded yogi had taught me once on the first floor in a tenement building halfway up the heavy stone steps in Wilses gate, between Deichmans gate and Fredensborgveien at the top. I was only seventeen then, it was twenty years ago, but now I couldn't do it. The yogi had given me a mantra, a word that was mine and mine alone to use when I meditated, which he claimed after fifteen minutes of talk had been specially adapted to my personality, and it was crucial that I told it to no one, especially not the one I had come there with, who also wanted to learn at the yogi's feet, Audun, my closest friend among the members of the human race. The only one, in fact. When we were back outside on the stone steps after a good half-hour altogether in the glow of two candles placed behind two oranges on a white cloth we'd been asked to bring with us, that for lack of anything better was my mother's biggest handkerchief, then right away we told each other which mantra we had been given, and of course it was one and the same, even though you'd be hard put to find personalities more different than ours. But I couldn't remember now which word he had given us, which mantra, so instead reluctantly I started to think about how I had lain in this same spot exactly one year ago, on the same sofa, in the same position, when one of Turid's girlfriends came in from the landing through the door which for some reason I hadn't locked. It was Merete, and she just walked right in without knocking and came in from the hallway with a big cardboard box in her arms and walked through the living room and past the sofa where I lay flat out on my back staring at the ceiling with nothing on besides a pair of boxer shorts and a singlet, for it was warmer then than it was now, a heatwave had flooded the city, an Indian summer, and she caught sight of me, and she laughed and said, so this is where you're hiding, God, how pathetic. But I couldn't answer her and couldn't get up, I weighed two hundred kilos and was glued to the sofa, and she laughed again and went out into the kitchen and began taking cups and plates out of the kitchen cupboards, my cupboards and my cups and plates, to the best of my knowledge. I'd not been informed that Turid still had things left in the apartment that were hers, in the kitchen, in the cupboards, or that she wanted more things than those we had agreed on, and if she did, had sent this friend of hers, Merete, on a mission all the way here, because she couldn't stand doing it herself. Because of me.

And Merete returned from the kitchen with a full box, and she glanced down at me as she passed, but this time she didn't say anything, she just laughed, she was pretty, she had kissed me once at a party, in a big house on Malmøya, we were both a little drunk, I could remember that she tasted good, even very good, and it wasn't that long ago either, it was more than a year, maybe two, but not much more, not long enough to forget a kiss of such quality, but I don't think she remembered, how good it was, or remembered the kiss at all. She was drunker than I was, but she kissed me more than willingly, that's for sure, as if it were something she had longed to do, to kiss me, and she well may have, but she didn't now.

The cardboard box was heavy with all the crockery in it, she had to rest it first on one knee, then on the other and

74

hoist it jerkily up to her breasts twice before she had got as far as the door, and then with much effort and very slowly I got up from the sofa, I have to help her, I thought, she can't manage to carry what is mine out of my home all on her own. And then I was standing and I raised my hands and said, here, let me carry that, and then she laughed again and said, Arvid, just lie the hell back down, God, how pathetic, and it confused me, how could she talk to me in that way, in my own home, so coarsely. She was not a friend of mine, but once at a party we had kissed each other, and I thought she was ugly, being so pretty and talking to me like that at the same time, and it was very uncomfortable, for she had brought me to my knees, and I couldn't understand why. I hadn't done her any harm, quite the opposite, but there was nothing I could say, nothing that she wanted to hear, I was nothing to her.

I let myself drop back down on the sofa. I could see her at the end of the hallway making her way out the door onto the landing with the cardboard box in her arms and her short hair cropped close at the nape of her neck like a boy in a very attractive way and heard the bang when she kicked the door shut with her heel. Someone must have been waiting for her downstairs and would come to give her a hand with the heavy box, for I lived on the second floor, and the ceilings were high and there were many steps, and maybe the yellow Caravelle that had been parked not so long ago in front of the building was back again, right by the bus stop, and maybe one or more of

Turid's friends were inside the car, waiting in their colourful clothes. Clothes I wouldn't be seen dead in.

The hallway fell silent. I could barely hear her steps fading down the staircase. I remained on the sofa. I looked down at my own body in its white defenceless boxer shorts and singlet, and I thought, I don't look the way I looked before. These heavy arms, this flat chest, these bony knees, all the things that together made up my body, I didn't recognise them, and at the same time I couldn't remember how I had looked at any other time, at any other age, before that day. It was confusing, but I didn't feel sorry for myself. I was a free man. I decide for myself when it will hurt, I thought, that's what I've always said and always believed, but suddenly I was not so sure. What force of will can pull me up out of this, I thought. Not mine, anyway. I'll let go, I thought, and let whatever happens happen. I'm letting go, I thought, now You take over.

And I let go. And it was just as I had always feared. A trapdoor with screeching hinges opened abruptly under my feet, and deep down the water was black as oil, and it was twilight, or dusk, and I fell down through all this moist and sticky grey disgusting swampiness and felt the ice-cold shock against my skin and could even hear the splash as I hit the surface, and it grew dark and silent around me, and there was nothing I could hear, nothing I could see, and when I woke up it was night and the room was dark. I was freezing infernally there on the sofa, and my first thought was, did He, did He take over while I was gone, while I was asleep. It didn't seem that way, there was nothing extra that I could feel, I had nothing now that I didn't have before, and then I felt an unexpectedly huge and until that day unnamed disappointment, for no surplus value had been added, no lightness, there was no suppleness in the body that He had granted me, on the contrary it felt stiff and almost impossible to shake up, and when I made an attempt, it hurt all the way down to my fingertips. And so everything was back in my own hands where it had always been, and my disappointment was enormous. I gazed up at the strangely drifting ceiling, and it was as I had read when I was young, Sartre, it must have been, in one of his books: We are condemned to freedom. Condemned. But I didn't want to be free, I was tired, I wanted someone to take me in their arms and lift me up, carry me forth, into a room I had never been in before, a serene balmy room where I could sleep and not dream.

A whole year had passed since that day when Merete came in through my door and slammed it shut behind her when she left, but I could recall how I froze so badly on the sofa that I stood up from it by my own free but reluctant will, I pulled myself together, as my mother used to say, for God's sake Arvid, pull yourself together, although I always hoped for something else, that she would say something else. And then slowly I made it to the bathroom and got the water running in the tiny, cramped shower cabinet filled with all the girls' unused, useless shower things and shampoos and stood under the hot, beating water in my singlet and boxer shorts until I felt the cold let go of my shoulders. But when I was out on the floor with the bath towel draped over my head, I thought, how old am I now. I couldn't remember any birthday party, but it seemed to be autumn already and a chill in the air, so there must have been, if not a party, then at least some kind of gathering, for it was sunny the day I was born, it was summer, there was clover in the grass and bumblebees, there were meadows, freshly mown after haymaking, there was ice cream and marram grass and salt water, I was a child of the sun. But that wasn't what struck you now. It wasn't what struck her first, who only a couple of hours before had kicked the door shut on her way out of my home. That I was a child of the sun.

CHAPTER SEVEN

That Turid was gone meant there was a fair chance the girls were not in the vicinity either, not at Bjølsen, anyway. The first six months they came every other weekend and an occasional Wednesday, and if I got out of bed and went into the living room and sat down on the sofa to smoke a cigarette or went into the kitchen through the hallway in the feeble fifteen-watt light of the ceiling lamp, most likely I would not run into any of them, not Vigdis, not Tine, not Tone, and all this emptiness stuck to my mind and made me uncomfortable in my own home. After a while it became difficult to get up at night and go to the bathroom, because the column of darkness crammed into the space behind the open doors could easily hold a grown-up person if that person squeezed himself into the corner and stood there, silent and mute, patiently waiting for me to come past on my way to the toilet or the kitchen and then attack me.

Sometimes in the evening, although it was still light outside and the TV was constantly tuned to a Swedish channel so I wouldn't miss a programme about August Strindberg they had announced but for some reason had postponed, I could still hurry out to the kitchen and take from the drawer the long knife I had bought in Crete ten years before from a man in traditional garb with all the trappings in a mountain village where most of the children to my surprise had blue eyes, and then pull the knife from its wooden sheath and shove it into a crack between the sofa cushions and keep it at the ready in case someone were to come crashing through my locked door to do me in. I placed it in different positions using my right hand, my left hand, to find the grip that felt most natural, most precise and efficient. The fact that the person who wanted to kill me might be able to wrest the knife out of my hand and instead use it against my person, my body, was a consideration I was forced to think through carefully, but the last years of restlessness had made me quick and erratic, also to myself, and in my judgement there would be time enough to get the better of him before he got the better of me, if my technique was good and I stabbed him in the neck.

Friday afternoons, every other weekend after school was out, I had stood in the parking space waiting for the girls close to the house at Skjetten. First they had to leave their satchels at home and then come out again with the bags that were already packed, full of clothes and things they didn't need which Turid was certain they needed, but I let that pass, it was nothing to argue about, we were only going up the stairs to the second floor, and to my thinking we'd had a fine time together and I was certain the girls thought the same.

*

Then after Christmas they didn't want to come for the weekends any more, not even level-headed Tine who was always fair wanted to come. It wasn't easy to take in. It was Vigdis who called, it was the end of December, between Christmas and New Year's Eve, my body hurt in more than a few places after an incident late on Christmas Eve I was certain no one had heard about. I had a small Christmas tree on a stool in the corner by the paraffin stove, and in the window overlooking the roundabout hung a semi-communist red Christmas star. Vigdis was twelve years old and the big sister, so she took it upon herself to make the call and didn't leave it to her mother. It turned out to be a formal conversation, she said, Daddy, we are not coming to stay with you for weekends any more, we have all agreed, we can come one more time before school starts, but after that it's not really convenient. Straight away I felt a burning in my stomach, but I didn't dare ask what the reason was, for I could not be sure that the answer I'd get was an answer I could live with, so instead I took note of it, and without batting an eyelid I renounced rights I was clearly entitled to and could claim with full justification, but I couldn't demand of them something that they did not want to give. I didn't have it in me. Oh, I said, that was rather a tough message for me to receive, but if you have all agreed, I guess I have to yield. I didn't know what else to say, she was so serious, and I didn't want to make it any harder for her, I just couldn't, but at least I said, is there anything I can do, or say, to make you change your decision. I don't think so, Daddy, and I said, I see. Now my stomach burned terribly, and it was as if I was falling and falling, with a rushing noise the way Saul had fallen on the road to Damascus, an unbearable blinding light in his eyes, and had turned into someone else, into Paul, and in the middle of that same dusty blazing hot road *I* too lost myself and became a different person from the one I had been, a different father, and I could not speak, and Vigdis said, Daddy, are you there, and I said, yes, now I'm here. But I wasn't. Someone else was. I have to hang up now, Vigdis said, goodbye Daddy, I love you a lot, maybe we can talk on the phone many more times, she said, but now very informally, I could hear she was about to cry, so I said as fast as I could, of course we can, I love you a lot too, goodbye Vigdis, and we'll talk soon.

I may have felt tired sometimes, standing out in the sun in the parking space by the house at Skjetten, my shoulder against the car door or my head against the window inside the car when it rained, if I'd been down in the city centre the day before, on Thursday nights, but it didn't happen often. I was never under the influence, and the way I saw it, I was careful, and I was pleased with the months that had passed since Turid moved out and with the winter so far, and that the girls did not share my opinion came as a blow right out of the blue. So after New Year everything changed, and I went out less and less often, not counting the evenings, of course, but during daytime, the working days, Saturdays. My life became very narrow.

*

For a time I thought about death a lot, that I was going to die, I couldn't help it. Not die 'in the end', as we all shall, but that I was going to die in not such a long time, in less than a year, or even sooner, in a few months, of some mysterious disease no one had heard of before, at least not in Norway, which had come here on board a ship from Africa or South East Asia, a tanker momentarily empty of Norwegian oil and a crew savagely decimated in the course of their journey, or that I would die in agony of lung cancer, which was more likely. I dreamed about that too, and when I did, I always woke with a start and got out of bed and went into the living room and rolled a cigarette, yes, a cigarette, and stayed there on the sofa smoking, looking out over the perpetual roundabout and the memorial, or I walked down the stairs and got into the car and drove away from Bjølsen through the night, to the city centre or out on the country roads in the half-dark, the full dark, almost always towards the east, and I didn't know whether I really was afraid of dying, no inner voice gave me a clear message but every time I passed a place that was familiar to me, a square or a street, a petrol station, maybe, where I had often filled the tank, or a café I'd stopped at for a Pilsner or two, then I couldn't help thinking, I'm seeing this for the last time, now I'm seeing this café with the lamps lit in rows through the room, I'm seeing it for the last time, seeing the people at the tables for the last time, the silhouettes by the windows for the last time, seeing them from outside in the darkness and into the yellow light, which was no longer my light, and

83

so I couldn't add that light to the sum of light, as Tolstoy is supposed to have said, add your light to the sum of light, for it was not my light, I had no light in me any more, and I could say it aloud to myself, this is the last time I will see this place, I'll never come here again. The fact that I said it out loud made it more powerful, more likely, although it was just a figment of my imagination. At least it made me melancholic, sad, sometimes so sad I was close to tears, and that sounds pathetic, I know, but the point was that soon I became convinced that it was true, that it would happen in the near future, I couldn't see any other way out of the state I was in. And being unable to get out under my own steam, it would take an accident, or an illness.

I had to shop for food, obviously, and I went for walks too, especially on Sunday mornings. I could walk up Bjølsengata, up the hill through the park with the tall sturdy old trees and past the allotments; it was nice there, sheltered, muted, as if in a room of its own, a world apart with only me behind a glass wall so far from the madding crowd, and after a while leave that room and walk down along the bustling Stavangergata, into Nordre cemetery from its northern gate and along the footpaths between the glistening gravestones with their names in gold and Gothic, walk up and down, back and forth, thinking, or trying to think, but I was not able to think forth a life that was different from the life I was living now, at this time, to see another world unfolding, I wasn't able to follow my train of thought all the way to the end, nothing left behind, until it stopped of its own accord in the fullness of meaning. I just couldn't do it.

I didn't know anyone lying in the ground at Nordre cemetery, no one from the families that were buried there. I couldn't find my own kin, which was not so strange since my mother was Danish and my father was born to Swedish parents in the district of Vålerenga in a city that was still called Kristiania and would remain so for another thirteen years until it was renamed Oslo, and that suited me fine, not for all the money in the world would I want to have a past here, nor did I come here to say hello to old acquaintances, but I could read the double, triple names out loud to myself, if they had something about them. Some did. What I did not do was go down to the city centre in the daytime, that would have to be for a very special reason. I didn't want to mix the days with the nights, I didn't want to meet anyone during the day whom I would rather meet in the evening, it had to do with the light, I thought, it would be too sharp and everyone would see me come up along Karl Johans gate without a stitch on my body and feel embarrassed on my behalf and turn their faces away, I could not do that, so when I had finished writing, or rather was done trying to write, I stayed at home. I slept. I stared out the windows, at Ole Dehli's verdigris silhouette on the memorial, at the buses and the people getting off, getting on. I tried to read. When the restlessness came over me and the pages mysteriously never quite came into focus, I would go down to the Mazda very early in the morning and drive to Sweden, far away to the small town of Arvika in Värmland county, the first county across the border, on Wednesdays or Saturdays, which were market days in that town, where I had often gone on talking drives with my best friend Audun in times that were long gone, when Turid still did not exist and we talked and talked, freely and candidly in his pale blue Ford Taunus.

The first time I went there alone was a few weeks after Turid's falling away. It took me well over two hours in the car, I burned enough petrol to fill a lake, but suddenly that was where I wanted to go. Out of the country.

They had a pastry shop there, in Arvika, named City Konditori, on the corner of Storgatan right across from the music school and the bus station, and apparently everything inside looked the way it had, shortly after the war, in 1947, when the pastry shop opened its doors for the first time, and it reminded me vaguely of Aunt Kari's Café, where my mother waited tables in the years right after the German occupation, on the corner of Bjerregaards gate and Uelands gate in Oslo, as I had heard it looked in the years before I was born, but had never seen.

I sat down where I always sat, at a table on the first floor with a coffee and a vanilla custard cake as similar to our own Napoleon's cake as possible and a view of the music school and the Swedes walking past in the street. They seemed strange to me, unpredictable, they felt foreign, which they obviously were, but they didn't look it, the way they dressed, they looked like *us*, in Norway. I had no idea why I thought like that. It was pretty childish.

By the wall stood a jukebox that didn't work, beneath a lamp with two lampshades of frosted glass there was a big picture of Marilyn Monroe in black and white, but with a fire-engine-red mouth, and a little further away James Dean in the rain on Times Square with his long coat and the cigarette between his lips. In the steep spiral staircase down to the ground floor there was an equally big picture of Elvis with a considerable kink in his knees and his hand curled around the microphone stand, his whole body lurching ominously to one side. The lampshades had turned yellow with age and the walls could have done with a clean and the chairs were upholstered in a burgundy material which the older of my dead brothers always called 'fake imitation leather', and on one of them the smooth hard material had cracked with age and a little of the old foam rubber stuffing poked out, but it really didn't look that bad.

I ate the cake, had another coffee and opened my book on the table by the window and sat reading for an hour, maybe more, without any problem. I felt such calm. Then I walked down the steep stairs and over to Systembolaget, the alcohol monopoly, on the other side of the busy square across from the railway station where the trains halted for a quarter of an hour before they ran on across the great plains towards Stockholm. At Systembolaget I always bought a half-bottle of Calvados, and on the way back I stopped in at The Book Tree, a small Christian book shop, where the man behind the counter always smiled broadly when he saw me come in with the bell chiming over my head and coins clinking in my pocket, if not literally, for he knew I always left money behind, sometimes a lot of money, but not for Christian books, he had other stuff too, almost everything by Selma Lagerlöf, who was from Värmland and, come to think of it, was a Christian, and Swedish classics I was more familiar with than with the classics of Norway; Strindberg, Hjalmar Bergman, Lars Ahlin, Nils Ferlin. You read a great deal, he said, and I said that I did, but still a good deal less than before, I'm too restless, I thought, too woozy. But I buy as much as I used to, I said, I can't help myself. I'm sure it will get better with time, he said, and I said, yes, it will probably pick up again. The reading, I mean. I hope so, he said, then you'll be back. I'll be back anyway, I said, and that made him happy. One time I bought Hjalmar Söderberg's collected novels and short stories on sale and read them all on a high, but then it stopped again. Another time I bought a Bible for my collection, in Swedish translation, in 'the original language', as the author Vilhelm Moberg once insisted it was when he was offered a Danish edition and refused to accept it, he wanted it in the original language, he said. That made the man at The Book Tree even more happy. You're the most Christian of us, Turid had said one Sunday when we were at a christening and

I didn't want to sing. I found it difficult, while she for her part could sing every psalm at the top of her voice because she was an indifferent non-believer and so was free to do whatever she wanted. But I couldn't sing. I wasn't free. I felt observed, not by the others in the church, who were relatives and friends and people I knew, but by God, who could see how false I was, how hypocritical, when I sang the psalms under the burden of doubt and at the same time insisted on my heathenism, and God laughed when He saw me sitting in the pews in despair, and His irony stung my heart, and I choked. I couldn't sing.

The trip to Arvika and back again took most of the day, which was the point.

Sometimes I tried to write at the Swedish, more than forty-year-old table on the first floor at City Konditori at the high end of Storgatan, with a pencil, most often on folded sheets of A4 copy paper, and not in notebooks, which were more problematic, they made it feel too much of a commitment in a way that undermined the writing. But still, it did feel a bit romantic; the classic author sitting in a café writing with a pencil in a foreign country, like Hemingway did in Paris in the twenties, sharpening the pencil and letting the pencil shavings fall into the saucer as he too had done, letting them fall on the napkin that had 'City Konditori' printed in sweeping green letters in one corner, but after a while I could feel my own sceptical gaze on the back of my neck, and most often it came to nothing, it was pushing it too far. I should stick to reading.

CHAPTER EIGHT

And then I drove home. Through the forests on roads that were tarmacked every three years, and every three years, but not the same year, were blown to bits when the ground frost thawed in April. The timber roads I passed were in surprisingly good shape, but still you could see the clear-cutting all the way up the hillsides in wide dead ravaged swathes, as in T. S. Eliot's *The Waste Land* in the ruins of the Great War; *April is the cruellest month*, he wrote. I didn't necessarily agree. And then the naked hills vanished as abruptly as they had appeared, and then the forest stretched out as it had done since what I liked to think were times immemorial. That was not the case. Large parts of the forest had been planted. But along the shores of the still lakes, along Rømsjøen, along Mjermen and Setten with their fine, half-hidden beaches, I could see Hiawatha of the Onondaga tribe kneeling in his white canoe gliding through the smooth water and on towards the river mouth on the other side of the lake and from there on down the waterways to the south to spread his message of peace between the clans. It was a heavy burden he had taken on, he was still young, but his dignity left no one untouched. If I paid close attention, I could still see him as I always had seen him, ever since I was little and read my first books and disappeared into them and somehow felt I *was* an American Indian, for when I was a child playing Indians, I didn't really want to *play* an Indian, I wanted to *be* an Indian. There was a big difference, that was clear to me, and when I was with the other children in the Dip then *they* were just playing Indians, I *was* one and could feel the whole time that I was not like them. And when their mothers came out between the houses and called them home for supper, they stopped being Indians and walked featherless back home to eat, their hands open and tomahawk-free, while I stayed where I was, prowling the paths, invisible in the dark night, between the trees with their high crowns around every turn multiplied in an endless row, and finally my mother too came out. And yet I have thought, what if she hadn't come, what if she hadn't called me up out of the dark shadows in the Dip, would I still have been an Indian today. What if she, for a brief but decisive moment, had forgotten that I was her son, would I then have kept moving along the paths and stayed there, would I have remained an Indian for the rest of my life. But you couldn't. There was no way you could be anyone else than yourself, but still I have always kept the possibility open, that I could disappear in that way if I wanted to, merely a brief glance back towards the house, and then be swallowed up and hear the door slam shut behind me, and enter a world beyond all reach, but then I had to let go of that thought, for now I was driving past the old log flumes which plunged steeply down from the lake to the river and were still in use up to the 1980s, it was not so long ago, but were out of play now, crumbling, grey and rather sad, and still further down the beavers had made ready for winter. On the slope towards the river the forest floor lay covered in woodchips and shavings of aspen and alder, of sallow, strewn like a golden carpet between the trunks, and several trunks were down for the count, and some stood half-gnawed, dejected on their toes, waiting for the winter winds to topple them over.

PART FOUR

CHAPTER NINE

The first woman I left with had slowly but steadily become impatient, why don't you just take me, she said, Jesus, why don't you just do it, but I didn't, and then she'd had enough, which is to say, nothing. She tossed the duvet aside and crawled naked over me right across the bed and slid down to the floor, elbows first, in front of the stereo at the wall there and pulled records from the shelf with her knees still up on the bed and bottom in the air and found the album she wanted, which was Mahler's ninth and last full symphony, with a Japanese conductor on the cover. The room was dark, but I caught a glimpse of his face and his half-longish grey-speckled hair in the narrow beam from the street light in front of the apartment building. The fourth movement, that's the one, she said, just listen to it and you'll see what I mean, measured against that you are a married man, do you understand that, Arvid Jansen, you are a married man. She was almost shouting. I had just got divorced, not many weeks ago, I had told her so, but I hadn't heard that movement before, I hadn't listened to Mahler much, to Gustav Mahler or any other classical composer for many years. After *Guns and Songs of the IRA* and folk music from Mali, from Telemark and Yorkshire in the seventies, there followed a lot of Nina Hagen and the Clash, David Bowie ten years delayed, the Police, ska music, the Specials above all, and for a brief period Sally Oldfield, who had very little to do with ska and in hindsight was embarrassing even thinking about, but there were valid reasons, at least I thought so at the time. It wasn't something Turid had been able to find on her own, classical music, before I came noisily into her life with everything mine and culturally speaking took up most of the space, she was too young, and then I too let the classical records lie, which she had never picked up. But back home at Veitvet I often listened to Beethoven, the violin concerto especially, and the fourth piano concerto, but also Bach's orchestral suites, and Rachmaninoff more than Tchaikovsky, and even Shostakovich in Soviet recordings on the label Melodia when my big brother was abroad and I had the room we shared all to myself. No one else in the family listened to classical music. If a symphony was played on the radio, a piano concerto, a string quartet, not least, the radio was switched off instantly, both the portable radio of the brand Kurér that stood in the kitchen and could be heard all day, and the Radionette cabinet in the living room which was turned on every Sunday after service and not a minute before, even though no one in the family went to church. No one except me, that is, during a limited period of panic.

The classical records I owned I had bought at Arne Gimnes's book shop in Prinsens gate, where I didn't have to engage with the experts behind the counter at Norsk

Musikforlag on Karl Johans gate, and since it was books I was meant to buy there, I always bought at least one, if I also bought records. But I hadn't caught on to Mahler. Now *sehr langsam und zurückhaltend* the first notes of the fourth and final movement of his ninth symphony unfolded in the darkness. I was naked and exposed and rather cold without the duvet, and she sat erect and white and suitably drunk in the middle of the bed, conducting the orchestra with her slender white arms, and unmarried in the sense of *free* was not the first word that came to mind when the music hit me. It sounded more like *me*, the way I felt just then, why couldn't she hear the same thing that I did, that it was me. It was so simple. But she didn't hear what I heard, she didn't know who I was. I didn't know who she was either. I hadn't seen her before the literary event in a room in the building known as the Flat Iron, a place I would never have found my way back to in daylight. But still, it had worked out well in the sense that we were where we were now, in her bed in an apartment the size of a medium shipping container somewhere not on the east side of the river, nor on the west, we were in one of Oslo's many intervals. I had spent almost all my life here in this city, I was born here, grew up here and had lived in several parts of it as a grown man, but I knew its intervals less well than many newcomers to the town; Oslo's dim districts, the bedsit quarters, almost only observed from a taxi window speeding past, mostly at night; the confusing lamplit streets in the damp, elastic air, disconnected from the common thoroughfares,

97

steeped in blue dusk and cold dawn, floating, undefined like Saramago's Lisbon in the Ricardo Reis book, that's where they lived, most of the women I tried to approach who were not married, or I thought were not married, in one of those neighbourhoods, and once I had left them, I was later unable to link them to other parts of town, in bird's-eye view, I couldn't locate them on a map next to an area I already knew from before, they were still disconnected. And I had thought maybe she was the one who could offer me the firm hand and the warmth I had never had but felt I was entitled to, and therefore not been able to pass on, to Turid above all. And although she had a, well, not exactly unfriendly but rather a tough look to her, there was something there which kept the door half open to my persistence, which was surprisingly intense and persuasive, including to myself, practically on fire, but when we had made it to where she lived, in one of these undefined areas, it didn't go quite so well. Right before I closed the door behind us going into the flat she lived in, it felt imperative to look back to where I had come from, which for the most part now lay in ruins, you could still see brick and plaster crashing down from the last walls left standing, dust rising like smoke signals from the floors, the busted beams, roofs collapsing, and I saw all this, and completely without warning I turned into a pillar of salt, and she understood at once. She could have stopped me on the doorstep for the good of us both, and instead she led me all the way in. It must have been out of compassion more than anything else. But yet she grew impatient, she

said, Arvid Jansen, what is wrong with you, but I was like
a mattress left out in the rain, sodden, heavy, impossible
to move, swathed in silence, and I couldn't stay, but if I
left, then who was I. So I played the highest card I had in
the pack. I exonerated myself. I used the burning ship as
a shield, I was shameless, I'm wounded, I said, that's why.
I didn't use the divorce, which confusingly enough felt
worse to me, but it didn't to her, it wasn't dramatic enough
to make me special, I was a married man, she had said,
although I no longer was, and maybe she said it dispara-
gingly, or maybe she didn't, either way I took it badly, she
diminished me, made me smaller than I deserved, that's
how it looked to me where I now sat, half upright in her
narrow bed about to bolt for the door. She lifted the needle
off the record and replaced the tone arm carefully on its
rest and bit her lip and sat there looking at me, lost, her
eyes moist, for everyone had the newspaper photos in
their minds that year and the year after, the furious flames,
the toxic smoke, the corridors of death and the fleeing
captain leaving the burning ship with most of the one
hundred and fifty-nine still dying passengers onboard, in
the middle of the sea between Norway and Denmark; the
yellow blaze upon the dark water, the grey smoke against
the dawning day, and the final motion of Mahler's ninth
symphony came to an abrupt end. And she sitting there,
with her white arms and empty hands in the dark and
suddenly so quiet room, and me thinking, death trumps
everything. Death was my queen, death was my ace.

*

When I was back out on the street, I had no idea where I was. It was still night, it would soon be morning and the asphalt damp, a drizzle in the air and autumn with slippery pavements and wet, viscous leaves on the ground between the trees in the little park across the way. Not a sound to be heard, only my own short breaths and the empty street glistening and the street lamp just outside the window on the second floor shining obliquely in on her who was now maybe already in bed, asleep and in her dream had forgotten who I was and would never again remember, or she was standing behind the curtain observing me, thinking, why did he come home with me, what on earth happened to Arvid Jansen. I didn't understand myself what had happened, I was numb from the hips down, I was like a man chained fast inside the muted room between pornography and bashfulness and had been there for a long time, no way out, impossible to think about, impossible to touch, and whatever it was she was willing to give me, I wasn't capable of accepting it.

I lit a Blue Master. The street I was in sloped faintly in a direction I didn't know, whether it was north or south, was east or west, but I thought, if I follow it all the way until it stops, then sooner or later I will end up in the city, down by the docks, by the fjord. I couldn't miss. After that I didn't have any thoughts.

There was a tram stop a little further down the street, so I walked over and stood there waiting. I stood for a good while, but no tram came. I dropped the cigarette butt on the ground, it hissed, and I snuffed it with my heel and started walking along the tracks, down the hills towards what I believed to be the centre of Oslo and was lost to myself and reappeared by Akerselva, the river dividing our town, as I was crossing Nybrua bridge, past the A&E and on towards the bus stop where I often stood, at the bottom of Hausmanns gate, not far from one of the few Baptist churches in town. In fact I was almost back where I started, in the place I had left a few hours earlier, hand in hand with the Mahler woman.

It had taken me nearly three-quarters of an hour to walk from her apartment and down here. Two of the three had vanished, I had no idea what had happened during that time, which way I had taken, but I finally arrived at the bus stop and halted there to wait for the bus. But there was no bus. It was too late, or too early, so I walked across Storgata, up past the Ankerløkka field which hadn't looked remotely like a field for fifteen years, not since the main bus station had been there and hardly even then, when the space was still open and not packed as it was now, with blocks of bedsits in trashy colours. I stopped by Jakob church. I had been to mass there once, a long time ago. It didn't help me much. I couldn't sit still.

There was a man lying on the pavement in front of the pub on the opposite side of the street, on the corner with Torggata. The pub was closed, I heard him faintly sing down into the asphalt, and I thought, I have to help him to the detox centre, to the Blue Cross just down the road, otherwise he's done for, for he was in a bad way there on the pavement, it was cold, and I remember the soft light from the window of the closed pub spreading over his back like a duvet, and as I stepped off the pavement to cross the street, I was gone again and didn't surface until the day after in the bed that was mine, on my side, one could still say, even though Turid no longer had a side that was hers. Not here, anyway. I gazed up at the ceiling and tried to figure out what had happened during the night that had now turned into day, between the Flat Iron where I had read from my third book for a sizeable audience with a microphone and all that went with it, and my bed here, whether I remembered the Blue Cross and the man in front of the pub, which I did, the man, that is, but not what, if anything, I had done in that regard, if I had actually got him to the Blue Cross, or to any place at all, or remembered getting back home. But I didn't.

CHAPTER TEN

A month had passed since Turid's abdication. Perhaps a little more. Vigdis and I had driven in from Old Hadelandsvei and stopped at a clearing right by Stråtjern lake. The nights had become cooler, the narrow leaves of the rowan had turned red, the leaves of the aspen yellow. It was really not a good place to park, just a wide path full of stones and thick roots crossing it like speed bumps when we turned off from the main road, but it was sheltered from the few cars that drove past and opened onto the water. I had been here before, alone, to pick lingonberries, and had managed to back out again. I had never seen anyone else here, not even wheel tracks. On the opposite side the lake ended in a bog that stretched in between the trees, you could see water lilies that had shed their petals, the course of a brook and a little way out from the bank two black ducks with some white near the wings, tufted ducks was my guess, that would soon migrate towards the southern coast of Norway when the final cold set in, but on our side the rock sloped down into the water, and it was nice and dry. It would soon be dusk. We had come from Jevnaker high up over the ridge to the east and down the steep hills towards Roa on the other side and driven past the Chinese restaurant they had there for some reason, and I suppose we could have stopped to eat, but I wanted to keep going a little further still, so we drove right through Roa, it took two minutes at most, and out onto the new Hadelandsveien a bit further south and turned off on the old one straight into the hills and then all the way up through the wide bends and past the abandoned cabins by the summer pastures almost at the top and on towards Maura along the narrow crest of the hill. There was forest down along both sides and yet in a way it was like driving in the mountains, you felt you were high up, and the air had a special clarity to it, a sharpness, when we stopped to stretch our legs, but it might have had something to do with autumn. The thing about the air. Are you okay, I said. I'm fine, Vigdis said. My legs hurt a little. Mine too, I said, but then we've been driving for a long time. And it was true, we had been driving for several hours.

We walked back and forth, stretching our limbs, and with knees straight we bent down and touched the ground in front of our feet, I with my fingertips, Vigdis with both palms, and suddenly she began to run, legging it away, shouting, first one to the tree stump. A bit further down the road stood a huge, crooked tree stump deep in the ditch, a spruce had once fallen across the road, and I made a dash for it, but Vigdis was quick, she had shot up in the past year, her legs were long and we were going fast, and I didn't catch up with her until we reached the stump, maybe a few centimetres ahead of her, or a few behind. You won, I shouted and at the same time I grabbed her under her arms and lifted her and swung her around, and to be honest she was a little too heavy, she really had grown, but I held on to her and set her down, and then she began to cry, and I said, were you scared. She shook her head. No, she said. Did it hurt, I said, did I hurt you. No, she said. Shall we go on, then, I said, it's not that far to the place I know of. Okay, Daddy, she said and dried her tears and got into the car, and I didn't know what to say, if I should do my best to drag something out of her. I chose not to. Sometimes you just have to hold back and hold your tongue.

When I got my grant and could quit the job at the factory, I had gone out to the car more and more often, not just to sleep, but to drive, after Turid's departure at all hours. I felt more at home behind the wheel than I did in my own bed, at least I was calmer, whether the car was standing still or I was driving fast, which to me was the whole point about a car, and it felt as if the Mazda had always been mine and no one else's, even though Turid used it too. She paid as much as I did when we bought it, and she was the first to get a driving licence. And yet she used to say almost as a joke, can I borrow your car, back when we both lived at Bjølsen, and out of sheer forbearance she was granted permission. When she moved out, the Mazda remained parked in front of the building as a matter of course, and she bought her own car, a Toyota, an almost new metallic-blue Corolla with red wheel rims. I had never seen anything like it, where did she get the money, what new money could there be, besides my modest child maintenance, she would never have come up with such a thing when we were together. A car like that. But it was a celebration. She hoisted the flag of the colourful.

Later the girls told me that most of the time the Toyota stayed in the shared garage where no one could see it or see its red wheel rims, and if that was not a comfort, it was something like comfort. You might say she lowered the flag to half-mast. But honestly, it gave me no pleasure. Who could have taken pleasure in that.

When autumn arrived in earnest and Turid was gone, I no longer went out to sleep in the car, not because it was growing colder, but I felt freer now. If I still had to get out, I took a sleeping bag with me or even my duvet, and drove to a less public place, up towards the hills behind Kjelsås, and sometimes the hills behind Tonsenhagen, Linderud, to woods I practically grew up in, where I still had a clear image of almost every tree's location, of every crag and every lake, the course of every brook, and still have today. I parked on grass-covered plains where hikers left their cars before disappearing into the woods on Sunday trails and timber roads, but at night there were never any cars there, nor was I seen by anyone.

A Mazda 929, a 1979 model and moreover a station wagon, was a pretty big car. You could push the back seats down, and I had cut out a foam rubber mattress that covered the full breadth of the boot and fitted around the arches over the back wheels, and then there was plenty of room for two persons to sleep next to each other, and so we had, Turid and I, a couple of times before Vigdis was born and the Mazda was still new, but then she didn't want to any more, she thought I was too needy.

Now the mattress had reappeared, and at some point or other I must have told the girls about this new invention of mine, for early one Friday which was not my Friday, Vigdis called and said, Daddy, Mummy wants us to go to Trondheim this evening. With the night train, I mean. Tine and Tone want to, but I don't. Can I stay with you this weekend. I replied without thinking, of course you can, I said, but that was not my plan at all, I had other appointments, I was still seeing people in those days, on the weekends that were Turid's, and I was supposed to meet Audun for dinner at Lompa that evening, but I would have to cancel, I couldn't say no, so I said, should I come and pick you up, then. Yes, she said, I suppose you have to. Now, I said, right away. Soon, I think, Vigdis said, Mummy says we must make up our minds fast, she's going to call for tickets, and she doesn't know how many. I see, I said, and Vigdis said, so maybe we can go on a trip just the two of us and sleep in the car like you do. In the back, I mean.

We could, I said.

*

She didn't have her own sleeping bag. I should have bought her one a long time ago, all three of them should have had one as they grew older, I ought to have encouraged the outdoor life, but I hadn't. I don't know why exactly, but I suppose I had felt it lay behind me, my own childhood behind me, every single day of it, my father in the forest and all that, the blue-marked hiking trails, the red-marked cross-country ski trails, every goddamn hill down into the deep and the snow coming at you. I'd had it up to here without really reflecting on it and it didn't even cross my mind that I was depriving the girls of a whole range of childhood experiences. But I did have two sleeping bags, the old one I hadn't touched since the summer camps in the Party when I promised myself I would never sleep in a tent again and in fact hadn't, and a new sleeping bag I had bought not long before the Friday we are talking about here, for the sole purpose of spending nights in the car with the best possible equipment, given how things had turned out. I had bought new woollen underwear and a new torch, I was armed for the cold dark autumn nights. I guess it couldn't really be called the outdoor life, but if I had to go out, I was prepared.

We were not there yet. When I picked Vigdis up at Skjetten, the weather was warm, inside the car we only had T-shirts on. Turid had been outside on the stairs when I arrived, but I didn't walk all the way over, I stopped near the end of the house where I had the car, and she waved, but I barely raised my hand to greet her. I had nothing to give. It was too early. It felt like it would always be too early.

Daddy, do you have a plan, Vigdis said when she climbed in. It was something they said, all three of them, practically every Friday when they came to spend the weekend with me at Bjølsen, they had rehearsed it beforehand, they got into the car and said in one voice, Daddy, do you have a plan, and expected precisely that, not simply that they would stay with me, be with me, there had to be something extra. It was my own fault. The first few times I picked them up, the mood in the car was tense. We were self-conscious and already felt a little foreign to each other, all four of us nervous and almost resigned to the situation we suddenly found ourselves in, but then I said, relax girls, I have a plan, which was a line they knew from watching some old Olsen-gang films on video not long before Turid and I got divorced, and that lightened the mood, but then I had to say it every single time we swung out of the parking space at Skjetten, just as Egon Olsen had to say it in every single Olsen-gang film when he came out of prison, I have a plan, and actually have one.

Vigdis was cheerful and light on her feet, as much for not having to meet a great-grandfather in a cramped apartment in Trondheim as for going on a car trip with me. But the look on her face was also expectant and wide open. I think so, I said.

It was hardly a plan. I hadn't had time to make one, other than maybe drive around Oslo in a circle big enough to contain twenty-four hours including a sleep-out, and I thought we might follow that circle in the same direction the clock moved, so if Skjetten was at 16.00 hours, we had to go west, first in a loose arc via the south and then up again towards 20.00, where Sandvika ought to be as far out from the centre to the west as Skjetten was to the east, and then head north, barely grazing the Tyrifjord on the way to Hønefoss, Jevnaker, up that way, towards midnight somewhere in Hadeland.

The plan is to go on an expedition, I said. That's great Daddy, Vigdis said. She was clever. She knew it wasn't a real plan, that it was something I had made up on the spur of the moment barely an hour ago, but she was fine with that.

A good while later we stopped at a Shell station not far from Lysaker to buy provisions. When we crossed the border to Bærum west of Oslo over the Lysaker river, I felt as always a flicker of unease, of 'let's get the hell out of here', for I was certain there were other laws in force on this side of the border that I would never be able to fathom, and it rubbed off on Vigdis, who said, maybe we should shop somewhere else. She looked reluctant, standing in the car park halfway between the car and the shop. There's no point, I said, it's going to be Bærum for a good while yet. We'll be fine, Vigdis. Okay Daddy, she said.

*

The young woman behind the counter wore the tight-fitting blue clothes favoured by the girls on the west side of the river; blue trousers, blue sweater, she was blonde with pink lipstick, pink socks and blue sailing shoes, but she was friendly and helpful and smiled in a way that made Vigdis feel safe and included. We filled two plastic bags with cinnamon buns and pre-packaged lefse spread with butter and sugar and crisps and an almond macaroon cake wrapped in aluminium foil and two bottles of Fanta, and I paid for a small sack of birch wood I could pick up on the way out to the car. You're really having a party this weekend, the girl behind the counter said. It's not a party, Vigdis said, we're on an expedition. Isn't that something, the girl said.

As we walked out with our full plastic bags, Vigdis turned around and said, goodbye, and the young woman behind the counter said, goodbye to you too my girl, although she was hardly more than a girl herself.

We came in towards Sandvika on the motorway. It felt cramped on both sides, Høviklandet and Høvik church on the left side close up to the road, the steep slope to the right and the not-so-grand houses in clusters behind the noise barrier, and then the fjord, suddenly wide open with all its islands, and the pedestrian bridge over to Kalvøya, where I had once heard Frank Zappa playing famously and Jens Bjørneboe reading his poems at one and the same concert. He wore a purple suit in the blazing sun, Bjørneboe did, it had been a great experience, it would never happen again. My youth would never happen again.

Right after Bærum's white town hall we took off to the right over the hill towards Sundvollen and the apple orchards and forests to the north.

I admit that on a few occasions I have claimed that Vigdis was born in a taxi on the way to the hospital, that I held her in my hands kneeling in the back seat between Turid's legs. It's not true, she first saw the light of day at the delivery ward nearly two hours later, but I thought about it going into the city and on through the streets in the taxi towards Frogner and the Red Cross hospital not far from Gimle cinema, that it might well happen that way. I could see it clearly, Turid's tanned knees sticking up from her wide skirt, one foot braced hard against the right front seat, the other against the car window behind me, and my slimy, slightly bloodied hands around the little head making its way out into the world, and the first faint scream and the driver's desperate glances over his shoulder, what will happen to the seats, he was thinking, how expensive to get them cleaned, and I could easily hear what we said to each other, hear my own shouts of encouragement, Turid's groans and grim determination, hear my words of comfort so loudly that in the years that followed, the birth in the taxi was the first thing that surfaced and at times the only thing. You tell lies so much you believe them yourself, Turid had said many times, and I can't rule out that she may have been right. I often believed the stories I told, although they weren't always entirely correct, to put it mildly, but I didn't lie, I just remembered it differently.

I was still working at the factory then, I had been there for five years. We had moved out of the city for a while, to a new area with new people, it wasn't long after the blow on Bentsebrua bridge, but it was buried and I didn't think about it any more, and it was Turid who wanted out of the city, it was better for children, was her opinion, and maybe it was true, but everything was half-finished up there at the edge of the forest, construction cranes still stood on the hillside, spindly, tall, pencil-yellow against the heavy shadows lining the woods at the back, and there were grey-flecked orange concrete mixers and circular saws on four legs and workers with tool belts and white helmets in full stride between the buildings and huge spools rolled out with cables for all things electrical, not even the shuttering boards were removed from the basement walls when we came out as one of the first couples in a borrowed van, the key in my hand. When, together, we carried the few pieces of furniture we owned into the ground-floor apartment, the scaffolding was still standing against the end wall of the building. I remember the long steep climb up the hillside and the nasty bend at the top. Already the first time I was on my way up I was sure the car would lose its grip and stop and slide back down again, that's how steep it was. It never did, not even in winter, not my car, but several others did, and I knew

I was going to hate that hill. After two years I'd had enough, Turid wanted to stay but I didn't, so we moved back to Oslo. Back to Bjølsen, to the same tenement, for more or less accidental reasons. I had nothing against it.

But that day Arne came running out on the shop floor. With a hundred decibels in the air no one could hear anything beyond the deafening machines, but he waved his arms dramatically, and I realised it was me he was trying to get hold of, so I started to run towards the door, towards Arne, where he was standing right next to Number Three which was thundering along, and he shouted that Turid was on the line, it's your wife, he shouted, it sounds like it's serious, and he flung his arms out, palms up, and I ran past him out to the staircase where the phone was mounted on the wall in a plastic enclosure against the noise, and there was a shelf beneath and on the shelf lay the receiver, so I picked it up and said with my breath high up in my throat, Turid, what's wrong, although I knew exactly what it was.

She thought she had wet the bed, but it was her waters that had broken. We didn't have a phone, and there was no telephone booth up on the hill yet, only wires sticking out of the concrete slab on the slope we could see from the balcony, and we didn't know anybody beyond nodding terms, so she got dressed and walked gingerly down the stairs to the garage beneath the building where our first Mazda stood and drove down the long, nasty hill to the next neighbourhood, which was older and had a telephone booth not far from the high-rise and the Co-op. Now she was standing inside the phone booth calling the factory, and I said, for God's sake, don't move, Turid, I'm on my way, and just dropped the receiver and ran back to the shop floor and over to Arne and shouted, you drive me, right, for I took the bus to work on the first shift, it was much simpler, almost door to door on weekdays, the late shift was another story, but enough of that, for Arne was happy to drive me, it gave him a reason to get out of the din for a while, and the foreman said it was all right, it was an emergency, after all.

When we got there, she was still standing inside the phone booth with one hand splayed against the glass wall and the receiver in the other and her feet apart like a sailor in a monsoon crossing the Indian Ocean, and I thought, how fearless she is.

I didn't want to be the one driving to town with Turid in labour on the back seat, but fortunately there was a solitary taxi standing there, right by the high-rise, which meant Arne could go back to work, I guess I have to, he said, and Turid and I climbed in, and all the way into town towards the west end I was thinking that the baby could just as well arrive in the car long before we got there. I had read about it, it often happened and especially in taxis, but it didn't happen. Vigdis was born in the maternity ward, and I was there to give support, and I pushed so hard every time Turid pushed that I was asked to leave the room.

I did as I was told and went out into the corridor and on to a roof terrace and lit a cigarette. After a single puff I almost fainted, but we were never again as close as we were on that day, Turid and I. And Vigdis.

We sat silently in the car, looking out at the lake. Not a breath of wind brushed the surface, not a ripple. Then Vigdis climbed out, and I got out and opened the back door on the left side and pushed the button close to the window and lowered the seat. Vigdis watched what I was doing and pushed the button on her side and lowered the other seat, and I walked around the car and opened the back hatch and took the rolled-up mattress I had fastened with a piece of string and a bowknot that was easy to untie, like a shoe-lace. I unfolded the mattress and moved it back and forth until it fitted perfectly into the boot space. There, I said. Then I unrolled one of the sleeping bags, and Vigdis unrolled the other, we were practically in step, and it was fun.

I built a circle of stones and started laying out the fire-wood from the little sack, and sent Vigdis out into the forest to gather kindling and tinder and soon she returned with enough to light the fire with the help of *Dagbladet*'s art pages. It was burning briskly, and with the fire going it got darker, and the glass of the car's headlamps sent the flames back and they wound their yellow way across the lake, and the shadows fell upon the other shore which silently, discreetly withdrew, and then there was just the two of us by the fire with our faces lit up as in a painting by Rembrandt.

We ate most of what we had in the plastic bags from the petrol station and drank the Fantas and tried out some Beatles tunes, to see if they would do as campfire songs, and that worked fine as long as they were slow. It was strange how well she knew the lyrics, but once in a while she stumbled in a way that reminded me she didn't have a clue what she was singing.

By and by night fell, if not for me, then for Vigdis. I helped her into the new sleeping bag and said, goodnight, see you in the morning, and she said the same, she was sleepy and tired after all the driving and the heat of the campfire. I rolled down both back windows, it was not so cold, and she could see me and see the campfire, and the whole time I had the feeling there was something she wanted to tell me, but then she didn't say anything. Maybe it was difficult to get started, maybe it made her shy, but there was nothing I could do to help. I couldn't interrogate her.

I sat there watching the small campfire slowly burn down and the flames on the water fade. I lit a cigarette. It wasn't so bad sitting there, in fact I was pleased we had gone on this trip, pleased that Vigdis had called me.

After half an hour alone I filled the Fanta bottles and poured the water on the campfire until it fizzled and died.

I had my usual difficulties falling asleep, but this time I couldn't go out to the car, as I was already in the car. All the same I slowly felt my body growing loose, and heavy, and perhaps it was something to do with the air, with the scent of spruce and the forest floor, of open water, some kind of generosity I could sink into, as in a gently swaying net that let me fall and at the same time carried me down in my sleep, so I didn't sink all the way into the wet greyness, and then suddenly I heard Vigdis say, I think Mummy regrets it, and at once I was back again, out of the net, out of the sway, and it was completely dark, and no matter which way I looked, I saw nothing. I thought she had fallen asleep a long time ago. What could I say. Finally I said, I'm not so sure about that. She cries at night, Vigdis said. Does she, I said. Yes, she does, Vigdis said. Well, so do I, I was about to say, but of course I couldn't. I see, I said. I don't know why it surprised me, I guess I had imagined she felt free and happy with her colourful friends, with a new energy. I hadn't really wanted to think about it. I'm sorry to hear that, I said. I thought Mummy was happy. She's not happy at all, Vigdis said. Well if you say so, I said, but that doesn't mean she regrets it. I really don't think she regrets it. You don't know what I know, Vigdis said. I'm the one who knows what I know. But she's probably just feeling sad, I said, everyone is sad once in a while, when they feel alone. She has us, Vigdis said, and she meant herself and her sisters, not me, and I almost said, yes she does, and I don't, but I couldn't say that either. She regrets it, that's what she does, she regrets it, Vigdis said, I know it, and her voice rose a notch, she was close to tears now, and then she began to cry, and I thought, is that why we are here, is this what she wanted to tell me, and I had to stop her, she regrets it, she regrets it, Vigdis shouted and struck the window, and struck again as hard as she could, it must have hurt her hand, and she wouldn't stop. I leaned over and put my arms around her in the sleeping bag and held her fast, I said, Vigdis, don't hit out any more, and she tried to hit out and she fought back, but I didn't let go of her, you have to breathe in Vigdis, I said, as deep down as you can and hold it there until you start to feel funny, and then you breathe out again. Do as I say, I said. And she did, she held her breath until I knew she was starting to feel funny, and breathed out again, and she grew calmer, and I said, can I let go Vigdis, and she drew her breath again hard and said, okay Daddy, you can let go, and I let go and said, maybe you're right, I don't know. I'm the one who knows, Vigdis said. Okay, I said, maybe so. But that wasn't why Turid cried, I was sure of it. I didn't know why she cried and didn't want to know, but that wasn't why. Vigdis was suddenly perfectly calm, she said, I have to sleep now Daddy, it's the middle of the night. I smiled, although no one could see it, I wouldn't have been able to see it myself, even in a mirror. You go ahead and sleep Vigdis, and I'll see you in the morning.

It was early dawn when I woke up. Against my habit I lay there for a while. I remembered the episode from last night, but it seemed so distant, so transparent now, that it had already lost its importance. It didn't make me sad thinking about it, nor uncomfortable. It had been dark last night and everything seemed more dramatic, now it no longer did. But how would Vigdis feel, now that it was light and she had managed to say what she wanted to say. She was still asleep, with her long hair coiled about her head.

The back hatch was closed and couldn't be opened from the inside, so I opened the back door on my side and wriggled out of the sleeping bag, out the door hands first onto the grass and then on my knees in the grass wearing only my briefs and stood up and took the clothes from the front seat and got dressed in the clean air and walked a short way into the woods to pass water, as my father used to say, and I remember feeling embarrassed, but I can't remember why, maybe because no one else said it like that. He couldn't do or say much that in my eyes was wrong, before I thought him foolish. It didn't bear thinking about, now that he was dead. I didn't give him many chances.

Not far from here, two neo-Nazis had executed two other neo-Nazis with shots to the neck and then riddled them with bullets from a sub-machine gun. Not for politics, but for money. It was ten years ago, it came to me while I stood there looking in among the trees, remembering how uncomfortable I had felt driving along this road for a long time afterwards, but now I felt nothing.

I walked down to the lakeside to wash my hands. The water was smooth as glass and the air milky white, the haze hung over the opposite shore, and you couldn't see the bog, nor the edge of the forest, but the ducks were in the same place they had been the evening before, dimly visible. It was a bit chilly, so I walked up and fetched a blanket I always had in the car, pushed the door quietly shut and walked back and sat on the rock right above the water and unfolded the blanket and draped it around my shoulders and lit a cigarette. Sometimes it's easy to think about nothing, other times your thoughts form an impatient queue. Now it was easy. So I thought about nothing.

I stubbed the cigarette and tossed it into the water and heard a car door slam, and I turned around, and there was Vigdis walking from the car past the campfire, and the sight of her was like a jump starter in my heart.

She came all the way down and sat next to me on the rock, and I lifted the blanket and wrapped it round our shoulders. Did you sleep well, I said, and she said, I dreamed a lot. One time I woke up and felt sad. I can't remember why. Then I fell asleep again. Are you fine now, I said. Yes, she said. I am fine now. Should we have some breakfast, I said. What do we have that we can eat, she said. Almond macaroon cake, I said. Vigdis smiled. We can't tell Mummy that, she said. No, are you crazy, I said.

CHAPTER ELEVEN

And then it was November, early in the month, and level-headed Tine asked, but what do you do then Daddy, when you're not with us.

Given that they spent only two and a half days with me every other week, this was a question of vast proportions and it was really impossible to come up with a meaningful answer. She knew that my job was to write, so that wasn't what she meant. But of course I couldn't tell her, tell Vigdis, Tone, about my nights in the city centre, so I said, I drive to Sweden, to a town called Arvika. Do you drive there every day, then. No, I said, not every day, it's a long trip, but quite often. Then Vigdis took over and said, so what do you do in Arvika. I read, I said, and she said, but you can read at home, can't you, you can sit on the sofa and read. No, I said. I can't. You can't, she said, and I said, no, I can't. Now she didn't know what to say. She thought I was different and not the same as I had been just a few weeks before, at Stråtjern in Hadeland, or was when we all lived together and I could read anywhere, any time, amid all the racket, I could see it in her eyes, how she was more cautious, and it made me sad. Just the same she said, so can we go there with you, tomorrow maybe. This was Friday, the night temperature had dropped below zero but no snow had fallen, we had just walked up the stairs to my flat, and now their bags stood heavy in the hall, as if packed and ready for a week on the Costa del Sol, or a Greek island, Rhodes maybe, but they were staying with me for only two hopefully fine days, and now all four of us were sitting at the kitchen table eating the traditional pancakes that Mrs Jondal had learned how to make in a different place than this, towards the west, in Telemark where she grew up and she had put them in a plastic bag from the Co-op and hung it on my door handle the evening before so I would have something to offer the girls when the girls came the next day and were hungry after school. She always had half an eye in my direction and my best interests at heart. I will never forget her for that.

I had other plans, really. If I went to Sweden, I always went alone. If I was with someone, I couldn't read. But I had to read. Or else I was done for. I had put up a rickety construction, you could breathe on it and it would collapse. So what would I do in Arvika in someone's company. Was I to show the girls the old table I used to sit at in City Konditori. And in that case how would the table look to me, feel to me, the next time I went there. Should I take them to System-bolaget and show them their assortment of Calvados, show them Swedish books they could not read, at The Book Tree, show them books by Strindberg, Hjalmar Bergman, show them Eyvind Johnson's *The Novel about Olof* in a fat pocket edition and maybe tell them something about it, and then show them Christian books I would never have bought. It was pointless. There was nothing there that I could share with them. Of course you can, I said.

We were sitting in the car. How long till we get to Arvika, Tone said. She was already whining a little. She wanted everything to happen fast, after a short while she always got bored, no matter what we did. It was one hundred and forty kilometres to Arvika on rough forest roads. It was Saturday morning. We had driven for half an hour, we would soon be at Gjelleråsen, Stovner lay behind us, Vestli too, barely out of Oslo.

We had gone down to the car early, Vigdis had been tired and unwilling when I woke her and at first she didn't know where she was and said things I could easily have found hurtful had I been her mother, which I informed her that I was not. Maybe it helped a little. But Tine and Tone jumped out of bed as soon as they opened their eyes. Now we were off.

We're not going to Arvika, I said.

There was a silence. Aren't we, Vigdis said. She was sitting right behind me. Her voice was very clear. No, I said. But you said so, she said. I know, I said. I know I said so, but it won't work. I'm sorry. We'll go somewhere else, I know of a nice place. It grew quiet again in the back seat. Then Vigdis said, I know why we are not going to Arvika. Tine and Tone said nothing. How can she know, I thought, she's only twelve years old. We are not going to Arvika because you don't want us to see it. You don't want us to see where you read.

You think it's daft. You just want to be alone there. You don't want to share it with anybody. I bet Mummy hasn't been there either. Which was true. I never went there in Turid's time. That's correct, I said. Tine said nothing, and Tone said nothing. They didn't understand. You are my daddy, Vigdis said. Yes, I said. I am your daddy. But you don't want me to see the place where you read. She didn't say *us*, she said *me*. That hurt. I waited a little. Then I said, yes, in a way that's how it is, I'm really sorry, but it just won't work.

When we had come all the way up to Gjelleråsen, I was getting restless. I turned left instead of going straight ahead, where the road dips down past Morten's Café to Hellerudsletta, but we drove north, through Nittedal, Hakadal where you could see Glittre Sanatorium for lung diseases hanging on the hill on the far side of the valley, to the east, up towards the forest there, like a Chinese fortress, a Greek monastery or a power plant in the foothills of the rising Alps. And we drove on, towards Stryken where the river came crashing down and was flung foaming up into the air on the left side of the road, in English they call it *rapids*, I thought, it's an apt word, in Norwegian it's called *stryk*, an equally apt word, hence the name of this place, one would assume, and then the valley was squeezed into a pass, at the very top, if not the Khyber Pass, then at least a gate you had to go through before you came out on the other side, as into another country. But of course it wasn't. It wasn't Afghanistan, it was Harestua.

*

It was silent in the back seat and had been since Gjelleråsen.
I tried to say something about what we saw through the
windows as we streaked past, to make it worthwhile
looking at, which I thought it was, the sanatorium, the
frisky river, but there was no answer. Vigdis was wrapped
in silence. I turned around and looked at her, to find her,
perhaps to coax her out between her wide-eyed sisters,
but she had closed her face, made her eyes dull. Was this
when she started doing that. It felt new. But I became
annoyed, honestly, I thought it was unfair. I rarely got
angry with them, never raised my voice, for the most part
I had no reason to, not even when the pressure of three
wills pushed me into panic and helplessness did I get loud
with them, something they obviously counted on, otherwise they would have held back. In most cases I would
have given up, given in, turned east through the forests to
Sweden and sent my brittle house of cards fluttering
sky-high to make them happy, but this time I couldn't, I
didn't want to, okay, I said, this is it, then, we're going
home, I'm fed up, in a tone of voice I had never used with
the girls before. I don't know what got into me. I pulled
sharply into a bus stop, almost grazed the shelter and spun
the wheel sharply to the left, straight out into a screeching
U-turn into the southbound lane, and it seemed more
dramatic than I had intended and sounded more dramatic,
and I was shocked to see a car come around the bend
behind us and another car come around the bend towards
us, and actually it wasn't really dangerous at all, the
distance was too big, as long as I got my speed up and

straightened my course, but I got scared and pulled too hard on the wheel, and the car with all four of us in it skidded across the gravel on the shoulder of the road for a moment before the laws of physics drew us down into the ditch, and the ditch wasn't really that deep, but it wasn't shallow either, and bang it went, with a nasty sound, and we tilted forward and stopped at an angle, each of us practically dangling from our own safety belt. Tine and Tone immediately began to cry, but Vigdis didn't make a sound. Vigdis, I said, are you okay back there, but she didn't answer. Damn, I thought, I need her on my side now, she must help me with the little ones, so I turned around, and there she hung forward in the middle with her eyes shut and only the safety belt around her hips holding her back. She must have hit the seat in front with her forehead and fainted. Vigdis, I said loudly, are you there, but she didn't react, didn't open her eyes, I heard a car stop and another car and a car door slamming, I said, Vigdis, can you hear me. Suddenly she looked straight at me, I have to go to school, Daddy, she said, I'll be late. Vigdis, I said, it's Saturday, no, she said, yes it is, I said, it's Saturday. Her head began to sink again, look at me Vigdis, I said, but her head kept sinking, and I said, Vigdis, do as I say, and then she lifted her head and looked at me, it's Saturday, I said. Okay Daddy, she said. She straightened up with her hand pressing against the front seat and looked to the sides, at her sisters who were crying low, did we crash Daddy, she said. Yes, I said, we crashed a little, it's nothing to worry about. I'll be right there. I loosened my safety belt and sagged a little towards the wheel and pushed the door open, and it was easy, because a man was on the outside pulling at the same time, and I got out knees first, and the man said, I saw the whole thing, it was reckless driving, do you understand, you can't drive like that with children in the car, and I said, I know, I'm an idiot. Yes, the man said. Help me with the children, I said, and we practically crawled each on our side of the car and helped the girls out of their belts and on up the little slope, up on to the shoulder of the road, where another man was standing at the ready. Are you all right, he said in a slightly syrupy way. We're fine, I said. Shut up, I said to myself. When we were all up on the road, I thought, it's not so bad, but I'll have to be towed out of the ditch, I think the car is okay except for a stupid dent, at least I hope so, and the girls are all right, Vigdis has to see a doctor, that was obvious, she had fainted after all, I have to call Falken, I said, I'm a member of Falken. There was a house on the other side of the road, I'm sure they have a phone there, I said and pointed to the house, it was yellow and far from pretty, and I started to walk over there, but then Tine said, don't leave us Daddy. I stopped and turned around and said, I'm not leaving you, I just have to call for a car that can pull us out of the ditch. I started to walk again, but after just a few steps Vigdis said, Daddy, don't go, with an emphasis on 'go', in a tone that was almost one of command, which made things a little difficult. I could understand them, they looked cold, frightened and alone. I can go, man number two said, I'll go and make the call. I looked at him, there was something about him, I didn't like him, he's sneaky, I thought, so I didn't answer, and then man number one said, no, no, I'll call, and he walked off at once, quickly across the road to the house, and I said, thank you, thank you very much, to his back, I liked him a lot better. Man number two walked over to his car, he wanted to save somebody, he wanted his picture in the paper, if someone came to take pictures of what had happened, of the Mazda in the ditch and him in front of the girls: the saviour. But now he'd been made redundant, and was clearly offended and got into the car and pulled out into the road and drove off, south, towards Nittedal and Oslo.

Man number one came back across the road from the yellow house. They're on their way, he said, the rescue vehicle was at Roa, it won't take very long. I know, I said, Roa isn't far. I knew that road, I had driven it many times, the last with Vigdis not so long ago, they had a Chinese restaurant at Roa, but not much else. Would you like me to stay here and wait with you, the man said. I can if you would like me to. It was a kind thing to say. He was ten years older than me, maybe fifteen, or more. He had a handsome overcoat on and a chocolate-brown suit underneath it, and his tie was an exemplary shade of beige. Striking and at the same time discreet. His fine suit trousers had got a stain on the left knee, he saw that I saw it, and brushed it as best he could, and it was almost gone. He thought I was an idiot, which was understandable, and it wasn't for my sake he said what he said, but for the girls', there was something he had seen, in Vigdis, in her face, I had seen it too, but she wasn't aware of it herself, she was too young. I was about to say, thanks for the offer, but we'll be fine until the Falken truck arrives, but then that's not what I said, I said, thank you, that would actually be nice, and it was true, I felt so tired all of a sudden, so alone. One more grown-up would be a relief. Maybe only one of us was grown up, in that case it wasn't me, but it was better for the girls, they would feel safer, no doubt, if he stayed a little longer, as long as I was there too, but only if it's no trouble, I said, not at all, he said, I am going to Gjøvik for a meeting, but I have plenty of time. Trond Sander, he said and gave me his hand. I took it and said, Arvid Jansen. The writer, Trond Sander said. That's right, I said, at least part of the time, and I thought, what does he know about that. He laughed, he could perfectly well hear what I was thinking, he said, I guess Dickens is my favourite, but I do try to keep up, and I said, it's not easy to compete with Dickens. No, he said, but then that's not necessary. I let it hang and swept my arm out towards the girls. These are my daughters, I said, Tone and Tine and Vigdis, showing them off in their full glory, as it were, and Trond Sander turned towards them and leaned forward somewhat stiffly, as a nobleman might do in a theatre or in a film, but not in real life, and it looked very solemn, for he took them by the hand one after the other and bowed politely and said, hello Tone, hello Tine, hello Vigdis, and said his own name each time, and each time he also said, it's going to be fine, and so the girls had to bow too, which I had never seen them do before, Tine actually curtsied, she had seen it in a film, and I remembered which film, but the mood became brighter, and Vigdis even smiled a little, and I thought, why wasn't I the one to make that happen.

And then the blue Falken truck arrived. The driver climbed out of the cab and greeted us, not with a handshake, all he said was hi. He placed two orange plastic cones in the middle of the road, one in the southbound lane and one in the northbound, closing off the traffic and creating a queue in both directions, and then he backed the tow truck into position by the edge of the ditch, got out and slid slid down in the gravel and fastened the cable with the hook around the tow bar of the Mazda, started the winch and pulled the car up without difficulty, it took only three minutes. Get in and check if it will start, the Falken man said, and I got in and turned the key in the ignition, and it started at once, like it always had.

I had to sign a form, he said you should have that front wing replaced as soon as possible, and I said I would. Or else it will fall off, he said, and he picked up the traffic cones and tossed them into the back of the truck, and then he lifted his hand to his cap and left. That was it. I had expected something a little more dramatic, to be honest.

Please, let me thank you again, I said, for your help, and I gave Trond Sander my hand, and he took it and said, it's not always easy, I have girls myself, though of course they're grown up now. Anyway, good luck. And drive carefully. I'm sure I don't need to tell you that. You don't, I said.

I drove carefully and almost too slowly the long way back over Gjelleråsen to Oslo, towards the Sinsen junction. On some stretches cars were piling up behind us and drivers leaning on their horns, but I stood firm and kept the same speed of well below sixty kilometres per hour all the way to the roundabout and made a full circle and drove up again to Aker hospital and turned off. They didn't really have a casualty clinic, but they helped me anyway. They concluded that Vigdis was fine and all in one piece, perhaps a slight concussion, I had to keep her awake for a few hours, I was told. You should be able to manage that, shouldn't you, they said, and there was something about the way they said it I didn't like, something condescending, but there was no way I could retaliate, so I pushed it aside and replied, of course, I can manage.

Then we drove out again on Trondheimsveien and turned left at the intersection. No one said anything. The only sound we heard was a faint scratching from the loose wing against a front tyre, but we pretended not to notice, and as long as it didn't get worse, I didn't want to stop and do anything about it. At Sandaker it fell off, we heard a sharp crack beneath the wheel when it struck, and Tone began to cry, and Tine began to cry, and Vigdis didn't. Still, it was not enough to make me stop and check.

CHAPTER TWELVE

In the month that followed, Vigdis fainted on two more occasions, once at my flat watching TV, just for a moment, then she was back, and once at Turid's flat, at the dinner table. Turid's parents were visiting, they rushed her to the A&E, but the doctor couldn't find anything. Turid called, and I said it had happened at my place too, and Turid said, I see. You didn't tell me. Didn't I, I said. No, you didn't. In any case Vigdis is going to Ullevål hospital to be examined more thoroughly. That's good, I said.

Turid never told me anything about what they found out or didn't find out at Ullevål, and I didn't ask, for some reason or other, and then it passed, Vigdis didn't faint any more, not in my care, nor in Turid's, that I was told of. But it was in the back of my mind, that it could happen again.

The girls couldn't possibly have said anything to Turid about the car in the ditch, for she never mentioned it, which she definitely would have done had she known, and so I didn't mention it either, it was probably stupid of me, but then Vigdis called between Christmas and New Years, and regardless of why they didn't want to come, I felt hurt, and I couldn't bring myself to talk to any of them for all of January. It was like a state of emergency. I didn't answer the phone when it rang. I knew that once in a while it had to be them, and yet I didn't answer. I don't know how they felt about that, but Turid more than willingly took it as a sign of my indifference. I met her by chance one afternoon in Kirkegata, she was on her way home from work, she looked good, and it made me feel uncomfortable. She smiled and said, I can easily understand, Arvid, if you want some distance now, it's fine with me, and I'm sure it was, but I didn't want distance, I just felt sad.

Later I found out that Tine had voted against, but she didn't want to go on her own, so she changed her mind in the second round and went with the majority. It was like in the Party, we voted over again until everyone agreed with the Central Committee. If we voted at all.

CHAPTER THIRTEEN

I met the Mahler woman again a few weeks later, not at the Flat Iron this time, but at Café Nordraak. I was often to be found at Café Nordraak, even though it always felt a little cold in there between the brick walls. It served as a canteen of the Academy of Fine Art in the daytime, in the evening it was a café and bar. For me mostly a bar. I couldn't remember ever having eaten there. It was also used for literary evenings. I had read from my work there a few times, but this evening was not one of them, and there was music, not literature, flowing from the loud-speakers, a lot of music, classical music, it must have been an evening for the dedicated flock.

To be frank I didn't meet her, I *saw* her, standing in front of the bar, and she saw me. We didn't exchange glances, but still she stared straight through me, right into my eyes without stopping, as if they were empty tunnels, and her gaze hit the wall behind my head with a bang and probably cut its way through that too, it was pretty advanced. I suppose she'd had some practice.

Instead I fell into conversation with a woman from Frogner. Frogner, Oslo, that is. She was perhaps a little older than me and lived midway between Gimle cinema and Hotel Norum on Bygdøy Allé. It was an impressive address. I had never been to that part of town, except for the Red Cross hospital, but she had grown up there. She told me about herself, and I told her about myself. Veitvet, she said, is that in Norway. It's in Finland, I said, pretty close to the Soviet border. She wasn't really listening, I didn't know a thing about Finland, and the Soviet Union didn't exist any more, but it did not register. We had been there for a while, we were drinking, and then they played Beethoven's only violin concerto quite loud, and we sang wordlessly along with the tune during the third movement, and it must have been more than the two us in there who knew that concerto, after all it was sort of an artists' café, but only she and I were singing, conducting the invisible orchestra. She knew that concerto by heart. So did I. I also knew every single Bob Dylan song by heart, I don't think she did. But that evening it was Beethoven, and I left with her willingly, up the stairs to her seven-room apartment. It's not very far, she had said as we left Nordraak in the rain, but to me it seemed far, I lost my bearings and sense of direction, and what I had to offer her in one of the seven rooms was not enough, she wanted more, and still more, and she didn't give anything in return. It was confusing, I felt rejected and used, completely numb and alone, and as soon as she had fallen asleep, I left Frogner, as cold as when I came, but sober now, in the back seat of a costly night-time taxi, and if the driver had been an amateur and asked me which direction to take, I wouldn't have been able to tell him. But he knew the way and drove through Majorstua, Ullevål, to Sagene and on up to Advokat Dehlis plass where the tall illuminated memorial in honour of the founder of the workers' Co-op stood on the other side of the roundabout, glistening in the damp night.

I never went to Frogner again. I didn't have to. For things went better after a while, and it amazed me how easy it was to make the women take me home, home to where they lived, how easy it was to get close to them, in such a short time, two hours at most. I didn't quite understand what it was about me that made them interested, what they saw, other than my new boldness, but my experience was that I succeeded, if succeeded is the word, and most likely it had very little to do with me, but rather with them, with why they were where I was in the first place, at the same event, and a little later in the same bar, and that I could see it. See them. Or it was because I had become lousy at small talk. Small talk made me restless, so when I approached them, and unlike the person I used to be, just dived right in, I might say, what's the best thing that's happened to you in your life, what's the worst, were you sad as a teenager, were you alone, did your father drink too much, do you believe in God, were you afraid of God when you were little, were you certain everyone else had sex before you did, which surprised me I had the nerve to ask, and most of them were certain everyone in their class had had sex before they did, and it made them feel trapped and anxious about what the future might bring, and it made everything worse. To my surprise many of them believed in God, some said, maybe. Maybe I do. And a few said, that's none of your business, and I said, you're right, I'm sorry, and made to leave. Then they wanted to talk after all. A handful just wanted to talk about this and that and all kinds of nonsense, but I couldn't do it, it made me irritable, so I excused myself and moved away, and then after a short while they might come over and say, I was very sad when I was a teenager, no one wanted me, I was so ugly, and I replied, in that case you've really changed a lot, and that of course often did the trick, although I didn't necessarily say it to flirt, but because it was manifestly true, if it was true that they had looked so bad. Who hadn't. One of them said, my mother was the one who drank too much, not my father. He did the best he could, I have a lot to thank him for. That's how it was in my family too, I said, but that was not really the case. My father didn't drink, that much was clear, he trained, he boxed, he went skiing, he ran in the woods every Sunday, but my mother didn't drink that much, at least I didn't think so, she just liked to drink when the occasion offered. So did I. When the occasion offered. Which was often, as it did on the evenings I am talking about here, in the centre of Oslo, in a bar on St Olavs plass, in Stortingsgata, in Tollbugata or at Grünerløkka, yes, even in the neighbourhood of Frogner, which I have already said I'd never set foot in until that year, except for the hospital not far from Gimle cinema. The films there were often Italian, or French, and I liked the thought of that, that the action didn't always have to play out west of Pecos, on Manhattan, or in Yorkshire, for that matter, but rather in the fountains of Rome, in Marseilles or Paris. But I had never dared go there. It would've felt like going to the theatre.

Was I afraid of God when I was little, the woman said and stared into my eyes so hard I had to lower my gaze. We were in a bar at St Olavs plass. She wore her hair up and drank double gins with Schweppes bitter lemon and four ice cubes, she was on her third that I had seen, it may well have been more, for she was already there when I arrived. She was standing at one of the busy tables leaning in with a lit cigarette between her fingers and her hand raised high and the glass in the other, deep in conversation with the young man on the chair closest to the window, he was younger than her, at least ten years younger. He was good-looking, he smiled politely, but didn't really say anything. No one at the table said anything, she was the only one who spoke. When I came in, she turned around and saw me walking towards the bar to order my first. She straightened up, made a theatrical bow towards the four people at the table, and steadily enough she walked the short distance across the floor and stood beside me who was closer to her own age. Hello, she said, hello, I said. Do I know you, she said. I don't know, do you. I am certain I do, she said. Do you remember Bjølsen. I live at Bjølsen, I said. Jesus, she said, are you still living there. We moved to the provinces, I said, but I couldn't stand it, so far from Oslo, we stayed for two years, then we moved back. It was me who wanted to, not her. Does she feel better about it now, said the woman with the gin. You might say that, I said, she moved out again and took my girls with her. All three of them. Poor you, the woman at the bar said, yes, poor me, I said and laughed. We clinked glasses, I remembered her now, but she had changed, and not for the better, some might have said, and I would have understood what they meant, but that's not how I would have put it. To me she was attractive. She wasn't back then, ten years ago. She was also so unhappy it was difficult to stand still next to her. Other people's misery can make you restless, above all because there is little you can do to help them. If you want to. Mostly you just want to flee. I had no idea what made her so unhappy, but I went home with her to a one-room flat at the top of Sars' gate, at Carl Berners plass, just one door away from the one I had lived in myself when I finally moved out of my childhood home, nearly twenty years earlier. She was pretty drunk, but she knew where Veitvet was, she had friends there, she said, and she said, come on Arvid, come, and dragged me from the landing across the threshold and on through the hallway. I suppose I wasn't too hard to ask, and I thought, this is the right thing to do, what I'm doing now, it was she who wanted to and badly, and I gave her what I thought that was, but when I stood fully dressed at the foot of the bed and saw her lying face down into the pillow, one arm over the back of her head as if to shield herself from a blow, it was more like walking into someone's home without knocking, just because they had forgotten to lock the door.

Of course I was afraid, she had said. My father had a thick book of Bible stories which he read to me every Saturday evening instead of letting me listen to the radio play on the Children's Hour, do you remember, *The Dung Beetle Flies in the Twilight*, those ones. Everyone else listened to them. I suppose I was past that age, I said, but I know the ones you mean, Maria Gripe, right. Yes, exactly, she said, but anyway I had to sit on his lap to look at the pictures in the book, I mean, he wasn't a pervert or anything, but he wanted me to see the drawings, a famous artist had made them, Gustav something or other. Maybe Gustave Doré, I said. That's the one, she said. I remember one of them in particular, it said *Mountain Lions attack Samaria* beneath the picture. And you know what. They ate people, in the picture they were eating people, and he wanted me to look at it. There were high walls everywhere, and they couldn't escape, the lions got them, and they ate them. It was God who sent the lions, as punishment. All those times I have dreamed I was down there. And was eaten. Because that's what God wanted.

CHAPTER FOURTEEN

I got on the tram at Birkelunden. There was snow in the streets. It was Christmas Eve, the first after Turid's defection. I was supposed to celebrate with her and the girls at the house of the mother-in-law I once had, in a block of flats over by the dip in the road after Strømmen station, not far from Skjetten. I had to say yes, because the girls wanted me to. Vigdis had called for that sole purpose, so naturally I had to mime that everything was all right, that my life was on track, and Turid's brother was coming and her sister was coming and her aunt was coming with her new husband. I was not looking forward to it.

I had been at the upper end of Grünerløkka to buy a pair of skis for Vigdis. It was the second time I would give her skis for Christmas. The previous pair was stored in the basement with skis and poles tied together with two straps in red and blue, not unlike the pair I held in my hands now, but the previous pair never made it out of the basement. Now they were too small. She didn't know how to ski. None of them knew how to ski. I always blamed the poor winters of the nineteen eighties, and it's true that they were poor, but not *that* poor, and really it was my fault. Not once had I touched my own skis after I moved to Bjølsen from the one-room flat at Carl Berners plass, in 1975. Turid was completely useless on skis, and I had just assumed the girls would learn what they needed in kindergarten and at school, but they didn't. On their school's annual ski day they brought sledges. It was embarrassing, not only for them.

Now I was on my way down from Birkelunden, past Olaf Ryes plass towards the city centre. I don't know why I had to go so far uptown, I could easily have bought a pair of skis at Gresvig or another sports shop with a wide assortment somewhere more central in Oslo, but most likely they were especially cheap, probably skis and poles and bindings all in one pack, a special offer someone had told me about that was worth the tram fare and the time it took.

I wasn't sitting down, but instead was standing next to the doors holding on to the rail, so skis and poles wouldn't jab anyone in the face when I turned around in my seat or got up. She was sitting in the carriage with her face towards me. I had turned away from the door and caught sight of her and realised that she had been observing me, perhaps for a good while, and her gaze met mine, and she held it fast for a moment longer than necessary and turned and looked out the window, and it was snowing out there in front of the stairs to Parkteatret, over the pavements, over the trees on Olav Ryes plass, and maybe she wasn't all that pretty, or she was, but in a peculiar outlandish and very nice way, something about her cheekbones, and when

143

I saw her profile, her nose looked more like Cleopatra's in *Asterix* than anything else, or at least made me think of it, remember it, it had something to do with how she was screwed together, and she glanced at me again, and this time it was I who held her gaze a little longer than necessary before I turned away, and I felt it in my throat, that she was sitting there, it moved me, it touched me. I looked out the window in the folding doors, and it had stopped snowing as we passed Schoushallen, the restaurant where several times I had ended up with a murky pint in front of me and a wild longing for the touch of skin or whatever else I could get hold of, and the room slanted a bit towards the bar, so it was difficult to get out if you wanted to, and when someone spoke to me, it was as if from the outside of a cupboard with the door merely a crack open, and there was a leer on my face that revealed a lack of direction. I had seen it in the toilet mirror when I'd been in that place, in Schoushallen, and the last time was not that long ago, nor was it easy to forget the woman whom I had left the bar with, how forthright I had been, how insistent. Through the windows I could see how today, on Christmas Eve, all the tables beneath the yellow lamps were full as the tram rushed past towards the junction where Thorvald Meyers gate and Trondheimsveien merge at Nybrua bridge and turn into Storgata on the other side of the river past the A&E and what was once the open space of Ankerløkka.

I turned around, I wanted to look at her again, for her face made everything else in the carriage dissolve, I could feel it even with my back turned, that she was looking at me, and when I lifted my gaze, she had stood up and was on her way out between the seats. She came straight towards me. I had been waiting for her, long before this day, and with one hand she held the same railing that kept me on my feet, with the other she set her bag on the floor, used her teeth to remove the glove, and lay her fingers naked and flat against my jaw, my ear, not hard, but not lightly either. I leaned in against her hand. It felt so good. But I held back a little. I didn't know why. Everything was fine. She smiled a little. You are not ready, she said. I searched my feelings. She was right, and it surprised me. No, I said. I wish you were, she said. Yes, I said, so do I. So what do we do, she said. I don't know, I said. I don't know what we can do. I wish there was something we could do. Yes, she said. We stood like that. We looked at each other. It's Christmas Eve, I said. Maybe that's why. Why it's difficult. It's not a good day, but then she leaned forward and held her cheek against my cheek, and with one hand still against my ear she said, it was meant to happen today, I think, but it is what it is. Only then did she withdraw her hand. At once my ear grew cold. This is where I get off, she said. Already, I said. She smiled. She lifted her bag, it was heavy, it was Christmas Eve. I looked out the window. I could have got off right after the A&E and taken the bus up towards Bjølsen on Hausmanns gate, Uelands gate, along that route, but I hadn't paid attention to anything outside, and now we were already past Teddy's in Brugata and the Gunerius department store, and the tram continued along the snow banks shovelled up against the pavements and the metal railing, and a little further down the street lay Dovrehallen with its two storeys, and Gresvig Sport, and the Opera Passage on the opposite side. It was Storgata. It was familiar territory. So you're not going any further, I said. No, she said, I have to get off here. The tram stopped, the doors slid open, and she said, happy Christmas stranger, and smiled in a way I would never see again and stepped gingerly down the two steps and on to the pavement with the heavy bag in her arms. I didn't dare to help her, and she didn't turn around, why should she, and I thought, if she turns around I'll jump off and follow her, and to hell with skies and Christmas Eve and let what happens happen. But she didn't turn around, and the doors closed. There goes my only chance, I thought. Now I have nothing. That was not true, I had several things. But I couldn't think of a single one.

A few hours later I was on the bus down to the Central station and took the train from there to Strømmen and the Christmas party of the mother-in-law that once was mine. I had always liked her, she had always been a figure of authority, good-humoured and loud in an engaging way, but on this Christmas Eve, all she wanted to talk about was how Turid and I should find our way back together, if that was at all possible, it would be so good and in everyone's best interest, she so much wanted to keep me in the family after all these years, we knew each other so well, and perhaps it was all due to a misunderstanding, what had happened, and so on and so forth, but I didn't want to talk about it, there was no way back, the glass wall had gone up, it was solid, and I got tired of listening to her. Clearly Turid did, too. Both of us kept our mouths shut and didn't look at each other unless we had to.

I felt out of place. Every time the aunt's new man spoke to me, I was on the brink of leaving. He sat to my right at the table and was hard to avoid. He so much wanted to talk to an author, he said, and he had clearly prepared for this evening, and he said he had often thought about it himself, that he would like to write, that he had a book in him, he felt it strongly, and he thought maybe I could give him the push he needed, the insight, the liberating words, and it wasn't really that difficult to understand, if he was being honest, that he wanted me to say something practically oracular which could lift him up on his way, but I didn't want to talk to him, I've stopped, I said, I've stopped writing, and I turned to my left where his wife sat, who was Turid's aunt, she was attractive, I had always thought so, she could have chosen me instead of her new man, was a thought that struck me. But then I remembered the woman on the tram. I would much rather have been with her. Actually I didn't know what I wanted. Each thing felt important as it came, but when it passed by and barely lay behind me, it had already started to dissolve. I couldn't stop it. And then the next thing came, the next person, maybe the next woman, and it didn't take me anywhere.

*

I had travelled by bus and train instead of driving. That meant I could allow myself a glass or two with dinner, it would be demanding too much of me not to, and there was beer and aquavit with the food, several aquavits, and the aunt to my left saw where I was heading, she smiled at me, she whispered, I know it's no fun, but you're doing fine. As soon as the first presents are over and done with, you can leave. It will do you no good to stay after that. Just don't get drunk. The girls would be upset. I'm not going to get drunk, I whispered. And I didn't, not very. I joked around at the table, and the little girls thought I was funny, so did the mother-in-law that once was mine, and Turid laughed, maybe out of relief, but Vigdis didn't. She could see who I was. I smiled at her, but she didn't smile back, she just nodded, as if confirming the secret we had between us, and that secret would be that I was not sober. She was still only twelve years old, and it was hardly an edifying secret to share with your father, that he wasn't sober, but she accepted the skis and said they were right on time, as the old ones were too small, and she didn't reveal to anyone that the old ones had never been used, for which I was grateful.

Tine and Tone were pleased with their presents, and more than that. They got Barbie dolls, which was the only thing they had really wanted and wanted strongly, and it turned out that I was the only adult who had caved in and bought one for each of them. It was an uncomfortable moment, for they all knew I was violently opposed to the second coming of those horrible dolls. Vigdis wasn't interested in Barbies.

148

On the other hand she wasn't that interested in skis, either. I could have given her a book, but I was under pressure and was certain the others would think I was getting off too easily. With a book.

But then I wanted to leave. It was before the coffee and cognac. Tine and Tone protested, but no one else did. It was a little disappointing. The aunt saw me out into the hallway. I bent down and put my boots on and tied the laces slowly while she watched me. I stood up and put on my reefer jacket and wound the long scarf twice around my neck. You take care, she said. I tried to look into her eyes, she was nearly ten years older than me, she had always made me a little shy. It will pass, she said. The hurt. It doesn't feel like it now, but it will pass. Believe me. She gave me a hug. I would like that, I said into her hair, for it to pass. I was touched by her wish to comfort me, it was the alcohol, it made me sentimental, I said, maybe we can meet some time. Why not, she said. But I knew she didn't mean it. She had a new man.

On the way to the station along the wire fence and the railway line it began to blow and to snow again. I didn't have a cap with me, but pulled one round of the scarf over my hair as a muffle against the snow, and the snow whirled around me in the wind and whirled over the closed-down factories by Sagelva river, over the shopping centre up the road, over the hills beyond and over Øyeren lake and the river Glomma, over the forests towards Sweden. And I imagined I could see all this snow whirling over the treetops and then slowly falling and new snow coming, covering the timber roads, covering tracks of elk and roe deer, of hare and why not the wolf now moving in from the forests of Sweden after a hundred years of absence, all this seen as if from a soundless helicopter, and I caught myself longing back to the Sundays when my father and I went skiing deep into the woods on the red-marked tracks in Lillomarka, his back broad and muscular ahead of me in the blue sweater my mother had knitted, just him and me breathing sharply in the sharp winter air and the dry snow and the dry cracking of trees leaning against each other in the bitter cold, and at the same time the longing for all this made me so weary. It wasn't going anywhere. It was just dragging me down. My father was dead. There wasn't any before. There was only now.

I got off the train at the Central station and walked out on to Jernbanetorget by the neon-lit Trafikanten clock tower. Now I felt strangely sober, perfectly clear, as if I was exactly where I was supposed to be, in a welcoming calm. Everything suddenly behind me. Turid behind me. The girls too, behind me. Cleansed, totally alone.

I walked up Karl Johans gate, up past Kirkegata, Kongens gate, and after the next block to the left on Nedre Slottsgate and down along the Steen & Strøm department store to a bar that was once a pharmacy at the intersection with Tollbugata. They were open. I knew that already, I had been there several times before. It had snowed quite a lot, it had blown through the streets, there was snow blown up against the low windows on both sides of the entrance, but in front of the door someone had swept the mat clean. I stood there. The light from inside sifted gently down over the snow on the pavement, and the street lamps turned everything yellow and each street lamp had its own circle and no circle touched another and between them there was silence. It was no longer blowing, it was not snowing, the street was silent, encapsulated as in a cave in its own snugness, and it felt intimate between the city buildings in a way I was sure it would not inside. Then I stamped the snow off my shoes, drew my breath and pulled the door open.

And it was very different. At once I felt a wave of human warmth surging towards me. The room was almost full. I closed the door behind me. Someone smiled and nodded when they saw me coming. It was Christmas Eve. Merry Christmas, they said, and I said, Merry Christmas and smiled back and went straight up to the bar without removing my jacket and ordered a pint and an aquavit. They came right away. I found a table by the window, hung the jacket over the chair and sat down. I drew my breath again, as far down as it would go, and only slowly exhaled. I felt myself smiling. I lifted my glass of aquavit and downed it in one go. Only then did I look around. No single women. It was just as well. In fact they were almost all men. Bachelors, probably, who didn't have anyone to celebrate Christmas with, and instead were sitting here rather than alone in front of the TV at home, and perhaps some of them lived in homeless shelters. In that case I couldn't blame them. For sitting here. At the end of the bar a couple was drinking shots. She in a conspicuous red dress, but by all means, it was Christmas Eve. They'd had a few already, he more than she, it was something about the way he was looking down at the floor. They were trying to speak discreetly to each other. It was difficult to be discreet when they were so intense, she especially was intense, but I couldn't hear what they were saying, and I was glad I didn't. Maybe it was a marital quarrel. Who wanted to listen to that. I hesitated, then I stood up, went to the bar and ordered another aquavit. I needed one more. The woman in the red dress looked up and saw me standing there waiting at the opposite end of the counter, and suddenly she said in a loud voice, you look like a man who has children, why aren't you with your children, why are you here, it's Christmas Eve, for God's sake. The man looked at me, he fell silent and turned towards the window, he seemed shy, and you could see why. I have my reasons, I said, and that should have been the end of it, but unfortunately I added, but you're here too, the two of you, why aren't you where your children are. I felt I had to get back at her. She closed her eyes, she squeezed them shut and squeezed her lips into a narrow line. I have no children, she said. Then I apologise, I said. It's really none of my business. The bartender handed me the brimming glass of aquavit, and I was about to return to my table, and then she said, he doesn't want to give me a child, it is the tragedy of my life. I'm sorry to hear that, I said. What else could I say, but I wanted to go to my table, I wanted that aquavit, and I couldn't drink it standing up, it would have looked shabby. He is so afraid of having a child, she said, that he doesn't dare make love to me, even though he thinks I'm on the pill. But I'm not. I haven't been for a year. Not that it's helped any. I stood there without moving, the man sat perfectly still. It's not fair, she said, I have the right to a child. All women have a right to have children. She suddenly looked me in the eyes as if there was something there she had only just noticed. *You* can make love to me, she said, but she didn't smile, she was serious, then I would definitely have a child. You look that way. It will be a pretty child. It will work, after all I'm not on the pill. I'm sure that once will be enough, if you don't think it's any fun. I saw the man slump down on his bar stool, there was a full shot glass of vodka on the counter, he took it and downed it and set the glass down, not hard, as I thought he would in jealousy and anger, but very carefully. I don't think it's such a good idea, I said. Why not. I don't know you, I said, and you have a husband, and I have a wife I love. Now she looked almost surprised, she flung her arms out, each of them in an arc, as if she wanted to pose in a classic dance act, the straps of her dress thin as twine, the red fabric smooth and pliant. She really did look great. I lifted my gaze. Don't you want me, she said, what in the world, don't you want me. It's not that, I said. It's just not how I am. But you would like it, she said, I guarantee you. I know a thing or two, I do. Yes, but the only one I want to be with is my wife. That's how I've always been. That got her annoyed, no men are like that, she said, I know all about it, besides I can pay you for a child, many do, you don't even have to like me, we could just make love and be done with it, but this was enough, I said, listen, I don't need your money, I'm an author, I make loads of money. Are you an author, she said. Yes, I said, I am. He's an author, she said to her husband, what do you say to that, but he didn't say anything to that, he had given up, he was drunk, he smiled senselessly, and I said, I'm sorry, but I have to go and sit down, and I tore myself from the bar and walked between the tables with the aquavit restless in the glass, and I felt a heat spreading from the back of my neck to my face, it was unpleasant, and behind me I heard her say, he is an author, what the hell do you say to that, but I didn't hear the man say anything, and as soon as I had sat down, I emptied the glass.

The evening was ruined, but I remained at my table. The calm I had felt was gone, nothing lay behind me, everything that had happened to me queued up and was *now*. Slowly I finished my pint. Now and again I looked towards the bar where they were still sitting. They had stopped talking. What more was there to say. I tried to think of other things, the other guests, they were fewer now, all single men. I looked out the window over to Tollbugata, it had begun to snow again, I could walk home, I thought, it was far, but it would be good for me, clarifying, I could walk off the alcohol, walk off the red dress. I wanted another aquavit, but if I had one more, I was done for, I wouldn't be able to walk anywhere. I turned around and looked up at the bar. They were about to leave. He was very drunk now, she had to help him out through the door, out on to the pavement, and I stayed at my table for five minutes, maybe more, before I stood up and slowly put on the reefer jacket, wound the scarf laboriously around my neck and walked up to the bartender and said, well, have a good Christmas, and gave him my hand, and then of course he had to take it, he said, same to you, and I didn't know why I had given him my hand, I normally didn't, I could have waved, it would have been more than enough.

And then I was out in the street. I stood on the doormat. I could walk all the way to Bjølsen, or I could take a taxi, the last bus had already left. I settled on a taxi, but there was no taxi to be seen, so I started walking towards the Central station. There were always some there. When I passed Kongens gate, I heard loud, angry voices from somewhere down the street. It was the couple from the bar. There was a taxi with the top lamp on, one back door open. She caught sight of me, she shouted, hey you, author, it's you isn't it, please can you come and help me, I'm in distress, please, can you come. I'd had enough of them, I wanted to go home, I could easily have walked on down Tollbugata towards the station, no one would have blamed me, but that's not who I was, and so unfortunately I went into Kongens gate to the junction where the taxi stood, and inside the car the driver sat behind the wheel staring out the windscreen without moving an inch. I can't get him into the car, said the woman in the red dress, and the driver won't help me, and from inside the car the driver said, I'm not getting out of this car, I just bloody won't. Can't you help me then, dear author man, but her husband didn't want to get into that back seat for anything in the world. I tried to bend his head in under the door frame, but he wouldn't bend either his head or his back, and I said, far too loud, come on man, just get into that goddamn car so you can go home, and I pushed him hard, but he wouldn't get in. Instead he turned suddenly and hit me right in the face, I stumbled and fell and landed on my back, and he threw himself at me.

He was stronger than me and used to fighting, but thanks to the alcohol it didn't hurt that much when his fist struck me. Snow had been falling for most of the evening, and now it lay high on Kongens gate, for they hadn't been out yet to clear the roads. It was still snowing, it was almost one o'clock, and there was no way he was getting into that taxi, but we kept at it, and after a while we forgot what we were fighting over as we lay wrestling in the snow, we just kept going aimlessly, and the taxi disappeared, and a new taxi had come and left again a long time ago without us noticing, and his wife too had left. We stopped and looked around, and the street was deserted. We stood up. My whole body hurt, my chest, my sides beneath the ribs, my face, close to my right eye. I wiped my nose and there was blood on my hand, it had to be from the first punch, and the sight of the blood made me strangely calm, it felt like a logical conclusion to the evening. We were both breathing heavily in the quiet street. At last I said, okay, I guess that's that, and he said, I hope so. It wasn't your fault, he said. What wasn't, I said, and he said, I can't quite remember, but I'm sure it was not your fault. No, I don't think it was, I said, I was really just going home, and we stood there with our arms hanging heavy at our sides, palms open, he was embarrassed, and I was embarrassed, we smiled sheepishly at each other and said, Merry Christmas, then, sorry for what happened, and then we each went our way, towards our taxi ranks, I down to the Central station, he in the opposite direction, up to where the taxis stood lined up behind the Parliament building. He limping, I limping.

CHAPTER FIFTEEN

The last evening we had together, the girls and I, was the day before New Year's Eve, on Monday school was starting up again after Christmas. Vigdis had called me a few days earlier, so I was reconciled to the state of things. I still had a black eye after the brawl in Kongens gate, it was turning yellow, but was still a little swollen. I hurt in several places, close to my eye, my left shoulder, my right knee.

And then all of a sudden I was not to pick them up at Skjetten. That was the message I received from Turid when I called the day before, to ask her when was a suitable time for me to come. You don't need to, she said, you don't need to come and get them.

They were supposed to stay with me just that one day, less than twenty-four hours, and my intention was for it to be a special evening and make the most of it, and I had also made a plan, so what she said made me uncertain. Why shouldn't I come to get them, I said, need, what does need have to do with it, why shouldn't I come to get them, and she said, oh Arvid, do I really have to tell you. She sounded like my mother, and that immediately gave me a feeling of guilt, a jolt in the stomach, the trapdoor beneath me creaked, and just as quickly I thought, goddammit, guilt, guilty of what, and was about to defend myself, but then I didn't know what to defend myself against, I found nothing in my memory, nothing she wouldn't have to tell me, and that made me anxious about what she might have taken it into her head to say, and I let it lie.

Instead Turid came to drop them off. It had never happened before. I stood by the window and watched her park her metallic-blue Toyota with its red rims close to my champagne-coloured Mazda in front of my apartment building, and the combination made the Mazda look derelict, hillbillyish, as if it was something Turid had planned beforehand, metaphorically to demonstrate the view she now held of our relationship, and that made it look ominous, and I thought, just a few months, and nothing is as it used to be.

I really did like picking up the girls. It made everything easier. In the car the mood always changed for the better on the way to Bjølsen, and they asked me what plan I had made for the next two days, and every single time I had one, and we sang twenty-five-year-old Beatles songs I had played for them countless times, and they told me about things that had happened in their lives since last I saw them, and I told them what had happened in mine, which wasn't very much if you took out my nights on the town, the successful ones and the not so successful. So I lied and made things up, which came easily to me, and it was easy to make them laugh at the stories they believed to be true. At least Tine and Tone did, but Vigdis laughed too. Now there was no transition, no awkward mood dissolved in the car, just all three of them plus Turid right in my face on the stairs, as if the girls needed a supervisor all the way to the doormat. But I didn't let Turid into the hallway. I had never been inside her flat either. It was probably messy there, she had always been messy, I would never have crossed her threshold, so I stood right in the middle of the doorway, this is it, I said, that's enough, I'll take over from here. Maybe you will, she said. Who knows what you do. And there was a hostility in her voice I didn't comprehend. Until now she had shown what I thought was relief that we were no longer together, and that hurt in many ways, but you could still say it was a friendly relief. You couldn't say that any longer. She wasn't friendly, and to be honest, I couldn't take it, that imbalance, it gave me a feeling of shame, and it was harmful to me.

When I opened the door, she noticed my black eye right away, and made a show of rolling both of hers, ironically, dominant, and the angry bruise on my cheekbone she also noticed, and that particular blow I couldn't remember, but it must have been one of the many I received in the snow there in Kongens gate, and it had hurt a lot in the days that followed, and still did. I couldn't touch it. Her look was easy to read, and it made me ill at ease, but also furious, I thought, how dare you look at me that way, how dare you judge me. I felt exposed, my temples were pounding, and I grew anxious again. It didn't bode well.

*

It's probably a good idea for you to stay at home this evening, she said. It's too late anyway, going for a drive.

So that was it. Of course. The thing about the car in the ditch and Vigdis fainting. I thought it was buried and forgotten, that there was an understanding, a consensus between the girls and me which had erased the incident, and yet in a flash I was back at Harestua and this time in a clearer light, and it was suddenly clear to me that the girls must have been more afraid than I wanted to admit on that day by the roadside before the Falken truck arrived, and that what had happened was more dramatic than I had tried to convince myself in the weeks that followed, even though man number one in the brown suit, Trond Sander, had helped me make the situation less tangled and had made Vigdis smile. He was the hero. The good person of Highway 4. And they had trusted him and his calm and his politeness, but they had not trusted me. And as soon as Trond Sander had got into his car and driven off on his way to Gjøvik, where he supposedly was to attend a meeting, they grew frightened again, all three of them, and were still scared when we drove the opposite way, back towards Oslo at a snail's pace, over Gjelleråsen, down Trondhjemsveien past Veitvet, but what had happened that day was never mentioned. Until now. Evidently.

Hello Daddy, Tine said, this is the last time, you know that, right. She was a strange little girl, small as she was, unsentimental, she meant no harm. I suppose it is, I said. Yes, oh dear, she said. She would soon be seven. Tone was five and a half. Vigdis had turned twelve. Hello Daddy, Vigdis said, and then she said, it wasn't me who snitched. She said it low so the others wouldn't hear, and if anyone had 'snitched', it was probably Tine. But Tine never snitched, she provided factual information if anyone asked. She didn't understand the concept of 'secret', why should anything be a secret. For in fact that's what had happened, our drive ended at Harestua, in the ditch, each of us hanging from our seat belt because Daddy got mad and made a stupid turn, and then Vigdis had fainted and when our car was back on the road and we were driving home, we had to stop at Aker hospital for Vigdis to see a doctor, and no doubt the girls had noticed how patronising the nurses had been, and it had made the trust between us even more fragile. At Sandaker the damaged wing had fallen off, and I hadn't said a word and just kept driving, and Tine had cried when she heard the bang, and Tone had cried, and Vigdis had not. Probably because she had fainted again. And I hadn't said a word to Turid. Tine probably didn't understand why, but she hadn't said anything either when I dropped them off at Skjetten, because Mummy hadn't asked. And then Mummy did ask, much later for some reason, and Tine told her everything in a simple and straightforward way, I was sure of that, and then Mummy got very upset because I hadn't told her, but instead had tried to hide it. I couldn't blame her. I couldn't explain why I hadn't said anything. It wasn't like me at all. I was pretty certain of that.

*

It's all right, Vigdis, I said just as low. It doesn't matter. Okay Daddy, she said.

I closed the door, Turid was still standing outside, she knocked on the glass at the top and said loudly, I'll pick them up early tomorrow morning, and then I heard her footsteps on the stairs on her way down, and I looked out through the glass, and Mrs Jondal stood on the opposite side looking out of hers. She knew what it was about this evening, I had told her the day before. She raised her hand and waved, and I waved back.

Early, I said, why early. I don't know, Vigdis said behind me. Mummy didn't even want us to sleep here tonight. Why not, I said. You always do. Mummy said it's not like always, it's the last time, Vigdis said. I turned around, she looked desolate, but she didn't challenge the fact that this was the last time. Why should she. After all it was she who had called to tell me, and I felt discouraged and suddenly dizzy. I felt dizzy more and more often, it came over me in the middle of the street, in a stairway where I was forced to stop on the first landing and lean against the wall, even in the car it could come over me. It was not a good thing. I said, Vigdis, I feel a little discouraged right now. I think I have to sit down. Okay Daddy, she said and followed me into the living room, where I sat down in the armchair close to the window. Vigdis sat down in the other. Tine and Tone were already on the sofa. Vigdis asked, does it hurt Daddy. She touched her face, so I did the same and lightly grazed the painful spot near my eye. Not so much any more, I said. Tine leaned forward with her hands on her knees, scrutinising me with a matter-of-fact, earnest expression. She took her time. And I didn't say anything. As if I were in her power. It felt a little uncomfortable. Finally she said, did you fight with someone Daddy. What could I say, that I had walked into a door, that's what people said in the movies when they hadn't walked into a door, so I said, I'm afraid I did Tine. Oh, she said. She sat up, her back stiff. There was a pause, and then Tone said, *did* you fight Daddy. Yes, little Tone, I can't deny it, I said, and then she shouted, oh no, oh no, and began to sniffle and kneaded her fingers together and lay her head back and looked up at the ceiling, and I said, Tone, it's not all that terrible, is it, but to no avail, oh no, oh no, she shouted and wrung her fingers until it must have hurt, and it looked strange, mental, if you like, and then she began to cry and not that low. For a minute her crying was the only sound in the room, and it filled the room all the way up to the ceiling rose, oh no, oh no, she shouted, but then Tine cut through, she cleared her throat loudly and said with what I could hear was hope in her voice, Daddy, she said, do you have a plan. It became quiet. Tone stopped crying, but to be safe she kept her gaze fixed on the ceiling. Vigdis hadn't said anything for a while, she'd been staring into the air with her face just barely open, but now she turned towards me, come on Daddy, her face said, come on, as if to coach me, it wasn't hard for me to see. Do you know what Tine, I said. I know I had a plan not long before you got here, but now I can't remember what it was. And it was true. I couldn't remember it. I'm sorry, I said, but I can't think of it. It grew quiet again, Tone was still staring at the ceiling, and then Vigdis said, it doesn't matter Daddy, and Tine said, no, it doesn't matter Daddy, she always found something to say, we can watch TV and eat sweets and that's it, she said. And that's it, I thought, and that's all and goodbye girls and I'm sure we'll see each other sometime, at Easter maybe, a week or two in summer. It was absurd. Could the girls have said something to Turid that they hadn't said to me. I had no idea, and I couldn't ask, and it was as if they gave up on me just then, at that very moment they gave up on me, they said, let's watch TV now and that's it, just wanting to get it over with. I was certain they'd expected me to put up more of a fight, a final effort to make right what I thought was wrong, a correction of the course we were now chained to, something they might be able to support, something they *would* support, if I made it possible, but nothing came. Not that day, not that evening, and there was no other evening. I sat in the chair feeling dizzy, searching for something to hold on to, something to say, but I couldn't find anything except the feeling of having been invaded, by the blue Toyota, by Turid on the threshold, and then in an odd way I grew tired of it. It came over me suddenly. Not sad. But tired of it all, including the girls, it was all too complicated, and even if eventually I had found something it was possible for me to say, something clarifying, even something cheerful,

I might just as well have kept my mouth shut. So they gave up on me.

It was eleven o'clock. The girls were asleep. They had gone to bed early. Vigdis too. I guess I had expected her to stay up a little longer. But what was there to stay up for.

I was still in the living room, but had moved to the sofa. With my hand under one of the cushions I held the smooth knife handle tightly. The bowl of sweets was empty, chocolate wrappers strewn all over the table, and the TV was still on. It was a Swedish channel we had switched to because their Christmas shows were better than the Norwegian ones, as in fact their programmes almost always were, and for all I knew what was on just then could have been the end of the programme about Strindberg I had waited for so long, but I didn't care, I didn't even glance at the screen.

As long as the girls were awake, I had kept away from the cigarettes, but in my reefer jacket there was an unopened packet of Blue Masters. I must have thought there was something to celebrate, but now it was hard to imagine what. I stood up and went out into the hallway and fetched the pack and went into the living room and was about to sit down on the sofa, but then I went back out into the hallway, took the Icelandic sweater out of the closet and pulled the jacket over it, and with the cigarettes in my hand I locked the door behind me out on the landing and walked down and walked out through the gateway to the parking place and got into the cold car. Only then did I pull the plastic film off the packet and stick an unfiltered Blue Master between my lips. The space next to the Mazda, where the blue Toyota had stood, was still empty, and the emptiness swelled, and in every other space a car was parked, and when I realised that, I got restless, it was difficult to sit still, and I didn't even have time to light the cigarette before I was back out of the car and inside the yard and on my way up the stairs.

When I was almost up on my own floor, I stopped and sat down with my back to the landing and finally managed to light the cigarette. It was probably the best cigarette I had ever tasted, at least the most welcome, but I hadn't smoked it even halfway when the door opposite mine was opened, and I knew straight away that it wasn't Mrs Jondal, if it had been I would have felt something in the chill air that I would have recognised, something alluring, intimate, and so there was only one other possibility. Are you sitting there, Jondal said. I didn't turn around. I blew a stream of luminous smoke out into the semi-darkness. I guess I am, I said. It's very late, he said, and I said I was aware of that, which made it no easier for him to understand why I was out on the cold stairs instead of in my warm bed, but then it came to him, and practically beaming he said, but poor Jansen, did you lock yourself out. Without turning around I took the keyring out of my pocket and dangled it from my index finger, which left him at a loss. Oh, he said, well, it's your choice. I suppose you can sit wherever you like, there's no law against it, I

167

guess, although it's the middle of the night, and I said my intention was to sit there for a while, so I hoped he was right. Oh, I can assure you that I am, he said. You just sit there. And have a good night now, Jansen. Goodnight yourself, I said. And please say hello from me. I certainly will, Jondal said. And I knew that he would. He had to. He was a Christian. He was bound to a life of righteousness and truth. I was not. Why should I be. I lied every day, about one thing or another, without exception. But he would tell his wife that I was sitting out there, and for a second I thought that if he did, she might come out on the landing. And then I thought that she would not. And then I thought of the staircase we had at home, between the ground floor and the first floor of the terraced house at Veitvet, where for many nights I sat as I was sitting now, on this night on these stairs in the district of Bjølsen high up in the city of Oslo on the west side of the river, but in every other respect on the east side, economically, cultur-ally, only it was now twenty years since I had lived at Veitvet. At the top of the stairs was the closed door to the bedroom my mother and father shared, and I was sitting outside because I was fifteen years old and the thoughts I had about the future had knocked me over, knocked me out with their full weight, and big boulders of bewildering impossibilities had tumbled down and blocked my path and with them came the fear of the years that lay ahead and the fear that I would never raise myself to meet the challenging dimensions of the future, and if still I tried, I would have to do it alone, and the conviction of this and

168

the conviction that it was really not within my power, squeezed the air out of me. I couldn't breathe, I couldn't swallow, and all this drove me out onto the stairs where I sat gasping for air and knew that my mother could clearly hear my hissing breath, and all I wanted was for her to come out and sit next to me, and maybe say something, or she didn't even need to say anything, but she didn't come out, and I couldn't ask her to, for what I must ask for, I do not want, it loses its value and turns to nothing, and anyway she didn't come out. She never came out. Instead she said in a loud voice, oh Arvid, go back to bed for God's sake. And then Mrs Jondal came out. She had probably already gone to bed and got up when Jondal came in and told her I said hello. She was wearing a dressing gown, it was blue with red scrolls, made of terry cloth, like a towel, a bath towel, then, and so I suppose it was a bathrobe, and it was well worn and might have been handed down to her, by her mother or an aunt with middling taste, that was just me speculating, I didn't have to. She pulled what in all probability was a bathrobe tighter around her and tied the belt with a bowknot and said, but Arvid, are you sitting out here. I didn't answer straight away. It felt a little awkward to say the same thing twice, but then it was a pretty silly question. I was sitting there. I could hardly say that I was not. So I turned towards her and said, yes, I guess I am, but it felt different when I said it to her, it didn't sound ironic. She came all the way out, pulled the door shut, but made sure it didn't lock and sat down and placed her hand on my shoulder. Are the girls all right, she said. They're asleep, I said. How all right they are, I don't know. I guess they're all right if they're asleep. How about you, she said. Well, I'm sitting here, I said, smoking. For now. I'm just fine. But isn't it cold, she said, and I said, I'm used to being cold, and she replied, that's true. She knew about the car and all that. She had seen me go out or come back inside, one of the two or both, probably several times, but she had never mentioned it, and I appreciated that. She let her hand stroke my shoulder a few times, is there something I can do for you, Arvid. Can I help you in any way. No one can help me, I said. No one, she said, and I said, no. But thanks for coming out, I added, I was glad you did, you have no idea how much. I wish there was something I could do to help, she said. I'll be fine, I said, I will sit here a little longer, and then go inside. It's no problem. She stood up, it was the middle of the night. Okay then, she said. Goodnight, Arvid. Don't sit up too long. I won't, I said. And goodnight to you too, but I didn't tell her to say hello. There was no one in there but Jondal as far as I knew, and she went in and pushed the door shut until it locked with a loud click.

Now suddenly everything was out of balance. I wasn't alone any more, I had been abandoned, and there was a big difference and I might as well have gone back inside in the first place, but I sat there a while longer, for appearances' sake, though there was no one there to watch me. I didn't want to go in. But then I couldn't stay, and I couldn't go down to the car. I had begun to feel cold, I was cold around the hips, my crotch felt numb, cold crept up my spine beneath the jacket. So I stood up stiffly and mounted the last two steps and locked myself into the hallway. I pulled off the reefer jacket, but not the sweater, and went into the kitchen and took from the cupboard one of the two whisky glasses my big brother had given me when he came by on the day before Christmas Eve, one for you, he said, and one for me, when I come to visit, and it rested pleasantly in my hand. I set it on the kitchen counter and poured a substantial drink of Johnnie Walker into it, the Grorud valley's spirit of choice all the way from Årvoll to Vestli. Then I went out into the hallway with the glass in my hand and sat down on the floor, on the threshold to the girls' room, my back up against one side of the door frame and my feet up against the other. The door stood half open as it always did. I took a sip of the whisky and took out a Blue Master and struck a match, and after each puff I blew the smoke away from the door into the hallway past the kitchen, and had another sip from my glass. I felt the warmth spread through my body and remained sitting on the threshold for I don't remember how long, with my eyes closed and the back of my head leaning against the door frame, listening to the girls breathing inside the dark room, each in her own rhythm, each in her own silent light.

PART FIVE

CHAPTER SIXTEEN

I opened my eyes. I was lying on the sofa with my two jackets on, and from there I looked up to the ceiling, the stucco, the plaster ornaments around the ceiling rose and the whole ceiling chalk white, freshly painted by me only a few months earlier, standing a whole week on a step-ladder with a crick in my neck, and it all looked pretty, but it wasn't my favourite place in the room. It was far from dark, but the light was different. Perhaps two hours had passed, the sun shone straight in through the window, and it wasn't warm, but too warm with both jackets on. I felt clammy in my armpits and down along my back. I looked at the clock. One hour, not two.

I rolled off the sofa and landed with my knees on the floor and stood up laboriously with my elbow heavy on the coffee table and sat down in the chair by the desk close to the sofa. I felt a little faint, a little grimy, as if I had been sleeping in the same clothes for several days instead of an hour and with a hangover. I lay my hands on the desk and looked at them. I no longer had a ring on any finger, but there was still a clear groove in the ring finger of my left hand, a whole year later, an obstinate groove that was one of the few visibles connecting my life to Turid's. It hadn't been to my advantage in downtown Oslo in the evenings. Many thought I took the ring off for that occasion only and the day after twisted it back on.

To the right on the desktop stood the silver Buddha. It wasn't really made of silver, but of something else, I didn't know what, and as a boy I often picked it up and ran my fingers over the smooth body until the metal became shiny with wear, while it still belonged to my mother and stood on the sideboard in the living room at Veitvet, it's mine, she always said, make no mistake, and none of us opposed her, her brother Jesper gave it to her, and Jesper was sacred, he was irreproachable, and he was dead. And I thought, what else do I have left from her that is of any value. To me. I have nothing. And then I tightened my fist hard around the Buddha and held it like that until my knuckles turned white and the incense bowl cut into my palm. Ashamed, I set it down again.

For years I had my desk in the bedroom, under the window facing the square. When Turid was asleep, I used a pencil, and it felt like the right place to keep it, a discreet place. To haul the desk out into the living room and let it take up space there would have been hubris, embarrassing and no good to anyone, but now, with the aching, half-empty bed behind my back, it didn't take long before I had to move the desk after all, and I pushed it into the corner where the TV had stood and placed the TV on hold in the opposite corner, and that meant I had to move the record player a notch closer to the door. It was the first thing I rearranged when I was on my own. I knew that it would seal the deal, there would be no way back, everything would be changed for ever, and it looked strange, radical, temporarily unbalanced, as if the floor, the whole room, sloped towards the door that she had walked through for the last time.

On the wall to the left I had hung the Chinese symbol for *no*, so I could easily see it in its silver frame when I needed to, and cleared a space for the Buddha right below between the gossamer-thin piles of manuscript. From where I sat at the desk I still had an oblique view of the bus stop and the parking space and the roundabout. I had kept that desk with me throughout all the years since it stood in the boys' room I shared with my brother at Veitvet, when my brother was in the country, at Christmas, in the summer and sometimes at Easter, my older brother that is, the other two were dead. Or, they weren't dead then, of course, they were dead now. Not back when I shared a room with my older brother. But it had become difficult to remember them between the four walls, to recall them sitting at the table in the living room on Sundays in front of the TV, having dinner there and not in the kitchen as we did on weekdays, because there was a speed-skating championship at the high-altitude rink in Alma-Ata or Lake Placid or Björn Borg playing John McEnroe in Båstad during the Swedish Open, and we all sat in a half-circle in front of the screen. It was difficult now to remember their weight on the stairs when the steps gave way beneath them, on their way up, on their way down, *that* weight, not my mother's weight, my father's, or the weight I myself had been assigned, remember their clothes on pegs in the hall, their high boots beneath, remember their voices from the first floor and the guitar chords spreading fan-like into the hallway in front of the toilet, remember their bodies present in any room, in flannel shirts, red, blue, coming in, going out. I closed my eyes tightly to force them up from the past, but I couldn't, I could no longer see them. It made me despair.

I went out into the hallway. First I took off the reefer jacket and then the James Dean jacket and hung the latter on the peg below the hat rack and put the reefer jacket back on and went into the kitchen and put on water for coffee, instant coffee, I was no gourmet, but I did not use hot water from the tap, as someone had once claimed. Before the water had begun to boil, I got restless and pulled the kettle off the hotplate and turned the hotplate to zero. I drank a glass of water, went to the toilet, washed my hands, brushed my teeth. I noticed the paraffin cans by the wall, where they had been for three weeks, and picked them up and remembered it was Sunday and set them down again. It's Sunday, I thought, they're not open. Instead I took the leather satchel I had from my father with the key items in it, folded A4 sheets of copy paper, my pencil case from secondary school, a book; it might be one of many I had laid one after the other on the floor to read again, *Alberta and Jacob*, *The Magic Mountain*, *Anna Karenina*, Steinbeck's *East of Eden*, which today was almost impossible to get through. This time it was John Berger's *G*. Then I let myself out of the flat and walked down the stairs.

It was half past one, the yard was deserted, on the cobble-stones you could see streaks of congealed soap. The double doors to the stable stood open, and it was dark in there, empty, so against all probability Jondal had already set off for Hamar in his own Volvo Duett. It was daring. It had rained up that way all night, in Hedmark, and who knew how muddy his car might get. It would pain him.

I drove along the ring road in a wide arc via Økern, as I had done all those times I worked the late shift at the factory, and entered the Grorud valley from the west on Østre Aker vei along the railway line at the very bottom of the valley with the tall red Siemens building in front of me on the slope to the left, on the right side Alnabru switchyard, which was incomparably more exciting in the dark with all its lights than it was during the day, and there, a bit further up the road, to the left behind the grove of trees, lay Veitvet school where I had spent the greater part of my waking hours for seven years, and I remembered every single one of them as painful, which surely they were not, how could they have been, but nothing else rose from my memory. Only a sudden, violent bitterness, certain teachers, certain pupils I would never forget and never forgive, and there lay the blocks of flats and terraced houses from the fifties like flights of stairs up the hills towards old Trondhjemsveien, and in the midst of it all was the dwelling

I grew up in, right below the telephone booth, and from the house that was my house you could see the luminous arrows pointing to any number of possible lives. Every day except Sunday my father would walk from the house down the road to Nyland train station a few hundred metres from Veitvet school, and then along Østre Aker vei.

It took half an hour, maybe forty-five minutes, to walk that stretch, and my father had walked it back and forth every single day except Sunday during the years when he went to work outside town, at Strømmen to the east, where a shoe factory lay on a plain, that was actually a barracks abandoned by the Germans when the war ended, and the factory had not yet gone bankrupt, but soon would, as most others already had, an army of shoe factories falling like dominoes behind the crumbling tariff walls. And at this very moment, in the Mazda more than two years after he died, I realised how big a part of his life he had spent going down the hills so early in the morning and nine hours later back up again in every kind of weather. There was always a bitter draught all the way down from the fjord and up on along the valley and it didn't stop until you were past Stovner and Vestli, and my father must have felt that draught, that cold against his back in the morning, and in the evening like darts of ice against his cheeks, and he may have been disheartened, his narrow eyes squinting against the wind, and also have felt helplessly alone, but it wasn't something I gave any thought to back then, I was too little, and to be honest, I never have.

*

I soon got to the exit where one road led up past Veitvet school towards Trondhjemsveien and further still, all the way up to the Nike battalion's camp and the football field we called Mil'tary field, for obvious reasons, and on along the paths through the big forest, but I didn't take that road, I drove around another way, in under the bridge on Østre Aker vei and then on down under the railway bridge and came up again on the opposite side, up the hill towards Alfaset cemetery.

It was a barren area with busy roads along both sides of the valley, there were petrol stations there with only diesel in their pumps, and the railway's workshops, locomotive sheds and switchyards and the depots of transport companies where delivery vans stood tightly packed in oblique rows, their accelerators stiff with expectation. There was an ironware factory there, and endless warehouses, but no dwellings to be seen down here with soothing green curtains, or yellow, only up on the hillsides did the blocks of flats stand each on their side, in each their cold mist, and it was steep, that final distance up to the eastern entrance of the cemetery.

It was a strange place to locate a cemetery, unworthy, it felt, you heard the roar from the heavy traffic no matter which way you turned, nothing to rest your eyes on, no gentle lines, nothing beautiful unless you found forklift trucks beautiful, or big lorries, or railway lines. I suppose some did. I liked railway lines. I liked endless goods trains with their bogies heavily loaded with timber, clanking over the rail joints. I liked power plants. I liked quarries and machines that did heavy work with elegant ease, but I did not like this hollow with the ice-cold river Lo running in the open and then underground and then in the open again towards the fjord, this windswept stretch with the cemetery abandoned in the midst of all the indecent nothingness of this place. That's why I hadn't been here since the funeral, or the funerals, to be precise. It was more than two years ago. I felt no pull making me want to come here, like in the movies, where the grieving falls to his or her knees before the gravestone and speaks to the dead, and the weeping grieving one declares the love that he, or she, failed to show the dead when they were alive. But I felt no need to fall to my knees. What they could no longer give me, they never gave me when they lived, and then I thought, that was unfair, I have just forgotten how it was, how we were, already I have forgotten. No, I said, you haven't forgotten, how could you have. I was confused, I didn't know what I had forgotten and what I could remember.

I locked the car and walked across the car park towards the chapel with my father's satchel under my arm and three hundred pages of John Berger under the flap, it was glued to my body on this day, and I walked past the chapel and down the footpath from the rise which my older brother two long years ago had called Boot Hill, and that's the way it looked. Anyway, it was this path I remembered from the funeral three weeks after the ship burned and it had finally been ascertained who was who in the burned-out corridors, in the cabins, in the toilets, and we came slowly through the rain that day, down the hill with the priest at the head of the long train of dark-clad people, adults and children and the four coffins on carts of the kind that are used in cemeteries because one assumes that people today are no longer strong enough to carry the coffins themselves, which probably has to do with our no longer being an agricultural nation nor an industrial nation and that children don't climb trees as much as they used to, et cetera, but either way I was moving along, holding on to a handle, pulling instead of carrying, as I would have done a generation ago, or two. Behind me walked the brother of mine who was still alive, we had been four, now we were two. He was staring at my back, I could feel it, and my gaze was fixed on the priest's back, and he must have felt it too, but clearly he was used to it, it didn't bother him, he was a fine priest. Many in the long procession carried umbrellas, but those of us who pulled the coffins, or the carts, could not, each holding our handle, and neither could the priest, and it probably never crossed his mind. I saw how the rain slowly soaked his hair and laid it flat against his skull and ran down his neck into his priest's collar, that had started to sag over his shoulder and practically dissolved in a way I thought proportional to what had happened. I felt the rain myself, in my hair, on the back of my neck and down beneath my white shirt and the charcoal-grey suit I had bought for this occasion only. I have to say, it had cost me dearly.

*

I came down the hill, and then I suddenly grew uncertain, on which side of the footpath was the gravestone, there were so many rows to choose between, and they all looked alike, and first I tried turning right, which felt most natural, and looked for a big smooth stone of red polished Grorud granite with room enough for four names, but most stones in this valley, in this part of the country, were carved out of precisely this material, and instead I tried turning left and walked in between the gravestones and headstones, and suddenly I saw the one that belonged to me, light red, practically pink, five graves in. A woman was standing a few stones further on before a simple white cross. She was pretty, it was easy to see, and I thought, actually there are few women who are not pretty. I couldn't think of any. In front of this woman the soil still lay piled up the length of a coffin, and the white cross told me the grave was new, that the engraving of the stone was not finished or the stone had not even been bought yet because death had been too sudden, completely unexpected by everyone around the now so deceased, that it had struck like light-ning, as once it did not far from our house when I was little, on the hill up towards the telephone booth spraying gravel to all sides, smashing windows one after the other and a man I didn't know went down for the count, and it must have perplexed them all who stood here not many days ago, their heads bowed, or that the woman here now, in front of the grave, could not get herself to make death permanent by carving it in stone.

*

As I approached, she cast a quick glance in my direction and abruptly began to move towards the footpath on the opposite side, as if she had been caught red-handed by a man who might tell on her, for maybe instead she was the dead man's mistress, if it was a he, and had not been present at the funeral, because she wanted to avoid the deceased's wife and the children they had together from seeing her standing there, and in that case speculating over who she was and how she had known the person in the coffin. And so she had come here on this day instead, to bid a final farewell and remember the secret, nervous, hectic, high-spirited moments they'd had together. It was not out of the question, but felt a bit over the top.

No one had tended the grave, no one had been there as far as I could see, to plant flowers, to weed and clear away the old dry and tangled scrub or light a candle for the dead. I felt bitter all of a sudden. That's not the way it was supposed to be. But I hadn't done it. My brother hadn't. Why should he come here to weed and tidy up, when I had not. And so I just stood there. The cold air from the fjord was in my back. The drone from the motorway leaned heavy against my body. The stone crosses of the fallen German soldiers stood at attention in straight rows behind the hedge a bit further up. I let go of the satchel and fell to my knees. Half a minute passed. It felt wrong. I read out the four names on the stone. It was strange to have them in my mouth, on my lips for the first time in a long while, but still it felt wrong. I felt God's gaze on the back of my neck. He said, what in the world are you doing. I despaired. I don't know, I said. I turned around. The mistress had stopped on the footpath. When our eyes met, she didn't drop her gaze, and so it was I who had to yield, as usual. I looked at the stone again. What little I was trying to hold together, fell apart. I took the satchel, and then I got up. The knees of my trousers had turned green and wet from the damp grass. What now, I thought. I looked over at the mistress. She could have been my mistress, I thought. But I didn't want a mistress. Or maybe I did, but it was too complicated, it was too late, my heart is not in it, I thought in English, not any more, and then I thought, English, you're so pretentious. But it was true all the same. My heart was not in it any more.

I walked out between the smooth stones towards the foot-path and passed the fresh grave. It was a man. He was thirty-five years old. It must have been an accident, perhaps while the two of them were together. Her, there on the footpath, and him, and only she survived. She didn't move. When I came abreast of her, I stopped. It may have looked a bit dramatic with the dirty trouser-knees, and embarrassing that she had seen me kneeling before the gravestone, but what's done is done. Hello, I said. Hello, she said. You're Arvid Jansen, she said. Yes, I said, that's me. I've read your books, she said. I like them. But why are they so sad. I don't know, I said, they just turn out that way, it's not really something I can control. That's odd, she said. Yes, I said, it's a bit odd. And then she nodded towards the graves, towards hers, and towards mine. Is it from the ship that burned. She said the name of the ship. It was a little difficult, hearing its name spoken. Yes, I said. That was terrible, she said. Yes, I said. Is that why your books are so sad. I'm not so sure, it started before that, I think, it really isn't that long since it happened, two years, a little more. Oh, that's true, she said, I wasn't thinking. And I turned and looked the same way that she was, over the gravestones and on down the row. Is it your husband, I said. No, it's an acquaintance. Was an acquaintance, she said. I felt like following up with another question, what kind of acquaintance, for instance, but I didn't. So we stood there. Her face had a calm I had never even been close to. Shall we walk up the hill together, I said. That would be nice, she said.

We walked shoulder to shoulder along the footpath in the cold draught and past all the rows with all their dead to either side and on up past Boot Hill where the urns with the ashes stood sturdily planted in the soil, and then up towards the chapel and the car park at the top. What a place to set a cemetery, she said. It almost makes you sad. Yes, I said, that's exactly it. I haven't been here once since the funeral. Until this day. My body goes all numb, I can't bring out a single feeling. But, she said, you were kneeling in front of the gravestone, it looked very powerful, to me at least, I couldn't leave. It was just something I did, I said, it was an experiment. Oh, she said, so, was it a successful experiment. No, I said, I didn't feel anything. How strange, she said, that you didn't feel anything. Yes,

I said, I wish I had felt something, but that's how it is, I felt nothing. I just felt odd. A little foolish, actually. She didn't reply, and I thought, why am I telling her something so private. What's it to her. Maybe it was the calm she had about her. If that's so, it's really sad, she said. Yes, I said, maybe it is. I wish it wasn't like that. How about you, I said. Did you feel anything. I have to say I did, actually, she said, and she stopped on the footpath and gave me her hand. Helene, she said. And she said her last name. I took her hand. Arvid Jansen, I said. I know, she said. Oh yes, I said, so you do. She smiled. We started walking again. May I ask if you're working on something now, she said, and I thought, why would I tell her about that. Usually I just replied, maybe, maybe not, time will tell, or something along those lines, but now I said, yes, I've started a new book. A novel, a novel of love. A novel of love, she said, that sounds nice, but does it end as unhappily as your other books. I can't rule that out, I said. How else could it end, that's all I know. It wasn't easy for her to respond, what could she have said. In any case I just made it up. The novel I was working on was something else entirely.

We came all the way up and stood there midway between the chapel and the car park. She gave me her hand again, and once more I felt how warm it was, and dry, and not at all reserved. I said, it was nice talking to you. Likewise, she said, although the circumstances could have been more cheerful. But I look forward to your next book. Don't expect anything too soon, I said, it's struggling to get out, maybe I'll never finish it, and she smiled again and said, I'm sure you've said that many times before. I didn't answer, maybe I was a little offended, and she noticed right away, oh, she said, maybe that wasn't the best thing to say, please don't get angry, it's really none of my business, but she didn't blush and she didn't stammer, she was just as calm. But you're right, I said, I have said it several times before, I say it often, I don't know why, so far things have worked out. They really have, she said, you can't say they haven't. Don't be sad, she said, and I replied, I'm not sad, and immediately I said, that was not true, I'm often sad, and again I thought, why am I telling her something so private. I'm sorry you feel that way she said. Yes, I said, so am I, and I said, you're a very calm person, aren't you. She was maybe about to leave, I thought I could see it in her shoulders, although she hadn't turned around yet, or maybe I was mistaken. I suppose I am, she said, and she smiled and said, but you're not, are you. No, I said. I'm never calm. That sounds exhausting, she said. Yes, I said. It is. Maybe you could talk to someone, she said, and actually it had crossed my mind, that I could, but I knew I would sit there mute, so it wasn't going to happen. There's no point, I said. Isn't there, she said. No, I said. It is what it is. I see, she said, if you say so, and in her eyes the goodbye-look came drifting, but I didn't want her to go. I tried to think of something to make her stay, and she seemed to hesitate, but I couldn't come up with anything, so she just smiled and said, take care of yourself, and good luck, and she turned and left.

I stayed where I was. I watched her cross the square towards the parked cars. She stopped at mine, and I thought I saw her peering into the driver's seat, but it was her own car that stood next to it, a black Mazda not quite as old as my champagne one. She could hardly know that the other one belonged to me. She got in, I heard the engine start, and at that very moment I began to run, it must have looked dramatic, with the satchel under my arm, and just as she was about to swing out between the brick posts, out on to the road that connects the two hillsides of the Grorud valley, she caught sight of me in the rear-view mirror and stopped, and I stopped running and walked instead very calmly the final steps over to her, a little short of breath. She rolled down the window. Hello, I said. Hello, she said. She smiled. Are you married, I said. No, she said, or, I am engaged, if it's still called that, but it seemed to me that she let it drift a little, she paused, and so I said nothing. Instead I waited. She waited too, and then she said, you remember my name. Helene, I said, and I said her last name. I'm the only one with that name, she said. I'm in the phone book. Thank you, I said. I gave her my hand through the window, and she laughed a little and took it, it was a bit daft, but what the hell.

She rolled up the window and started driving, and I walked back to my own car and got in and sat there behind the wheel without moving. I could still feel her hand in mine. I thought, is it her. I wasn't sure. I had imagined it to be easier, that I would see it at once, feel it, like a punch in the stomach, but not like the punch Turid gave me on Bentsebrua bridge. Nothing was easy, though, you had to make a decision, you had to make up your mind.

CHAPTER SEVENTEEN

It may have been in February, and if so at the very end of the month, there were flags flying the whole day in town and at the harbour. In any case it was well after Christmas, and it was not January. It was a bright day, it was brighter than it had been for a long time, there was a wind, and in the hills and woods surrounding Oslo there was snow, but not along the fjord, what had fallen was melting. I sat at the back of the bus with the leather satchel on my lap on the way down from Bjølsen to the city centre and felt expectant, but not happy. I thought, there must have been some good days these last few months, this last half-year, days when despite everything I had been content with the situation I found myself in, or at least approached it with stoic calm. Maybe this was one of those days, but now I no longer knew how to measure them, measure them against what, which other days. But I didn't see the girls so often now. If I were to compare, that too would have to be considered. It would have to carry some weight. How could it be otherwise. I felt no calm.

I lifted the flap of the satchel and got out the book I had brought with me that day. I opened it and read the first sentence: *I was born at four o'clock in the morning on the 9th of January in a room fitted with white-enamelled furniture and overlooking the Boulevard Raspail.*

I was seventeen years old when I took it home with me from the library, and I never returned it. It was her name that fascinated me. No one I had ever heard of had a name like that. It took nearly the whole book before she met Sartre, but that didn't matter to me, it was the way there, it was her I was interested in and the open hand she reached out to me, she said, come along, Arvid Jansen from Veitvet, come with me to Paris, across all borders, across time, let's walk together along the Seine, walk together down rue Jacob, walk on towards the Boulevard Saint-Germain, you have to meet my friends at Café de Flore, and she lifted me out of my boy's room, out into Europe, and gave me a powerful feeling, an intoxicating feeling of living *the big life*, but also a lonely feeling, for I knew I couldn't talk to anyone about it, and now, sitting in my usual seat at the back of the red bus twenty years later with the first volume of Simone de Beauvoir's autobiography in a Swedish translation open on my knees, thinking there had never really been anyone I could talk to about it or about anything else I was reading, but I got used to it and eventually it didn't occur to me that it could have been possible or even there being any point.

The bus sped down Uelands gate, with Ila and the Ila valley to the left down the long hill after Lovisenberg hospital, on a green wave across the intersection at Alexander Kiellands plass and on down along the knife-shaped park, it too to the left, and a block further down, on the corner with Bjerregaards gate, lay Aunt Kari's Café, which wasn't named Aunt Kari's Café but something else, I couldn't remember what. Maybe just Café. It had been closed down a long time ago, no one could remember it any more, but my mother waited on customers there in the years after the war, it was her aunt who was called Kari. My mother had come up here to Oslo via Copenhagen and Stockholm to look for work and freedom from the town she had lived in as a child and grown up in. Wearing a white apron and a knee-length dress made from shiny black waitress cloth she served lunch and dinner in the booths, and coffee and Danish pastries, with an almost mysterious smile on her lips and a jocular affability to which many were unaccustomed, a North Jutlandic motherliness, despite her young age. From the outermost booth it was easy to look out through the windows, in between the trees, at an angle through the park all the way over to the other side where the Jewish Salomon brothers' shoe factory lay between Maridalsveien and Akerselva river, right below Sannerbrua bridge, where my father stood on the inside by one of the machines and still hadn't treated himself to dinner in the café where he would meet his wife-to-be. Eating out was unheard of in my Baptist family, it was bordering on hubris. But now I could easily see him from the bus window as he came walking slowly for the first time through the trees in the park, with his slightly too thin winter coat and woollen gloves and his double-buckled leather satchel under his arm, which was identical to the satchel I had on my lap inside the red bus forty years later, but that day *he* was carrying it on his way down towards Aunt Kari's door, we're now in November 1948, less than a year before my oldest brother to nearly everyone's great surprise was born way out of wedlock, four years after the end of the Second World War. They were grown up, my parents, and more than that, but I still think it came as a surprise to them that a child emerged from the brief togetherness they'd had, this one short night, and it was certainly not planned. They were so different, not only of different nationalities, they lived in different worlds, in different cultures, and those cultures would never meet and create something in common, a common space, and in fact they never did, they were for ever set on separate paths.

I looked up from the book, there was a drumming on the roof, it was February, but it was not snowing, it was raining, it came on suddenly and intensely in the bend in the road at Fredensborg, a cloudburst, rapids, stage curtains of falling rain against the windows of the bus, the first act was over, something new was waiting in the wings. Let it come down, I thought. I lowered my head again and read on and didn't want to leave the book just as Simone had received the second-best grade at the university, but then I did anyway and looked out at the road again, which was Hausmanns gate now. In the almost dissolved air the bus floated past the heavy Baptist church at Number 22, where my father often came on Sundays on the tram down from Vålerenga with his brothers, four in all, but not Benjamin, the fifth and youngest, who died of consumption at the age of ten, nor with his sisters

Esther and Ruth, who were still living, but all that aside, down here on the tram they came, to hear the word of God of the Baptist brand and meet people they knew, young people, who gathered on the steps after the service to plan hiking trips in the mountains, bicycle trips across the high plains to the west and the deep fjords, with boxing gloves in their rucksacks and the Norwegian flag stitched on to the flap. But it had been a long time since the tram came into town from Vålerenga, few people know about that line today, but from my seat at the back of the bus it was easy for me to conjure up the heavy blue wagons clanking along the tracks from Galgeberg, past the Salvation Army's War Academy and the little petrol station on the corner with Strømsveien and on up Vålerenggata towards the tram loop at Etterstad, mostly observed from above, where in my third year I could be seen practically dangling on the window ledge three floors up in Number 5 before we moved to Veitvet. But now, past Jakob church behind the rain and the tall wide maple trees, my bus swung into Storgata, past Cordial pub and on down the familiar stretch of road in my father's city.

I stuck the bookmark in at the right place and put de Beauvoir in the satchel, tightened the old belt I used to hold the worn leather flaps together, tucked the satchel under my arm and stood up from my seat. My father carried the satchel in the same way, tight in his armpit, every day he went to work, to one of two shifts, or three. Carrying his satchel was not so difficult now, since he was dead. I would never have touched it while he was alive. And then he died, but he didn't die alone. I didn't know if it meant anything, if it gave any meaning to him in the moment before he died, that they died together, all four of them, whether they held each other's hands as they realised what was about to happen. They never did normally, while they lived, in life they hardly touched each other. Or if it gave any meaning to me. What meaning might that have been. Who would have dared give it meaning, what had happened, beyond the simple fact that it had. No priest would have dared, no government representative. It had its own heavy non-meaning and was closed within itself, inaccessible to me and to all others. But now, nearly two years later, I often took my father's satchel from the closet and filled it with books I was fond of and my pencil case and writing paper and the notebook from my youth with all the sad entries and the anti-nuclear sticker on the black cover and carried it with me under my arm to remind myself that he had in fact lived a tangible life. He had always been a quiet man, and it was easy to forget my father among the din of the others.

CHAPTER EIGHTEEN

It turned out to be one of those evenings. I got off the bus at Jernbanetorget. As I set foot on the pavement, it stopped raining, but I don't remember where I went after that, where I had my first beer, whether I talked to anyone, I must have, and I don't quite remember how I ended up there or how, if anyone had invited me, which was unlikely, but to my surprise, I found myself at a party for Nigerians, for Nigerians and companion. It was an odd way of phrasing it, but I saw it through the haze on a sign by the door. I was not Nigerian, nor was I anybody's companion. Not that I remembered. I hadn't been at the party for very long, or I didn't think so, that's not where I was first, but the transition was unclear. I remember asking for the toilet. A Nigerian laid his hand on my shoulder as if I was his little brother, and I might well have been, he was a big man, and I felt lost and in want of a brother, although I still had one left. I must have forgotten. The Nigerian man leaned forward with his heavy body and his heavy hand and set me on the right course, and it was a long walk, the room seemed enormous. When I came back with my satchel still wedged under my armpit, it felt like returning from an expedition. I felt a little woozy, and a woman who was not Nigerian took my hand and towed me out of the room and pushed me into a taxi which someone must have ordered. I thought I was being kicked out because my skin was not dark, and I said so and protested, but then she too got in. A little further down the block she asked the driver to stop and wait and got out of the car and crossed the street, over the tram tracks with the light from a street lamp on her hair, mahogany brown, my humpbacked grandfather would have called it, for he was a cabinet-maker and knew a thing or two about wood and its nuances and hues, he was dead now, he had died a few years back, it was a bit sad, really. He hadn't said much during his life, not that I had heard, and it wasn't easy to remember his voice, not even while he was still alive, but the world felt different now that he was gone, as if something of particular importance had been lost, and I missed him and the workshop he had had a few hundred metres from the dairy shop on Danmarks gate in the North Jutlandic town. When I was little his workshop had been golden and unending, there was the whine of the band saw and the mild hum of the hand drill cork-screwing shavings towards the floor on both sides of his workbench, and all the boards and stakes and lengths of wood stacked on brackets along the walls, and all the mouldings, the worn tools, the mirror frames, the cupboards, the chests of drawers that were fashioned by his hands, and when he was safely in his grave and evening came with sandwiches and beer served at the wake, my mother began to cry and slammed her fist on the table in front of the whole family, and to everyone's surprise said, he was a hard bastard.

I had never noticed. He wasn't like that towards me.

On the other side of the street she went into a kiosk where you could bet on horses, at the corner of an old tenement building, right before Bislet stadium. She wasn't gone for long, just a few minutes, and came back under the light of the street lamp with her hair still mahogany brown, and from the car window I could see her face for the first time as it was when she thought herself unseen, and she looked focused in a way that moved me. It really did. There was a slight stoop to her back, or it was something about her shoulders, that she bent forward, over herself, embracing herself, that she held on to herself, and that gave her an even more focused expression. She glanced quickly to both sides before she crossed the tram tracks coming back, and when she was next to me again, she took a small flat pack from her coat pocket and placed it in my hand, it was Mamba, the green condom. That's all they had, she said, I hope it's all right. Sure, I said. She leaned forward between the seats and said, you can drive now, and the chauffeur put the car in gear and drove on down the street, it must have been Pilestredet, I thought I saw it on a sign. But really it was difficult to see anything clearly that wasn't brightly lit, and not much was, for in the streets a strange haze drifted above the asphalt which erased most signs and shop windows and bus stops, even the colours of the buildings' walls were dissolved and everything was the same wet grey on our drive through the city, dream-like, swaying and silent, so I closed my eyes, and I may have slept a little, but I wasn't gone for long, and I was certain she didn't notice.

And then we were out of the taxi, which she paid for, and on our way through a gate in yet another old tenement in a street I was sure I knew the name of. Again she took me by the hand and led me, but there was no need to, I followed her gladly, and I wasn't that drunk either, I didn't stagger, but walked straight as a rod across the backyard and through a corridor and all the way down that corridor, and through yet another door we walked into a small bedsit behind all of this, at the heart of the building, with a bed set high up on the wall, unusually high, like a bunk bed without a bottom bunk, only higher, to make more room on the floor for the few things she owned, a sofa among them.

But then nothing came of it. I liked her, I thought she was pretty in every way, it's true, she was likeable too, and kind, that was easy to see, and I needed that, for someone to be kind to me, for someone to wrap me up and take care of me, for someone to put me in a bag and carry me with them, on visits or excursions, to places by the sea, the wind there, for no one had been kind to me in a long time, except maybe Mrs Jondal, it wasn't healthy living like that. Maybe someone had tried and I had stopped them oblivious to their intentions, but I really didn't think so.

*

And nothing happened. Nothing in my body responded to her call. It was an odd feeling, to sense her hand on my skin and not be able to respond, it was distressing, and I found it difficult to just lie there, but then she said, don't worry, it's all in your mind, it's of no consequence, she said it in posh English, but I was sure it was of some consequence, for she was lying on her stomach now and not on her back as she had done only a moment before, and I couldn't quite see her face, if she was sad, for her hair was long and mahogany brown. I was sure she was sad, and she who'd spent money on condoms and all, and it didn't seem fair that I should draw the highest card, it would have been insensitive, so instead I said, you may be right, that it has to do with my life, the way it is now, even though she hadn't said anything of the sort, I can't get any air, you see, I said, and that makes it difficult to do sensible things. You can't get any air, she said, not even up here with me, and I said, no, but it's not your fault. Now she grew worried, it was the maternal instinct, it could strike at any time, right out of the blue. She hoisted herself up on her elbow and looked at me, she had been crying, but she wasn't crying any more. You can't breathe, she said, is it like with asthma, and I said, maybe a little like that, I mean, I can breathe, or else I would have died, but I can't get any air, you see. Isn't that the same thing, she said, no, not quite, I said, and she said, it sounds like that to me, and I suppose it was easy to think, then, that she was a little, not simple exactly, but that she asked me things in a way that seemed a bit childish, but that's not how it was, it was she who lowered herself to my level. No, I said, it's not quite the same thing. Maybe not, she said, but it's all up here, she said, this is where it happens, and she tapped herself lightly on the forehead. And I'm sure she was right, although it didn't feel that way, that it was there. But then she smiled faintly and said, come, and she turned with her back to me and lifted the duvet, and I lay close to her, and she was very warm, it flooded through me, oh Father, I thought, who art in heaven, how warm she is, and she laid the duvet down again over us both, and with my chest to her back she fell asleep at once, and I fell asleep.

When I woke up, she was still sleeping. I knew where I was straight away. I had fallen asleep as if on a Persian rug hovering under the ceiling deep inside a tenement I was certain lay on Nordahl Bruns gate in the centre of Oslo city. I was floating there close up against an unfamiliar body which was not itself unfamiliar to this bed, two metres or more above the floor with a steep ladder down and an untouched pack of Mamba, the green condom, by the headboard. And then she woke up, and I felt it against my stomach, that she froze, held her breath, and went soft again, and I wondered if she knew who it was lying naked up against her back, if she remembered, and then she said, hello, without turning around, and I said, hello. I don't know your name, she said, and I thought, she doesn't say 'know' the way I do, we're not from the same part of town, my name is Arvid, I said. Arvid, she said. Yes, I said, I'm from Veitvet. Where is that, she said, but this time I didn't answer. Instead I said, my body feels quite different now. But are you getting any air, she said, and I said, yes, now I am. She turned slowly over on her back, and I gave her the space she needed, and not long after, when we were drifting, far out, I could see the flames moving across her face, and she didn't look focused in the same way now that she had the night before, instead her face looked mild, smooth, almost, and with her eyes closed and her mouth slightly open she let herself go, that's what happened, she let herself go, she accepted me, she trusted me, she just let herself go, I thought, and she smiled, but she didn't know that she was smiling, and I saw the flames moving across her face, and she breathed very deeply, and every time she drew her breath in, it seemed to lift her a little, and it lifted me, and I thought, she is giving herself over, this is what they call giving oneself over, and I hadn't seen it before, not in a face like the face beneath me, and I thought, Jesus, what courage, and it impressed me and moved me and made me happy, and it made me proud because I was the one she trusted, and it made me sad too, for I would never ever be able to do what she did, give myself over with such trust on my face, it was not possible for a man in my situation.

Before I left, she found a beer coaster from Frydenlund breweries, and she broke it in two and wrote her phone number on the back of one piece, and I was to write mine on the other, which I did, and then we swapped pieces, and in the weeks that followed she called me a few times, but it wasn't possible for me to take the phone and answer her, or rather I did pick up the phone, if I hadn't it would have been unlawful, but I didn't give her an answer, and so I didn't call her either. I didn't know what to say. When I left her bedsit that morning, I felt almost certain. It was her. But after a few days I was in doubt, and then I grew certain again, it was not her. I wished it was, but it wasn't. And so she stopped calling. It felt like a big relief. Not just for me, but for her too, was what I thought, so she didn't have to beg, it's not good for anyone to have to beg for love and not receive any.

But then she called one last time, she said, I'm not calling to ask you for anything. I understand. It is what it is, and you are who you are. There's not much I can do about it. But my dear Arvid Jansen from Veitvet, I want you to know one thing. You have no idea what you're missing. You really don't. It suddenly struck me. And that's sad for you, I mean it, but you have absolutely no idea.

CHAPTER NINETEEN

It's March, deep into the month. That much is clear. Seven months have passed since Turid departed, nearly two years since the ship burned. It's late in the evening, the ditches are bare on either side of the road, it's bare and dark up the hills towards Disen. It's dark between the street lamps on the way out of town, dark between the windows of the houses, the blocks of flats, but inside, behind the windows I can see the bright living rooms, flickering TV sets, lit-up kitchens filled with laughter where bottles of wine are opened, it's Saturday. I see lit bedrooms, fluttering curtains despite the cold season, but also bedrooms in darkness, in many of them acts of love unfold under extinguished lamps, in others their absence prevails. Most of them stay dark, it's quiet in there, someone is sleeping, calm and safe, in other rooms the lamps are lit again and someone rises from the bed and walks across the floor, drawing the fingers of both hands through their hair, why do I freeze when I should have been soft, why do I never let myself go, what's wrong with me, is there something wrong with her. Is *that* it. It can't be, it's me, it's me, someone says in the room, and it's cold outside on the roads and there is snow in the air, at least an expectation of snow, you can feel it easily, on the rising wind. The sky is clear, a few stars, and yet. Something is going to happen. I drive out of town from Sinsen along Trondheimsveien towards Grorud. On the hills going up, right after the roundabout, lies Aker hospital where I was born, where my father almost died and my mother almost died, and then she died, and my father died, but none of them in the hospital. On a shelf at the top of the hill lies the racecourse. From the tower there I could often hear the voice of the announcer through the crackling loudspeakers, but I never saw the horses, never the sulkies nor the drivers in their silks, not until I made my own money. My father never went there. He didn't care much for horses.

After the long bend at Lunden, there is Linderud Manor, a white plantation-sized building in behind the smooth pond between the birches, none of them visible now, not the pond, nor the birches, just a few lights on in the main house, and then down to the right Veitvet with Northern Europe's first 'shopping centre' steeply down to the right as you drive past, and the Underground line also to the right before it switches sides under the bridge close to the women's penitentiary and heads left towards the hill and the horse fields and Rødtvet farm, which is not a farm any more, but still was when I was little. Anyway I wouldn't have been able to see it now, or where it lay, but I remember the man in the boiler suit, the cows calmly in a row on their way home from pasture. I remember them as being dappled, brown and white, maybe black and white. I always saw them from a distance. They were from another age. It's we who are here now, my father said.

*

At Grorud I pass the church and the churchyard where Audun's father was buried, the wild man of the forest with a Luger in his rucksack, and Audun, who hated his father, began to cry between the gravestones against all the odds. With the churchyard behind me the cliff drops steeply down towards the secondary school which was once my school for two years until I dropped out a year early and never looked back, the flaking plaster, the wilted ivy, the faded buildings at the bottom of the valley by the railway line and the yellow station building and the Star Blocks where Henrik and Erik grew up. I could have driven down there out of curiosity or dubious nostalgia, but instead I drift on up towards Gjelleråsen and down again to Lillestrøm along the airport and the hangars and the jet fighter mounted on a plinth and then Åråsen football stadium and further still, across the plain, across the Glomma river on the bridge with Fetsund timber booms way down to the right, the red log drivers' cabins in the shadows and the asphalt black over the bridge and dry and yet strangely glistening, polished. Outside the car everything is moving. Everything swaying. On the bridge along the railing the lamp posts all have a banner from the bend at the top to halfway down the pole with the log drivers' silver peavies on the green cloth whipping on the wind, and the wind comes from the north, rushing down along the dark river close to the water and is sucked up under the bridge, and I can feel it high up in the air on my way across, the sudden gusts, the car rocking, but we stay in our lane, and we are not we. We are not several people in the car, we are just me. It's near to midnight, it's still today, soon it will be tomorrow.

After the bridge I turn off at the petrol station behind the bus shelter in the orange light where the flag ropes snap against the poles, and stop at one of the pumps and switch off the engine and sit there behind the wheel looking into the shop. I thought it was open all night, all week, but it closes at eleven. No lights are on in the shop. I have a full tank. It's not that. Maybe I could sleep here, in the shadows behind the car wash, I know someone who does every time she's on her way out to Høland, but she sleeps during the day and only for half an hour. In any case it won't work. There are houses right across the road, everyone is at home, it's the weekend, and I'm not tired enough. So I back up in a U-turn between the petrol pumps and drive out again and up the hill and to the right on National Road 22 at the junction. *Mysen*, it says, *48 km*, and for long stretches it's completely dark, kilometre after kilometre of dark forest on either side towards the south, no street lights, wide bends, sharp curves and down into third gear, down into second at the worst. In brief flashes towards the west I sense something open, a surge which may be the sky above the big lake that Glomma flows into, an emptiness, an expanding space and the feeling of height and the sudden fear that comes with it. I can't see but I can hear the rush of the wind in the trees on both sides of the car, the trees bending, chafing and striking against each other, everything's in motion.

There is hardly any oncoming traffic, but that doesn't make me cut corners so I keep to my side of the road with a good margin, my headlights on full beam and the white line along the crash barrier in the corner of my eye and the longer stretches have no barrier at all, only the white line faded in some places, in others almost worn out. I hold on to it, what little I can see, until my eyes hurt, a prisoner of the white line, according to Joni Mitchell.

In the long hill up from a hollow, where a closed-up deep-frozen-looking house lies forbidding and all on its own at the bottom of the V in the shadow of shadows, I suddenly see the orange stripes of a sign for a turn-off to the left, a side road with a name in the spirit of the explorer Helge Ingstad, and on impulse I turn there and cross National Road 22 into the smaller road named Vinlandsveien maybe too fast and skid as if there was snow under my tyres and not gravel, but manage to correct my course and then ease off the accelerator. From the car I see a tumbledown barn on an escarpment and a house with its outside light on, but no others. I drive past. The sky is no longer clear. What earlier had a shine to it is hazy now and woolly at the edges. I drive along a small lake, the headlights sweeping open water, the wind whips the water into foam, a few more outside lights, and then nothing. Only woods and darkness and the narrowing road, and the wind, and I drive until I see a lay-by where I can park my car and stop, but let the engine run and the headlights shine. I open the door. My body feels fine. There's no panic. I swing my legs out and walk over to the edge of the beam and do what I have to do, and return and put the back seats down, spread my duvet out on top of the fitted mattress and turn the key in the ignition, and it's quiet. I switch on the light in the back and keep it on while I undress, lower one of the windows halfway and lie down under the duvet. Then switch off the light. Like in a ship's cabin. I lie there for a while listening to the powerful wind sweeping the valley and the even bigger sound of what might have been the Skagerrak sea, on the way across to Denmark, and have that feeling of comfort I always have onboard a ship when it rolls with the sea, lifts and sinks, striking the waves, a sense of freedom, an exhilaration, almost, though many would have thought it to be the other way round, for me. And I fall asleep.

I wake up, and it's completely still. No wind. It's not light, but it's lighter. I hoist myself up on my elbow. It has snowed. Not a huge amount, but still a good deal. It has snowed in through the window, there is snow in my hair. It's no longer snowing, it's a little cold, even under the duvet, so I fumble around in the half-light and find my sweater over the seat in front and pull it on and lie down under the duvet again. And fall asleep.

The next time I wake it is light, it's half past eight, that's late for me. But I feel fine. I turn over on my stomach, lift my head and look out. White everywhere, the spruces white, the road white. In the middle of the road there is a horse. It's not big, more like an Icelandic horse, only more harmonious, its legs and body fit together as they do not on the horses from Iceland, its fur is woolly and yellow. I can see from the tracks it's been close up against the car, peered in maybe, now it's standing still in the road with a dusting of snow on its back, and the snow melting against its warm fur, and its white breath emerging in even thrusts from its nostrils. The horse has no harness whatsoever, not even a halter. I try to get dressed very carefully so it won't see me and run off. I get my trousers on, but my socks and shoes are under the seat. It's too complicated. So instead I open one of the back doors as quietly as I can and wriggle my way out head first and get up and stand there barefoot in the snow. It doesn't feel very cold. The horse turns its head, watching me, but stays put. I walk calmly towards it. It's a mare. Hello, horsey, I say. What are you doing here, I say in a light voice, and she doesn't move, she snorts and shakes her head and sees me coming through the snow. I walk close up to her and lift my hand and stroke her under the chin, and she likes it and stretches her neck, so I stroke her down along her neck several times. I lay my hand on the horse's back and it's wet from the melting snow and I lean my forehead against her shoulder, lightly at first and then with my full weight and whole self, I would have fallen had she moved, but she doesn't move. With my nose pressed into her fur I cry a little, for it's a very touching woolly horse, and I think, she and I have something in common, here in this valley, all alone with no harness on, and I cry a little more, and then I say, that's enough, and stop. I straighten up, I stroke my hand along the horse's flank and say, thank you, you're a fine horse, and I blush as I say it, I can feel it in my cheeks. It's pathetic, like in a Disney movie. On the other hand, how pathetic can it be if no one can see you or hear you. Not very.

Suddenly my feet feel urgently cold. I let my hand slide off the horse and turn around and walk back to the car hopping on one leg in the snow, open the back door and find my socks and shoes under the seat and sit down and put them on. I look up. She has followed me. My feet are so damn cold, I say, almost expecting an intelligible answer. Perhaps that's not quite what I get, but she comes all the way over and lowers her head and pushes me with her forehead almost into the car, takes a step back and does it again, not hard, but firm, what the hell, I think, what is this, and then I think, maybe she wants something, maybe she's hungry and the snow makes it difficult and nothing green has appeared yet. Hold on a moment, I say. I walk around the car and open the door to the passenger seat and take from the satchel the wrapped sandwiches I have brought with me for breakfast and walk back around the car and open the wrapping and take out a slice of bread and give it to her. She takes it and drops it in the snow in front of her and eats it from there. Horses like peanut butter. I take the other slice and get into the seat with my legs stretched out of the car, and in that way we have breakfast together, it gets warmer around us, steam rising from the snow, from the horse's back, just a few scary steps from the car a steep cliff drops down towards a long, narrow and dim lake I didn't notice last night. I can barely see it through the haze which thickens fast and soon hides the lake entirely. I have to get home, I think, it's daytime, it's nice here, she's a nice horse, but I have to get home.

I put my jacket on and say to the yellow horse, I have to go now, and so do you, to where you live, we don't have wild horses in Norway, you're not supposed to be alone, you're a herd animal, do you understand, and I'm not your herd. I slap her rump, not hard, but firm and shout, giddy-up! to get her to move, like in a cowboy movie when someone is about to be hanged from a tree. She ambles away, but stops only a few metres out on the road. I get in and start the car and turn it carefully away from the cliff and out onto the road in a half-circle through the snow. The horse is standing right in front of the car and refuses to move. I drive slowly towards her and just barely push her with the bumper, and she makes way reluctantly, only a few steps at a time, and when at last I am leaving the valley, I can see her in the rear-view mirror still standing there, pale and yellow in the white haze.

CHAPTER TWENTY

I remained in the car in the car park behind the chapel at Alfaset cemetery. The mistress had driven off. Helene. My mind had gone blank. I looked at my watch, it was odd how the hours extended on this day, they stretched, they got longer, they were elastic, it seemed they could contain everything. I still had plenty of time. I turned the key and drove out on the road and straight down under both bridges, the railway bridge, then the bridge below Østre Aker vei and didn't turn to either side but went up Veitvetveien past the school, which still looked as it did when I was a pupil, and on up and parked in front of the bowling alley right below the Underground station and got out of the car and walked up the little hill, into the upper deck of the shopping centre and past the kiosk we used to call the Invalid when I was a boy. There was nothing wrong with the man behind the counter that I had seen, but then I had never seen him anywhere else than behind the counter. It could have been anything wrong. The kiosk was open now, but nothing else. It was Sunday.

By the statue of the naked pigeon-lady I ran into Magnar, he was sitting on a bench, smoking, I hadn't seen him in twenty years, not since I moved, but I knew him at once.

Hi, Magnar, I said. Arvid, he said and smiled, it's been a long time. He got up, he had filled out, but he was smartly dressed. He was back then too, twenty years ago. He had a mother from Finnmark and a father from Bergen and they didn't let him forget it. Maybe they were still alive, mine were not, but he didn't mention them, and I was grateful for that. He seemed happy to see me, we were in the same class in primary school, he always sat in the last row, not because he was long-sighted, but because he wanted his back to the wall. We shook hands. So you are riding the old hunting grounds too, I said a little flippantly, but in fact I wasn't, this was not where I was headed. No, I live here, he said, I moved back three years ago, I was always homesick for Veitvet. Wow, you were. Yes, he said. Weren't you. No, I said. Or yes, in a way I suppose I was. I've missed the sledges, but that's not something you can move back to, and I've missed Inger Johanne, to be honest, her I have missed, and Magnar said, you mean her in our class, Hanne, who sat up front by the door. Yes, I said. But she sat by the teacher's desk, didn't Øyvind sit by the door. Yes, maybe you're right, but Jesus, Arvid, Hanne wore glasses, Magnar said. So what, I said. No, maybe you're right. There was something about her, Magnar said, but what was it. It was her mouth, I said. What was it about her mouth, then. I don't know, I said. But it was definitely the mouth. Magnar stroked his lips with two fingers, then he nodded, it was pretty, he said, but it must have meant more to you than it did to me. And that had to be true. How could it have meant more to anyone than it did to me. It could not. And how she got so mad at times, I said. That much is true, Magnar said. He laughed. He offered me a cigarette. Prince with filters. I didn't really like ready-made cigarettes other than my party smokes, Blue Master, without filter, but I said thanks, broke the filter off and stuck the cigarette in my mouth, and he lit it for me, with a match and a cupped hand, as in a *film noir* from the forties, we always did it that way. I drew the smoke down and slowly let it flow out again. It tasted pretty good. Prince was a strong cigarette. So how was it, moving back, I said, did you find what you were homesick for. He wasn't laughing any more, you know what, he said, I had forgotten how miserable I was, it's so hopelessly stupid, how could I have forgotten, I, who dreaded going to school every single day, and to put it grandly I have walked up and down along the paths of childhood, and to tell you the truth I didn't find one fucking metre that gave me any joy. God, the things that happened on those paths.

He wanted to be poetic, but it was true, I too remembered, they wouldn't leave him alone. I was not one of them, but I didn't protect him either. You weren't so bad, he said. Maybe not, I said. We stood there in silence, he said nothing, I said nothing, and then I said, how could you forget, but it wasn't really a question, and he said, how could I forget, and it wasn't really an answer. It's incredible, he said, how could I forget. Now I just want to get away, it's the only thing I want, but selling the flat is difficult. Are you back on Beverveien, I said. Yes, he said, in the same building, I live just two doors down from the flat I grew up in. It's so stupid. And what a dump. I didn't quite agree. Audun had lived on the floor above Magnar before he moved in with Abrahamsen, in the bend where I lived, and I had liked it at Audun's. I liked walking along the Sing-Sing balcony with the wire mesh fence and the doors all in a row, like in a prison, to ring Audun's doorbell at the very end. I liked the opera records his mother played, but would never have played them myself. And I liked his neighbours just as I liked my own neighbours, they were the same kind of people all over Veitvet, there were shuttering carpenters and bricklayers, brewery workers, there were sailors and lorry drivers, tinsmiths and plumbers and office workers and two or three teachers, and a doctor, actually, in the same building as me, but he moved. Down the road there was a journalist, a deacon or two, and a sexton in purple stockings, even though he was a man. Several old *Nasjonal Samling* members lived there, they had supported the Norwegian Nazi Party during the war, they were the exception, I guess, and I knew well who they were, but there were even more communists. Why wouldn't I like them, they were the same as me, my father was a factory worker, my mother a factory worker, and I felt more at home among them than I did at the university, which anyway came to nothing. I had passed the preparatory exams. I had registered for a basic course in history and turned up at the faculty along with students from the whole country speaking different dialects, and the lecturer delivered a short introduction about Africa in the colonial era, which was the theme we had chosen, and when he had finished, he said, next time it would be good if you split up into colloquium groups. Colloquium groups. I looked around me, they were all young, as I was, unfinished, keen, and wanted nothing more than to get started, to move on, first degree, another degree, maybe a Master's, and they wrote down in their notebooks which books to buy, and they laughed and helped each other with the spelling. I didn't know any of them. And I realised I wasn't going to ask anyone in the room what a colloquium group was. I didn't have it in me. Okay, I thought, that's it, then. I slowly withdrew from the crowd and walked down the corridor and down the staircase and quietly out through the glass door on the ground floor, across the big wide cobbled square and all the way to the loop where the trams turned, and sat down at the very back of the first blue one that arrived and rode it down all the hills into the centre of Oslo.

The week after, I got a job at the main post office in Prinsens gate, in the package sorting department. It was a half-time position, but I didn't need much, just money for books and food.

You can look back, Magnar said, you can long to go back and make yourself believe things, but you can't go back. To me that sounded fairly obvious, but maybe it was easy to forget all the same, and I said, you have a point there, no doubt, and decided not to walk down past the red telephone booth and the house where Inger Johanne had lived, which I easily might have done being already at Veitvet, and then walk along the flagstones past the doors at the back of the eight-family dwelling I grew up in at the bottom of the hill and maybe meet an old neighbour or two and talk to them about what had been and how life had turned out for this one and that one, for Ellen and Uno, for Johnny and Rita, for Tor Erik, but they would definitely want to talk about the burning ship too, and I did not.

I bent down and put out what was left of the cigarette against the plinth where the pigeon-lady stood, just as I had done twenty years earlier, and blew the ashes off the stub and put the stub in my jacket pocket, which I also did back then. I looked at my watch. Suddenly I was short of time. I said, Magnar, I have to go now. I hope you manage to sell that apartment soon. I took his hand and said, hopefully we'll see each other before too long. I'm sure we won't, Magnar said. Who knows, I said, why not. But he was right, and I asked myself if I minded, but I didn't. I couldn't remember thinking about him a single time in twenty years and was certain to forget him and forget his despair.

CHAPTER TWENTY-ONE

The babysitter lived in a block of flats I knew well, in Rælingen, on the hill east of Strømmen and Skjetten, at the very edge of Østmarka forest. It took twenty minutes to drive there from Veitvet on a Sunday.

She had lived in a house with an orchard at Tåsen, but had moved here because Turid lived here, but Turid didn't live here any longer by the time she arrived, we had moved again, Turid must have forgotten to tell her. I knew who she was and I didn't like it. It was Merete, the colourful who had once kissed me at a party, but who probably didn't remember the kiss, nor the taste of it, and if she did, must have tried to repress it and had even entered my apartment at Bjølsen uninvited to fill a cardboard box with cups and plates on a mission for Turid and had seen me lying defenceless, half-naked on the sofa, and took pleasure in it. But that was a year ago. I wasn't that me now.

I parked in front of the building in the space reserved for guests. There was just one slot free, and probably none of the other cars belonged to a guest. They hardly ever did. I turned the rear-view mirror until I could see the upper part of my face, and I closed my eyes and rubbed my whole face with flat palms many times and pulled my hair tightly back with my nails scraping against my scalp and opened my eyes and couldn't see any difference. I twisted the mirror back into place, but stayed in my seat. I was dreading this, I had to admit, and I regretted the offer I had made earlier that day. But at the same time I longed to see the girls. We had been together for a week that summer, in the Danish house. I had ended up drinking too much on the first evening. That was stupid of me, I was alone with them, something might have happened, but I don't think the girls noticed. The morning after I had a headache, but I got up early anyway and went out into the kitchen and poured the remains of the bottle of Famous Grouse into the sink. It was a litre bottle, I had bought it on the boat on the way down, as I always did, but it wouldn't do. I couldn't, and without remorse I let the expensive drops run down the drain, for things had turned out all right, I was relieved, and it would not happen again. I was about to screw the cap back on the empty bottle when Vigdis came out of the room with the bunk beds which the three of them slept in, as they had done at home, at Bjølsen, when they still came for weekends. She saw me at once and knew what I had done, and she didn't say anything, but nodded faintly as she lifted her gaze from the bottle and met mine, and just then, for a brief moment, she was above me, she was the more adult with an insight and a command of the situation which I lacked. It couldn't be true, it *wasn't* true, she was not yet thirteen, and still, a feeling of shame and inferiority came over me. But the rest of the week it all went well, I couldn't remember better days, and Vigdis was a child again. I hadn't seen any of them since.

I got out of the car and walked across the lawn taking the shortest route where after many years there was a path across the grass, the same path I had walked so many times up to my own entrance and in past the door to the flat on the ground floor which had once been ours, Turid's and mine, in the two years before we moved back to Bjølsen. Because I insisted. I couldn't live there any more, I refused to.

I walked up the stairs to the first floor and stopped in front of the door to the right, where there was only one name on the door plate. Or, there had been two, but the other name, the man's name, someone had scratched out, or attempted to scratch out, with a nail, by the looks of it, or a screwdriver. I didn't know who that man was or had been. I stood there for a while, I hesitated, I thought stupid thoughts, then I said half out loud to myself, come on, for God's sake, just ring that bell, and pressed the button.

At once someone came running in the hallway, I heard quick steps and a bright laughter, and the door swung open, and it was little Tone, she hung onto the door handle and went with it a way out and stood there surprised beyond the threshold, is that you Daddy, she said, red-cheeked and breathless, that's right, I said. Oh, she said, Vigdis, she shouted over her shoulder, it's Daddy who's here, but it wasn't Vigdis who first came into view, it was Turid's friend Merete, with her boy's haircut, her motorcycle hair, except her hair was long now and fell to her shoulders, and was even a different colour than when I saw her last. It was a bit odd, I thought, like a wig, and it didn't make her look any younger. She was far from pleased. Is that you, she said. It is, I said. I can't deny it. If I'd known, I wouldn't have let Tone open the door. Is that so, I said. Turid was supposed to come and get the girls, she said, we had an agreement, it was not you. Maybe not, but here I am. I don't think that will work, she said, and I said, of course, it will work out fine. And then Vigdis stood there, and finally Tine came and peered out and said, Hi Daddy. Hi Tine, I said, are we leaving, she said, and I said, yes, you are. That suits me perfectly, she said. I had to smile, that's good, I said, and Vigdis, why don't you just get dressed and we'll leave. Okay Daddy, she said. She looked happy to see me. Then she took their clothes from the pegs in the hallway and handed them out and started getting dressed herself. I don't think this will work at all, Merete said. Vigdis, she said, hang those clothes back up again, please, and we'll wait for your mummy. She's not coming, I said. What nonsense, Merete said, she'll be here soon, why wouldn't she. She simply isn't coming, I said. Trust me. Vigdis stood, her jacket in hand, and looked at me and looked at Merete and looked at me again, and I smiled and nodded, and she smiled back, and Merete said, put that jacket back, Vigdis, right this minute, but then Vigdis turned and started pulling the zipper up, and now she was staring straight down at the floor, she said, you don't decide over me. You don't decide over Tine and not over Tone and not over me, we're going with Daddy. No you are not, Merete said, do you understand, we are going to wait for your mummy, and she wanted to pull the jacket off Vigdis and took hold of one sleeve and pulled on it hard, but the zipper was up to her neck now and Vigdis lost her balance and fell as if from a great height, I could see her closed eyes and her tight lips on her way down before she struck the shining parquet with her left shoulder first, and her fair hair swept like a wing across her face and spread out, fan-shaped, on the parquet. That fall must have hurt, but she didn't cry, she pressed her lips together and got up slowly, still staring at the floor. Tine stood there rigid with her trousers up to her knees, and Tone with her head barely poking through her sweater, they were thinking, what will happen now, what can happen now, anything can happen now. I was on my way into the hallway to lift Vigdis up off the floor, but I was too late, she was already back on her feet, and with her hand in a fist and her eyes closed and all the force a twelve-year-old girl is able to muster, she hit Merete in the side, right below the ribs, where the kidneys are supposed be, and Merete hunched up, but it was shock more than the blow itself that made her lose her balance, she opened her mouth and was about to say something, but instead she had to put her hand out and grip the peg rack to stop herself from falling backwards, and with the other hand she struck out before going down on her knees and she hit Vigdis in the back of neck, and Vigdis fell again, and this time tears began to run down her face, but she didn't utter a sound. Just then I felt sorry for Merete, for she would never forget this day, and every time she thought back, she would have this unpleasant feeling in her stomach and remember that this was the last time she was allowed to see her friend Turid's daughters and probably Turid herself and would for ever after put the blame on me. I didn't mind so much, but for her there was no way back, the bridge was in flames behind her.

I walked quickly into the hallway and helped Vigdis up from the floor and took hold of her the way I'd done before, and she was heavier now than the last time, at Hadeland when we ran along the hillside, but I had worked out a lot over the past six months, I wanted to look present-able with my shirt off too, and now I lifted her high up off the floor and set her down again on her feet and whis-pered in her ear, it's all right, Vigdis, and she whispered back, okay Daddy, it's all right, and dried her tears with the back of her hands, her skin white under her eyes. Do you have your rucksack, I said. It's behind the door, she said. Then take it and go out on the landing and wait there, I said, and she did as I told her to and took her rucksack and went out on the landing and stood by the railing to wait. I took her sisters' clothes over my arm and their little rucksacks, and right next to me Merete was on her way up off her knees, and then I said very loudly, like hell you're getting up until I've gone, and she sank back down. I hadn't expected that. She wasn't herself any more than I was me, and then she started to cry with her hands covering her face, and why shouldn't she, I thought. And with one little girl in each hand I crossed the threshold through the wide open door, and at the same moment the neighbour on the opposite side of the landing came out of his door and stood there stiffly holding his house key up as if to show me how rare it was, how valuable, and he knew me from the old days, from the Party, his name was Olavsen, I saw it on the door plate, in the Party he was Konrad. He didn't live here when I lived here. I said hello, and he said, hello Jansen, it's been a long time, and I said, likewise, but how did you know my name, I didn't know *your* name, I said, until now, and he said, I do read the papers you know. Shit, of course, I forgot. I keep forgetting. You've done all right for yourself, he said. I guess I have, I said, and suddenly we heard Merete shouting, Olavsen, he's kidnapping the children, you have to stop him, you have to call the police. Olavsen and I looked at each other, are you, he said. I shook my head, no, I said, and he said loudly, as far as I know, Merete, these are Jansen's children, they're not yours, and then he locked his door, gave me a nod and walked calmly down the stairs. Merete was still on her knees, crying. With a kick of my heel I slammed her door hard into the frame.

CHAPTER TWENTY-TWO

I had driven the girls from the block of flats in Rælingen to the terraced house at Skjetten in Skedsmo, a little unsettled, but otherwise safe and sound. Vigdis must have felt it in her shoulder and neck, but she didn't say a word. At Strømmen station we had stopped at the car park right after the railway bridge. There we sat in silence beneath the big wide tall trees behind the station building, breathing, each in our uneven rhythm, as if we'd all been running, but none of us the same distance. Then I said, Vigdis, I guess it's up to you whether we should say anything about this to Mummy, about what just happened. It was quiet in the back seat, all three of them sat there looking out the windows. Vigdis sat in the middle, but it was Tine who said, no, and then Tone said, no, too, and Vigdis didn't say anything. She probably thought further ahead than the two little ones and considered what a 'no' might lead to at the next crossroads, but at last she too said, no, it will make things so difficult for Mummy. I agree, I said. I turned the key and the engine was running, but then Vigdis said, Daddy, do you have any small change. She was looking out the back window, and I looked out the window to where she was looking, and there was a telephone booth by the bushes along the side road. I turned the engine off. I found some coins in the pocket where I always kept some and dropped them into her open palm, and she got out of the car and walked over to the booth. She stood on her toes and put the coins into the slot and waited, holding the receiver in both hands, and then she began to speak, and waited again, and nodded forcefully several times as if the person at the other end of the line could see her, and then she hung up the receiver, opened the heavy door and walked back, crawled over Tine and sat down. It was all right, I said. Yes, Vigdis said. Then we drove slowly up the hills towards Skjetten. It wasn't far.

We parked at the end of the terraced house, and I followed them over to the footpath and stopped there and helped them put their rucksacks on, I said, take care girls, and they said, bye Daddy, and Vigdis turned around, she gave a slight smile and said, it will be all right Daddy. Yes, I said. It will be all right.

Before they had reached the last flat the door opened and Turid came out on the steps, her hair wet, she must have run through the shower after Vigdis called. She said, hello girls, how great you're coming just now, it's perfect timing, and all four of them went in, one after the other, and she slammed the door behind her. She saw me, or she saw me not.

CHAPTER TWENTY-THREE

It was spring, it was April. Nothing had bloomed yet, but you could feel it in the air, even within the city the sweet fragrance of restless birches drifting through the streets, in the parks the lime trees stood sated with their own scent, and it pressed against the bark from the inside so hard the bark burst open in big gashes, and in Nordre cemetery you felt the warmth of stones and granite slabs when you held your palms against them. I did that, I couldn't help myself. It was as if there was something deeper within the stones, a deeper warmth, not deeper in a geological sense, but deeper in its wholeness, its stone-ness. What a short while ago had been frozen crystalline tissue in the soil, now rose as steam in the milder air, it was Oslo, now. April is my choice, said the writer Bjørnstjerne Bjørnson. We stood shoulder to shoulder.

Dark fell later now, and the days were clear. I'd been up on the heights, past the Torshov valley at Sinsen, on the doorstep of the Rendezvous restaurant, also known to us as 'Renna', at the top of the hill, where I was supposed to meet a woman I had struck up a conversation with on the way out of Eldorado cinema after watching the fifth movie about the boxer Rocky Balboa. The conversation was not about Rocky, not about boxing either, but I always went to see boxing movies the few times they showed one. I had seen *Raging Bull* with De Niro and *Somebody Up There Likes Me* with Paul Newman. I never got started myself, but boxing was the only sport I had ever wanted to practise. It probably had something to do with my father, with how he looked in the ring when he was young, his dancing, wiry body and his dancing red locks of hair, his confident smile even in adversity, the soft tight-fitting shoes with the long laces, my father swaying on his toes in full control, all this long before I was born, on photographs in black and white, I only knew that his hair was red, it no longer was when I grew up. I had felt a sympathy for Rocky in the first movie, it had a surprising freshness, a warmth, against all expectations, despite the obvious ending, and then they got worse and worse, and the fifth was so bad I felt sad and embarrassed.

But that evening I couldn't go through with it. I couldn't bring myself to enter 'Renna' and instead I stood by the door I had just opened, and unlike all the times when the din had pulled me in, the compact noise from the inside, the laughter and the jolly singing from every nook and corner, the cigarette smoke and the dense warmth, the smell of beer and cheap food, turned into a wall I didn't have the strength to penetrate alone, and I was always alone when I came, although I was often not when I left. The woman I was supposed to carry on a conversation with had not yet arrived. I suddenly got anxious that I wouldn't recognise her, but if I closed my eyes, I could easily summon her up, and when I opened them again, she was nowhere in the room, and I didn't wait. I turned on the threshold and went back out onto the pavement and started walking down the long hill to the centre of town, all the way to the harbour, which was where I went when I went alone, and for the most part I walked along the docks from City Hall, past Kontraskjæret and the cliff below Akershus fortress, where the monument to the one hundred and fifty-nine dead would be erected so many years too late, and when it was finally put up, I would stand there cold and tired amid the crowd, listening to the speeches and not shed a tear.

Just as often I came from the opposite direction, from Østbanestasjonen, which was no longer called Østbanestasjonen but was called Oslo Central station and had been for ten years, and walked along the ponderous, majestic harbour warehouse, that was no longer a warehouse but a fashionable office block, on my way out to the crooked pier at Vippetangen, where I stopped at the short end of the quay the ferries docked at when I was a boy, and the gangway didn't go up, but stuck straight out and sometimes a little down with a railing of coarse rope and nothing more. Then it wasn't more than three or four steps forward, and you were over the narrow sickening rainbow-coloured strip of water and safely aboard the boat, where a man in full uniform bid you welcome with a bow and a smile, even if you were well under twelve years old and had a free ticket, and still smiling examined your passport if you were an adult. I knew everything about those boats, I had run up every staircase and down again, run up and down every corridor with my brothers, my big brother, my little brother, my littlest brother, when we were all alive. I knew every square metre of deck and knew exactly which crannies and corners behind the lifeboats you could hide in if you had to. And it was not without its dangers, I had read *Captains Courageous* and knew how badly things could turn out and was certain that no fishing boat would come and pick me up if I fell overboard, as the men on the fishing boat in Kipling's story had picked up Harvey, the spoiled upper-class boy. I wasn't rich enough, I thought, which took away the whole point, at least for the script, and so I would drown.

On this particular evening I walked down along Trondhjemsveien, across Carl Berners plass and finally over Karl Johans gate and on between the ramparts at Akershus fortress at the end of Kongens gate where the girls stood waiting their turn up in the shadows beneath the wall and the cars rolled hesitantly past. It felt awkward to be walking down the street without being a customer, and being one was unthinkable to me, and it didn't exactly make me anxious, but I felt very shy, for it was as if the girls beneath the stone wall were members of a secret society which pushed me away, a secret sisterhood, a masonic order of prostitutes, if you like, and I could feel

233

a sudden sorrow over not feeling what they felt, and not being able to be where they were and see the world from their place, and this because I was on the outside, while they were on the inside of real life where important things were at stake, and what timidity I felt walking past them in the middle of the street with a good distance to either side, made me feel ill at ease.

And at the same time each one of them could have been a girl I had grown up with and knew well, or someone else had grown up with and knew well and went sledding with in the wintertime and played split the kipper with in summer.

I came out onto the quay much later than I usually did when I ended up there. It was almost midnight, it was dark, the tall grain silo rose unseen into the low night, as did the turrets of Akershus fortress. It was a little cold now, despite it being spring. It was completely still. The naval college lay massively still on Ekebergåsen hill. You could disappear in time and hardly notice and struggle to get back.

I didn't see her at once, but instead I stood there gazing at all the ships that had set sail from this port more than thirty years before and vanished for ever, the hollow space they left behind, the empty darkness, I sniffled over my lost childhood.

She was standing in the lee of a stack of Euro-pallets that came up to shoulder height, and her head barely showed above the top and might easily have been an object placed on the uppermost pallet by someone working at the docks, but I quickly realised it was not, and then I thought she might be one of the girls who had come down here from Kongens gate, along the containers and out onto the quay, and even had a customer at this very moment, behind the pallets, that I couldn't see. But it was not like that, for suddenly she strode alone across the pier, out of the shadows where she had been standing for a good while, and came out in a green coat into the yellow glare of the lamp on the wall of the terminal building. It lit up her back, and her shoulders, but not her face. She stood only ten or twelve metres away from me right at the end of the pier, and she didn't see me, but looked down into the oil-slick water, leaning forward at an ominous angle, and I didn't think and didn't wait, but walked quickly straight up to her and grabbed her arm and pulled her away from the edge. She gave a violent start and turned half towards me and struck me hard in my face with the flat of her hand, and then I started too, it was not what I had expected, and it hurt, she was strong, or very desperate. Let go of me, dammit, she said, and I let go. What the hell were you thinking, she said, that I was about to jump in. Yes, I said. That's how it looked to me. Did it. Yes, I said. Definitely. She let her hand drop. I don't want to talk about it, she said. That's fine with me, I said. It's none of my business. But it would be nice if you didn't jump in, at least not when I'm around. I smiled, but she didn't smile back, not that I could see, it was too dark. I touched my cheek where she had hit me, and rubbed it carefully, and it still stung. The water's not especially clean either, I said, that ought to count for something, but she didn't respond to my bit of witticism and said instead, does it hurt, and I said, yes, which was true. I'm sorry, she said. I guess maybe I could have said something before I attacked you, I said, and she replied, yes, you could have. Anyway, I'm sorry, I didn't mean to hit you so hard. Oh yes, you did, I said. There was a moment of silence, then she gave a short laugh and said, maybe I did. So then, what is it that you don't want to talk about, I said, what is it that makes you stand out here with me in the middle of the night instead of being with someone else or at home in your bed, sleeping. She shook her head faintly. She didn't want to talk about it. She'd already said so. Fine. Did your boyfriend break up with you, I said, and so you've come down here all miserable to throw yourself in the water, and that would have served him right, and I thought, that was a flippant thing to say, you idiot, now she'll be upset, but she just ignored it, she said, it wouldn't have bothered him one bit. Believe me. I had no reason not to believe her, so I said, in that case he's a fool, and she said, fool is a very weak word for that man. Anyway, I don't want to talk about it, are you not listening, and he has nothing to do with this, with me standing here now. Okay then, I said, that's fine, I won't ask any more, and then I kept silent, and then I said, but it's not easy to hold back. You'll have to, she said. Or else I'm leaving. I hadn't assumed she would do any different, why would she stay. Don't leave, I said. Can't we just stay here a little longer. Sure we can, she said.

We stood at the edge of the quay practically shoulder to shoulder and looked down into the water and over towards Hovedøya island and the lights from the small marina out there, and to the left we saw the lights from the Postgiro building, high up, from one of the offices. It felt fine. We didn't say anything for a while. Then I said, did you really not intend to jump, and she said, would I throw myself into the water because of that idiot, and I thought, maybe not because of someone, but something. Not for anyone else either, she said, in case you're interested, and suddenly I was, I was interested, so now you don't have a boyfriend, then, I said, and she laughed a little. It doesn't look that way, she said. No, I said. I guess it doesn't. But then why are you standing here, I said, if not for love lost. Is that why you're here, she said. Yes, I said, what else. Then why don't you go ahead and jump in, she said, and I was certain she was smiling, though I couldn't actually see it, the light still fell on her back and shoulders, which made her face indistinct, shadowy, almost enigmatic, although we were standing so close to each other. Of all the ways to die, drowning must be the worst, I said, and she probably agreed, but I couldn't see her face or what she was feeling, it was too dark; I can't see your face, I said, it's too dark, I don't know what you look like. But she didn't move, didn't turn towards the light. I'm quite good-looking, she said. Are you, I said.

Yes, she said, I have to be honest. I had no reason to doubt it, but I didn't know if it was important, I didn't really think so, you could kiss me, she said. That was a bit sudden, it wasn't what I had expected her to say. Yes, I said, I guess I could, or, why yes, of course I can, absolutely. She still had the light from the lamp on her back, and her face was unclear despite the short distance, but it was a very fine kiss, very soft, it touched me, a lot, and I thought of all the kisses that hadn't been like that, so full of good will, so open without reservations, I've changed, I thought, it was easy to kiss her, I wasn't used to it, and I didn't give it all I had, that would have implied something more later on, and I didn't know if I wanted that, not this night. But the truth was I never gave all I had, not ever. I didn't understand why, but it was as if the trapdoor could open at any moment if I did, and in any case it was too late, for she felt it at once, that I held back, and we slid apart, out of each other's arms, she let go of my elbow and said, all right, I guess it stops there, and I said, yes, I guess it does. That's okay, she said, and then she fell silent, maybe she was waiting for something, her arms hanging limply on either side, and at last she said, you go first, then, and I'll wait here. I thought for a moment. I don't know, I said, you came first, so maybe you leave first. All right, she said, that's fine, then I'll go first, and she turned around at once and started walking, and the shadow followed her and spread around her shoulders like a shawl, erasing the green of her coat, and still I didn't have a clear picture of her face, if it was pretty or not, it probably was, but I would never recognise her in the street, and it felt bad knowing that. Thanks for the talk, I said rather loudly, and thanks for the kiss, it was a very fine kiss, I will remember it. She could hear me perfectly, but she didn't turn around and didn't say anything, just walked quickly on along the terminal building towards the containers, while I stood at the edge of the quay with my back to the dark water and the naval college on Ekebergåsen hill, and I thought, it was a lot worse seeing her walk away than I had imagined.

As she was swallowed up by the darkness, I called out, you were going to jump, weren't you.

I didn't know why I said that. I was far from sure. Maybe she was just like me. Why was I there.

CHAPTER TWENTY-FOUR

When I came back from Skjetten for the second time that Sunday and swung up from Bentsebrua bridge towards Advokat Dehlis plass and parked by the bus stop, I felt a little shaken. The day hadn't turned out the way I had expected. I didn't know what I had expected. But something other than this.

It was afternoon. It would soon be evening. As I was about to let myself into my flat from the landing, I heard the click from the neighbours' door and the door opening and Mrs Jondal on her way out and the click of the lock as she closed it. With my face half turned towards my own door I only caught a glimpse of her face, her body, and she was all dressed up, and she looked good, even from that angle. I didn't really want to say hello, I felt depleted, confused, but out of politeness I turned around anyway and said, hello, Mrs Jondal, you're looking really nice. And so she was. Mrs Jondal, she said. After all this time, Arvid, you still call me Mrs Jondal and not Mary. Her name was Mary, pronounced the English way, Mary, Mary Jondal, and I said, I guess I'm a little old-fashioned that way, and when you're looking the way you look now, it's probably safer if I use your last name. Don't be silly, Mrs Jondal said, but she blushed a little and smiled, and on her way towards the stairs going down she said, and you, Arvid, are you doing all right, and I said, no, I can't say I am, and then she stopped abruptly. Oh, she said, is there anything seriously wrong. Strictly speaking there was, but nothing I could talk to her about, nothing I wanted to talk about. She turned towards me, we were standing chest to chest, and she really did look great, why does she have to go now, I thought, dressed like that, and leave me behind. I suddenly felt bitter. I held my left hand flat against the half-open door, the key was in the lock, but I didn't go in, and as long as I remained, half turned towards her the way I was, it wasn't easy for her to leave either. I guess I'm just feeling a little low today, I said, it's nothing to worry about, actually I'm fine. It doesn't seem like it, Mrs Jondal said. Doesn't it, I said, no, she said, you look very sad. So what do we do, then, I said and thought, *we*, did I really say *we*, why did I say *we*. She bit her lip, I was supposed to be meeting some girlfriends, she said, we get together one Sunday a month at Regnbuen, that's why I'm a little dressed up. You look really great, I said. Do you think so, Mrs Jondal said, and I said, absolutely, haven't you looked at yourself in the mirror. Well yes, I have, she said, thank you, and then she said, maybe I could call and cancel, she bit her lip again and said, or I could have it postponed. I'm the only one who turns up every time anyway, one of the others always calls and has to pull out at the last moment, so why can't I do the same, she said, I can call. No, no, you don't have to do that, I'm perfectly fine, I said,

I'll manage, honestly, Mrs Jondal, I didn't mean it that way, but no, I'm going to make that call now, she said, I think it will be for the best, and she turned and unlocked her door and left it open and walked straight into the hallway where the phone stood on a low chest of drawers below the mirror, as phones still did back then, and she lifted the receiver and dialled a number, and I heard her say that she couldn't come to Regnbuen that evening because she wasn't feeling very well, if you know what I mean, Mrs Jondal said, and apparently the girlfriend at the other end did, for there was no protest as far as I could make out, and while they talked, my key was still in the lock, my hand flat against the door, and I hadn't moved a centimetre for several minutes. I thought, Jesus, that was fast, it was just a whim, what do I do now. Is it like with the cake last year. Is it just a cake.

I stayed where I was and she hung up in there and came back to the doorway and said, Jondal went to Hamar this morning, to see his father again, he seems to be ill, my father-in-law that is, it's something to do with his stomach, he's in hospital apparently, he's coming home on Thursday, Jondal I mean, my husband, she said, but I knew that already, and then she blushed and opened the door all the way and took one step to the side as if to invite me in, and I said, yes, but that won't do, I can't come into your flat, it's his home after all, you see, even though he's in Hamar, you have to come into mine, I said, everything in here belongs to me, no one else has any say in my home except me. All right, then, she said, I will, and she said it resolutely. She shut her door, pulled it firmly to until there was a sharp click from the lock and pulled out the key and dropped it into her coat pocket, and I held my door wide open for her, and she walked the few metres across the landing without hesitation, and the sound of her high heels clacked up into the floor above us, sending echoes back down, and she walked quickly past me, ahead of me, and then I too went in and dropped my father's satchel on the floor with John Berger's political Casanova under the flap and shut the door, there was no way I could talk myself out of this.

I helped her out of her coat, and I did it gallantly, almost formally and perhaps a little hectically, for suddenly we were behaving in a way they only did in movies from the forties and fifties. I wasn't wearing a suit, but I might as well have been, and it could have been powder blue, as they often were back then, even when the films were in black and white, with something red on the tie, merely a detail or two, and we were a couple and had just got home from the premiere of a merely passable play at the National Theatre, we had talked about it in the taxi on the way up, Norwegian contemporary drama was in a poor state, we both agreed, and actually it was a bit strange, after all quite a few years had passed since the war, you'd have thought it would be on its way up, full of new energy and to hell with everything that had set the world on fire, that it would be angry, but that was not the case, not Norwegian drama, it was more or less pathetic, the war didn't exist, everything was feather-light and entertaining, and my thoughts kept wandering like this as they often did and still do and could have done for a long time yet, but in fact I knew nothing about contemporary drama, it could have been anything, and besides this Sunday was more than forty years after the war, and I had been to the theatre only a few times in my whole life. The problem was the cloakrooms, was I supposed to tip or not, and if I was, how much. Everyone else knew. I wouldn't know how to handle myself, I wouldn't find my seat, I would get so nervous that they realised I was from Veitvet and therefore made mistakes, and then they would laugh at me the way they laughed at me when I said cacao instead of cocoa, and laugh at me the way they laughed at Charlie Chaplin at his clumsiest, but I didn't want to be like Chaplin, so instead I simply refrained from going to the theatre.

I took out a hanger for her coat and quickly found a place for it in the row below the hat rack and took off my own jacket and hung it on the peg over the paraffin cans that still stood empty by the wall. It's a little cold in here, I said, and she said, I don't mind.

She walked into the living room in her high heels, and now it was definitely Mrs Jondal and not some black-and-white woman from 1949. And I looked at her back, and her skin at the nape of her neck beneath her pinned-up hair and the pretty dress and the zipper running all the way down, and she turned around and looked at me, and I said, are you really sure you want this, and then I thought, maybe she doesn't understand what I mean, maybe she'll say, what are you talking about Arvid, want what, but she said, yes, or else I would be on the bus on my way to Regnbuen, and then I said, would you like me to pull down that zipper. Yes, would you, she said, and didn't smile and turned her back to me again, and I pulled the zipper down, and she stepped out of the dress, and I thought, right now it's better not to look her in the face, and in the bedroom I was glad I had changed the bedclothes and made my bed up so impeccably that morning, and she was much more active than I had expected, she was eager and surprisingly sure of her herself, and at first that made things a little complicated, we practically collided at both ends, but then it was just a big relief, and once she said, Jesus, Arvid, which I suppose was a reasonable thing to say at that moment but then she was quiet, and I closed my eyes and took my chances.

And the phone rang. I was almost asleep, I thought, I don't want to, I don't want to open my eyes. But I had to. Next to me lay Mrs Jondal, also known as Mary, on her stomach with her forehead into the pillow and my only duvet barely covering her bottom and she didn't smile, though she might well have, there was every reason to, I could have smiled myself. It surprised me that it had gone so well, it should have been more complicated, it always was. Go ahead and take it, she said into the pillow. I don't mind. As long as it isn't Turid. And she smiled as she said it. But I was pretty sure it was Turid, who else could it be, it was something about the phone, it was ringing in the same way it had this morning, as if an extra shrill tone had been added. The dialling tone was A, you could tune your guitar to the dialling tone, but this ringing didn't have a key, you couldn't place it on a scale, I'm not going to answer it, I said, it *is* Turid. How do you know, Mary said. I can hear it, I said, I can always hear who is calling. If you had been calling, I would have known it was you. If I had forgotten to pay my rent, I would have known it was the landlord calling and not my mother. Your mother is dead, Mary said, so that would be easy. That's true, I said. Vigdis, then. That I would have heard. That's an odd skill, she said, that you can hear who's calling. I was born that way, I said, and she said, but in the nineteenth century that skill would have been wasted, you could have been born then, with the same skill, that you could hear who was calling, except there were no telephones. That wouldn't have been any fun, would it. It wouldn't, I said, and it felt so good lying there, and my body had a weight, a calm it hardly ever had, and Mary said, if we hadn't just had such a nice time together, we wouldn't be lying here talking rubbish. I know, I said.

It was she who stood up first. She was naked and pretty and not shy at all, she hadn't blushed a single time in here the way she blushed on the landing. I stayed in bed while she got dressed. She studied me all the way up and then down again and said, I've always wondered what it would be like with you. Have you, I said, last year too. How do you mean, last year, she said. That chocolate cake, was it more than just a cake. She laughed, oh, that. That was actually just a cake. Was it, I said, I was hoping for something more. I felt a little cold without Mary Jondal in my bed, I wanted to pull the duvet over me, but I couldn't while she was watching. Did you, she said and laughed again, but anyway, now I know, she said, now I know what it would be like with you. You're a fine boy, Arvid Jansen. She had all her clothes on. Now the shoes. Boy, I thought. I am thirty-eight years old, she must be younger than that, I didn't know how old she was. She bent down and kissed my shoulder, and I thought, she doesn't really think I'm all grown up, that's it, and then she said, I suppose it will have to be just this one time, otherwise we'll end up waiting for each other and getting upset, and I said yes, I think we'll stop here, and a weight was lifted off my shoulders, but she was the one doing the lifting, I didn't lift it myself, and I thought, I never get ahead, why am I never ahead, is it a weakness in me, it has to be.

Now she was fully dressed and said, I just might make it to that dinner at Regnbuen after all, at least the dessert, we usually have a drink first, and that often takes quite a while, the way we talk, so maybe I'll make it if I take a taxi. Goodbye then Arvid, I hope you're feeling less troubled. She smiled and went into the hallway and took her coat from the hanger and walked quickly out onto the landing and pulled my front door shut with a loud click, and I could hear the swift clatter of her heels on the way to the ground floor and all the way out onto the cobbles in the backyard. And boy or not, in fact I did. Feel less troubled.

CHAPTER TWENTY-FIVE

I pulled the duvet over me and lay there waiting. Maybe a quarter of an hour, maybe more. I almost fell asleep. Then the phone rang again. I let it ring. I knew who it was. I had the gift. But then I couldn't ignore it any longer, and I had to get out of bed, into the chilly room without a stitch on, and cross the cold floor towards the half-open door to the living room where the phone stood on the desk in the opposite corner, halfway in front of the window with the curtains I hadn't drawn, because I'd forgotten. It rang for the fifth time. I could easily be seen from the other buildings where I stood naked by the desk, if anyone happened to be interested. I lifted the receiver, and it was Turid, I could hear it at once from her breathing, I knew it by heart. I didn't say anything. She said, Arvid, are you there. I still didn't say anything. Jesus Arvid, she said, I know you're there. Shit, I thought. Yes, I said, I'm here. But I didn't say, why are you calling, instead I waited. That will make it harder for her, I thought, so I didn't say anything, but then I had to, are you feeling better now, I said, are you less troubled. Is it of any interest to you, she said. Not really, I said, but that was not entirely true. Or, maybe it was. I had spent the whole morning helping her and might have done the same for any other person.

I didn't know. Either way it was her tone of voice I didn't like. I searched for the sudden desire that had been there that morning, but I felt no desire. That was not quite true, I said. Of course it is of interest to me. I find that hard to believe, she said. Okay, then, I said. So why are you calling. I'm not coming to you with my life, she said, you should mind your own life, you will not interfere in mine. All right, so why are you calling, I said again. I don't need you, she said, do you understand that, and I thought, that's not true, she doesn't have anyone else, she doesn't even have her friends, the colourful, she didn't call any of them when she was in distress, she didn't go to any of them with her life, she came to me. But I wanted none of it. That's not what you said this morning, I said, and she said, oh really, what did I say this morning. You said you have no one else but me. I don't remember, she said, why would I say a thing like that, and I said, I have no idea. I felt completely calm inside, it was almost strange, for the floor was cold now, I was freezing, I couldn't stand still, like a boy who needs the toilet, I couldn't help it, even though I was so calm on the inside, like the surface of Bunnefjorden on a day without a breath of wind, but now I had to get some clothes on. Arvid, Turid said on the phone, are you there, are you listening to what I'm saying. Of course, I said, I'm listening Turid, can I call you back in five minutes. There's no need to, she said and hung up. All right, I said.

And that was it, really.

CHAPTER TWENTY-SIX

Then I too hung up and walked naked across the floor and found my clothes and put them on, even my jacket and shoes. I had to get warm, right now, but I needed air too, yes, that was it, and it was in and out all day, I thought, in and out of the building, up and down the stairs, out to the car, in from the car, and it must have looked conspicuous during this past year to those who hid behind their curtains and used the brief time we have on this earth to keep an eye on all that happened at the junction and roundabout on Advokat Dehlis plass, those who went in, those who went out, and who did what and when they did it. Maybe a little like me. At least I didn't hide. In any case I walked down the stairs and out to the square and over to the Mazda, but I didn't get in. I leaned against the bonnet and lit a Blue Master. It felt as if there was cause for celebration. It was a movable feast. I looked up the road, a bus was coming down from Voldsløkka and pulled in at the bus stop a few metres away from me, no one got off, two got on, but not me. I wasn't heading downtown. Why would I.

I walked along the pavement with the perfectly formed cigarette between my lips and came around the corner of my building, from the parking space up towards

Bergensgata. Inside the paint shop I saw Tollefsen standing with his back to me in his brown, paint-speckled coat. I had never seen him without it. He was standing by the workbench with several cans of paint without lids lined up in front of him, but it was Sunday. I looked at my watch and went over and tried the door, and it wasn't locked, so I opened it and called in, are you open, it's Sunday, isn't it, and late too. I know it's Sunday, Jansen, he said without turning around. And no smoking in here, if you don't mind. I dropped the half-smoked cigarette on the concrete slab by the door and crushed it with the tip of my shoe and said, but are you open, then, and he said, no Jansen, I'm not open, it's Sunday, and it's late. But the door is open, I said. Jesus, I know the door is open, he said, can you please be quiet please, I need to concentrate. He was mixing colours. There are people waiting, he said. I couldn't see anyone waiting, but they might have been waiting somewhere else. Maybe the paint was supposed to be delivered somewhere, what did I know, to Sagene, for instance, it was right down the road, it took three minutes. Any chance of filling my jerrycans today, I said. His back was still turned, you could see he was impatient, he was irritable, he said, then you'll damn well have to hurry. I let go of the door and half ran back around the building, took the steps two at a time up to the second floor, picked the jerrycans up from the floor in the hallway and ran down again and back around the corner and entered the shop, the bell jingling over the door. Wow, you're pretty fast when you want to be, Tollefsen said.

That's right, I said. I went over and set the jerrycans on the counter. Only then did he turn around. He smiled. But you should have come a long time ago, all the others have filled theirs. He looked at me over his powerful glasses and said, you know what, Jansen, I've had this bet going with my wife. About what, I said. About when you'd come to fill those jerrycans for the first time this year. About how much closer to zero it would have to get before you dragged your feet down here. It's colder now that you live alone, you've known that for a whole year, especially at night it's colder, it's colder in bed, if you're alone you need paraffin, that's elementary. Sure, I said, it's elementary. I screwed the caps off the jerrycans and handed him one of them, one of the jerrycans, that is, and said, so who won. Who won what, he said. Who won the bet. I won, said Tollefsen. I know you.

I had to laugh. I gave him the other can and got the first one back. You don't know me. Jesus, he said. Everyone in this building knows you, Jansen. He had his back to me and his hand turned the tap of the paraffin tank all the way to the left. Slowly can number two filled up. Everyone in the building, I thought, that adds up to about sixteen people, plus children, including Jondal. No chance did he know me. Don't fool yourself, Tollefsen said. He gave me the other can. The till is closed, he said, you can pay tomorrow. He had spilled a little, so I got paraffin smeared over my palm, I lifted my hand to my nose, it would take a day to get rid of the smell no matter how often I washed my hands, but Tollefsen didn't care. Now get yourself up those stairs, he said, and fire up that stove, you've been in the cold for long enough. Okay, I said, and he said, I have to get this paint mixed, if that's all right with you. That's all right, I said. There are people waiting, he said. I still couldn't see anyone waiting, but I turned around and was on my way out of the shop when he said, and don't you worry now Jansen, there is not a person in the building who has anything against you, on the contrary, as far as I'm aware. I'm not worried, I said. Good, he said and turned around again and lifted one of the cans and poured paint from that can into another one which was not as full. Damn, he mumbled, and he stood there with his back towards me as he had been the first time I came in.

CHAPTER TWENTY-SEVEN

There wasn't much left of Sunday, but I had not gone to bed yet, I didn't want to. It had been a long day, an eventful day, now it might as well last a little longer. I was tired and dazed, but also strangely calm, and I didn't want to let go of that. I suddenly feared the coming day. I knew it would be emptier. Just me and the typewriter. Today I had been *in* life, in spite of it all, tomorrow I would be pushed back out of gravity. Or rather, let myself be pushed out. And float away. I could see no bridge from today over to tomorrow other than sleep, which was a doubtful bridge. Suddenly I wanted to be where I was, in what this day had been, I had to postpone sleep for as long as possible. If I fell asleep, anything could happen. Anything could *not* happen. Absolutely nothing, and then I would remain where I was. I didn't want that. I felt less troubled. I wanted it to stay that way. What if it didn't last the night, what if sleep was not a bridge, but an eraser.

I had eaten. I had got the stove started. I went out into the kitchen and reached for a bottle of red wine from the shelf I had fastened to the wall above the kitchen counter. I had wanted that bottle for a long time, but hadn't touched alcohol for a week, except for the couple of Pilsners I'd had the evening before this Sunday in September, in a bar that was once a pharmacy, where I had been several times before, one of them on Christmas Eve. I fetched the cork-screw from the top drawer and opened the bottle and took a sip straight from the neck, it must have looked pretty shabby. It can be a good discipline, watching from the outside, what you are doing, as if you were someone else, and what you would think if you saw that person, who was you, drinking red wine straight from the neck of a bottle before even having looked for a wine glass in the cupboard. As if it was a matter of life and death.

I felt the effect at once, so I took another swig and went into the living room and sat down on the sofa and stood up again and pulled out a record with a symphony by Mahler that I had just bought from Kjell Hillveg at Norsk Musikforlag on Karl Johans gate, the fifth symphony conducted by Leonard Bernstein, not the ninth with the grey-haired Japanese conductor, not the Mahler-woman's Mahler. To me the fifth was the greatest, with the funeral march and all and the fourth movement flowing calm and acutely mournful and yet so uplifting, although Bernstein could be rather sluggish at times, you grew impatient, it was as if the piece of string he held the notes together with could snap at any moment and a gap would appear that you could tumble into, but at his best he was supreme. I was a Mahler expert now.

I sat there listening until the first movement, the funeral march, was over. Then the phone rang again. I was growing weary of it. And this was not Turid. I had no idea who it was. I had lost my gift. It might be the alcohol. I took the bottle I held on my lap, the one I had taken a third sip from while I listened to the music, and set it on the coffee table and went over and switched the turntable off and went over to the desk and lifted the receiver and said, yes, it's Arvid, it's actually pretty late. And it was Audun. It's Audun, he said, I know it's late. Hello Audun, I said. Hello Arvid, he said, it's been a long time since last I saw you, and it sounded like a song, with the words in that order, and maybe it was a song, I tried to think, in that case which song. Is there something wrong with you, he said. Is there, I thought, is there something wrong with me, and a long time since last I saw you, is it dum dum, da dum, it was definitely the wine. Is it that long ago, I said. It is, he said. Yes, I know, I said, and he was right, how long could it be, it's been four months, he said. Oh, I said, that's a long time. Yes, it is, he said, in fact it's more like five, come to think of it. He had been my best friend for most of my life, ever since he moved from the countryside with his mother and siblings and started seventh grade at Veitvet school with a bang. When together we looked back, we were often unable to separate his life from my life, no matter how different they had been, no matter how different *we* had been, but we had shared each other's lives, and he was still my best friend. Nothing had happened to make that friendship end. Maybe things had been a little difficult in the past year, not the friendship, but everything surrounding it, and the truth was that I had forgotten him, my best, my closest friend, I had forgotten that he was my friend.

After the ship burned we were together nearly all the time. Not Turid and me. Audun and me. Maybe I shut her out, shut the girls out. He called every other day to talk, we went to the cinema together, we ate out as often as I thought I could get away with, mostly at the restaurant in the shopping centre at Veitvet, in the corner on the second level where we had been out for our first Pilsners together, other times at Lompa on Grønlandsleiret in the centre of Oslo. We travelled up to old Gardermoen airport to watch scenes being played out in the departure hall before the plane to America took off. The kisses were long, many cried, and some yelled at each other. We sat on the balcony alongside the cafeteria each with our Coke or coffee gazing out over the hall and saw two women saying goodbye to the same man; one close up, hanging around his neck, the other with her hand raised a bit further away, under the balcony, so the first woman would not see her. But we saw her. Another time we saw a woman making a show of turning her back on the man who had come with her to the airport and carried her suitcase and checked it in for her, and on the way towards security she slowly opened her hand and let an object drop to the floor, and we turned to look at the man who saw the same thing that we saw, and I said, what the hell did she drop. She dropped her wedding ring, Audun said. Are you taking notes, Arvid, he said, you have to take notes. And one time he drove in to Advokat Dehlis plass and picked me up off the floor where I was lying flat out on my stomach. Turid and the girls were in Trondheim, and I had no intention of getting up for a good while, but rather preferred to lie there with my forehead ground into the hard cold dusty floorboards, and I thought, how does one measure grief, is there a yardstick for grieving, is there any difference, say, between grieving for one person as opposed to two or three persons, or even four, as in my case, did all this fit on a yardstick, or could the level of grief register as on an instrument, such as a Geiger counter, and the closer the instrument got to the full power, the full height, the full number, the faster and louder the instrument would emit its familiar beep. And how was I to know when there was grief enough, and if grief was liquid like melting silver, could one then pour the grief into a litre measure and conclude, under these circumstances eight decilitres ought to be sufficient, and let the silver congeal hard and shiny not far below the rim. How was I to know. And how was I to know it really was grief I was feeling, it didn't seem to resemble anything I had seen on film, or what others told me they had felt when their people died, and I was bewildered, for I didn't cry, and when did one cry really, when you were alone, or in the company of witnesses. And if one were alone, what was the point, when no one would see it, how was I to know, I didn't have that yardstick, that litre measure. I had to deal with it myself, was that not so, I let no one else inside, no one else's yardstick was of any use, no one's litre measure, and in a way it felt strangely irrelevant, no, not irrelevant, but rather beyond my field of vision. I could barely glimpse a dark swishing tail disappearing, and when I grasped it and held it fast, I was left with nothing but the tail in my hand. The rest was gone, like a lizard sacrificing its tail for freedom. I did try, and hard too, with open eyes to face what had happened, but I didn't know what to do with what I saw, I had already watched most versions of the issue acted out on TV, they were used up, and I couldn't think of any others. So then I simply tried not thinking about it at all. That didn't work either. And so instead I wanted to find an image that could cover all this, after all it was my job, to turn the whirling liquid into something concrete, turn the waves of distracting electric shocks to the stomach into solid surface. But I didn't have any images that were large enough, firm enough, and after a while I found it pretty exhausting. So I lay there until Audun arrived. He walked straight in, the door wasn't locked, I had forgotten as usual, and before even seeing me, he said into the hallway, hello Arvid, for Christ's sake, why don't you answer the phone when I call. And it was true, often I didn't answer, it was a breach of every rule, but I was afraid there might be an undertaker at the other end, although I knew the funerals I was supposed to attend lay behind me for now. And there came Audun, in through the living-room door and he saw me on the floor and said, what the hell are you doing down there. I'm thinking, I said. All right, he said, so what are you thinking about. Litre measures, I said, yardsticks, that kind of thing. Okay, he said, that sounds practical in a way, but you can get up now. I'm not sure I can, I said down into the floor, my lips cold against the cold planks, covered in dust, the vacuum cleaner hadn't been out for a good while. Yes, you can, he said, just do it, and I'll go to the kitchen and put the kettle on for coffee.

Ten minutes later when he came back with two full cups of coffee and milk and sugar on a tray, I was sitting on my chair at the desk. It wasn't exactly Mont Blanc, but it had been a long climb.

And now, with the receiver in my hand and Audun at the other end, I couldn't think of what to say. I had forgotten him, it was a little odd, but I hadn't had time to consider it yet, what was there to consider, I didn't know. I've been busy, I said. That's just it, he said, I have more than one witness telling me they've seen you downtown, quite often in fact, hanging around bars and whatnot, looking like you'd had a few, always with someone, I mean with women, a different woman each time. That sounds familiar, I said. But it might tell you something about your witnesses too, doesn't it, I said. You're right about that, he said, it does, but what are you up to, what goes on in your life, and in a way I could understand why he was asking, and it made me glad too, for he did it out of concern, no one else showed me any concern, except Mary Jondal, who maybe still was at Regnbuen with a late dessert on the table before her. I just didn't want to talk about my life. And still, it was Audun, so when he asked, and I'd been lucky enough to have him return from oblivion, I had to give him an answer. It's not easy to explain, I said, it's all a little hazy. Well, you can try, he said. But do you have the time, I said. Of course I have the time, I have all night. Do you, I thought, aren't you going to work tomorrow, are you no longer a typographer, have you shelved the alphabet, and I hesitated, and it didn't escape him, but he was not offended, he said, Arvid, you can sit down now. I am sitting, I said, and he said, no, you're not. And I wasn't, it surprised me, I thought I was sitting. I let myself down into the chair, lay my left arm on the desk and leaned forward. Now I'm sitting, I said. That's good, he said, no, wait a little, I said and put down the receiver, hooked the cord around the Buddha so the receiver wouldn't crash to the floor, and stood up and walked quickly out of the living room and into the kitchen and fetched a glass without a stem from the cupboard above the sink, and on my way back I picked up the bottle from the coffee table and passed the *no* in Chinese characters framed on the wall, and I thought, *no* to what, I had forgotten that too. I set the bottle and glass on the desk and poured a sizeable amount, it was wine, after all, not spirits, it wasn't that bad. I took the receiver in my right hand and set my left elbow on the tabletop in front of me, and I leaned forward and rested on said elbow. There, I'm sitting again. That's good, Audun said. Are you comfortable. Yes, I am, I said. Are you drinking, Arvid, he said, and I said, yes, I am drinking a little, but it's wine, not spirits. That's good, he said, that it's not spirits. Just take your time, I'm not going anywhere. Or maybe a quick visit to the toilet first, he said, so I won't have to interrupt in the middle of everything. Don't hang up, he said and put the receiver down and left, and I didn't move, just sat there waiting. I won't, I said and took a long sip of the wine.

When he came back, I could hear him set a glass on the table, but he didn't say anything, and I didn't say anything, I could hear his breathing, and it would have been strange if he couldn't hear mine, and we sat like that for a while, and finally he said, hey Arvid, I'm waiting. Oh, I said, sorry, it slipped my mind.

It wasn't true, though, it hadn't slipped my mind.

CHAPTER TWENTY-EIGHT

You remember we moved from Bjølsen out to the provinces, I said. That was in 1979. It was after the blow on Bentsebrua bridge. Of course I remember you moved, Audun said. But which blow are we talking about here. Forget it, I said. Turid was supposed to stay with her grandfather in Trondheim for nearly two weeks, and we had to spend the night at her parents' in the suburbs. We hadn't bought the first Mazda yet, we were young, we didn't need one, not inside Oslo, but there was still no bus to the city on Sundays from the place we had moved to. There weren't many on weekdays either. I remember that, Audun said.

I woke up when the alarm rang, a little before six in the morning, and the room I was lying in was unfamiliar. It had been her room before we moved in with each other, her home, but I didn't feel comfortable, I didn't like to sleep anywhere without my things around me, my books, my records.

I sat up on the edge of the bed, the sun was already out. I glanced out the window straight over at the Underground station where I had stood waiting for her so many times, looking over at this block of flats at the bottom of the slope and straight in through this very window on the third floor when she didn't know I was there. I liked it, I liked to watch her moving around when she thought herself unseen. She was so fine, it was like watching a dance, you could sense the music.

Her father was up wearing slippers and pyjamas and had breakfast ready for us when we came out into the kitchen. He was an older, taciturn man who occasionally burst into sudden attacks of rage. It always had to do with the war, but he never took it out on me, and I was glad he didn't, but others got an earful. He had been active in the resistance and had to flee his home when the Gestapo stood on the doorstep, the wrong doorstep, fortunately, it gave him the few minutes he needed. When the war was over and he returned from exile, a former member of the Norwegian Nazi Party was living in his house, and he didn't get it back.

Now he was just silent. He had got up at five o'clock and had breakfast ready for us, and it surprised me, I was touched, I hadn't expected it.

We ate the food, we were tired and didn't say much to each other, but still we sat there for too long and had to take a taxi to catch the train.

It was going to be warm. It was only a little past seven as we sat in the car on the way downtown, but it was already twenty degrees. I'd seen it on the thermometer before we left.

The concourse of the Central station was dark and gloomy after the sun-bleached streets outside and yet full of hustle and bustle, there were lots of tourists in there under the tall ceiling, Germans and Americans talking loudly as they waited for the train to Bergen or Trondheim over the Dovre mountains, barricaded behind their huge bags and suitcases, fortress-like behind their sunglasses.

She searched the sign above the barriers for her train, and found it at once. She was always fast that way, thorough, as opposed to me, who had a restless mind. I walked ahead of her along the platform in the shadows with her suitcase in my hand, and then out of the shadows from under the big glass vault into the sun, the light was blinding, and there was a lot she had to bring with her, papers, books, rain clothes, that kind of thing, which made the suitcase pretty heavy. I thought maybe I should say something, but every time I opened my mouth, my mind went blank. I didn't know why. So instead I walked ahead of her.

We checked the carriage number on the ticket, and when we got in, I lifted the suitcase with both hands and pushed it all the way in on the baggage shelf by the door. Then we walked together between the rows of seats. The carriage was half full, and a woman was sitting in her place. We compared tickets, and she had got it wrong and moved one row further back, she blushed and apologised, and I said thanks for taking the trouble, and then we walked out again onto the platform.

We stood there in the sun which was shining intensely, making every detail stand out. I could see the tiniest fleck on the train windows. The woodwork in the carriage behind us oozed tar in the heat, and the iron fittings on the door were rusty, the whole station vibrated and yet she was trying to button her jacket, it was a habit she had developed in the last month, but it was not possible any longer, her belly had grown too big, and I said, you should have had a new jacket. I know, she said, but it's just for a short while, in three months this one will fit again, and it's summer, I can easily do without a jacket if I have to. You still should have had one, I said. Maybe so, she said, but it won't be long now, and anyway it's so warm. Besides we can't afford it, a jacket like this costs over four hundred kroner. I know, I said, it was me who bought it for you. I knew we couldn't afford it, but I didn't like the way she put it. Caringly. I wanted none of it. That's true, she said and smiled.

The train was leaving in a few minutes, it was announced over the loudspeakers. First in Norwegian, then in poor English. You have to get in now, I said. Yes, she said. She climbed up on the first step, turned around and held my hand. Arvid, she said. Yes, I said. I won't be gone long, she said. I'll be back in no time at all, and then we'll go on holiday, right. It wasn't no time at all, it was fourteen days, to me that was a lot, and I couldn't understand how she could talk like that, as if we were okay, but then so did I, and I said, that will be nice. She leaned forward and gave me a hug. Her cheek was soft and warm, and I swallowed hard as one's supposed to do in railway stations. Take care, she said. Take care, I said. You could write a postcard, I said, but it was just something I said. Frankly

I didn't give a damn. It was a strange feeling. Of course I can, she said.

The conductor blew his whistle and came over and closed the heavy door right in my face. He didn't even bother to look at me. I saw her walk into the carriage, it was dark in there and a sharp light outside and there was a windowpane between us. Yet I could see she was waving, she was smiling, but most of all I saw my own face reflected in the glass. I could have been anyone. I waved back, and the train shuttered and began to roll, and I left.

The local train to Lillestrøm didn't leave for another twenty minutes, so I bought a newspaper in the Narvesen kiosk and sat down on a bench to read away the time. When my train pulled in, I found a seat by the window. We hadn't lived out there for more than one long month, and there was plenty to see along the route, but I wasn't interested.

I got off at Strømmen station, but there was no bus on Sundays. I had already forgotten. I started walking, but quickly changed my mind and walked back again. It was a four-kilometre climb, and I just didn't have the energy for it now. There was a solitary taxi parked by the station, I got in and said, the Eagle's Nest. The driver grinned, the Eagle's Nest. That's a good one. You don't like it up there, then, he said. Those who do, call it Soria Moria, even though it's not called either of those things. He was Pakistani, or Indian. I know, I said. Of course you do, he said, and after that he didn't say anything, and neither did I.

The flat was completely silent when I came in. I heard the alarm clock ticking in the bedroom. I turned on the radio to fill the living room with sound, but it was the Sunday service, so I switched it off and put on a record instead. The first Led Zeppelin, the first track. 'Good Times Bad Times'.

It smelled empty. As if someone had been there who was not there any more. To feel that empty there must have been someone there first. It didn't cross my mind that it was us. I walked through the living room and out into the kitchen and put the kettle on for coffee. I tried to think of her. I sat down at the living-room table with the cup of coffee and thought about how I looked forward to her coming home again, but I didn't know if I did. On the table there was a list of things I was supposed to do while she was away. She had made it, I picked it up, sat like that for a while, as if I was reading, and put it down again.

I emptied the cup and went out into the kitchen. The counter was spotless, she had cleared away all the dishes before we left. I set the cup down on the metal top, dried my hand on my trousers and picked it up again and threw it hard into the sink. It exploded. I leaned forward and looked at all the tiny shards and thought of her mother, how she used to stand in the doorway every time we came to visit for weekends. Her happy smile. Dammit, I said aloud. Then I went into the bedroom and took the rucksack from the top of the wardrobe, opened the wardrobe door and stood there for a long time with a pair of trousers in my hand, it was brand new, and put it into the rucksack and took out a few other random pieces of clothing, a couple of books and a bottle of Upper Ten whisky we hadn't touched yet because she was pregnant. I turned off the record player, I didn't like Led Zeppelin any more, I didn't know why, I'd always liked them. I pulled out all the plugs except the one for the fridge and turned the knob on the boiler to zero.

Some way down the hill I saw a taxi heading up, and barely a few minutes later it came back down again having fulfilled its mission. I raised my arm and waved. The driver slowed down, pulled to the side and stopped the car just a few metres ahead of me. I took my rucksack off and opened the back door. I threw the rucksack on to the seat and slid in after it. Strømmen station, I said. Strømmen station it is, he said. Our eyes met in the rear-view mirror, it was the same driver.

I sat quietly as we drove through the housing development at Løvenstad and peered out the window as we crossed the junction at Gamle Strømsvei and down Stasjonsveien where later they converted the Strømmen steel factory into a big shopping centre down on the plain before the railway, not far from the shoe factory where my father worked after Salomon had gone bankrupt. There was no trace of it now.

*

We drove along the tracks, then across the narrow bridge, and turned in behind the station building on the opposite side. He took it for granted I wanted to travel towards Oslo, and maybe he was right.

I paid and wriggled out of the seat dragging the rucksack after me, slammed the door shut and began walking towards the platform. The driver got out too. He lit a cigarette and leaned against the open door, smoking. He left the engine running. I stood there. I had no idea when the train was coming. If it was coming. There was a timetable posted on the wall of the station building, but I didn't go over to look. I saw the driver flick his cigarette butt to the ground and get in behind the wheel. He revved the engine and put it in first gear, I could hear it click into place, and the car slowly began to move, and I turned and started to run and caught up with it just when it was about to enter the road towards the bridge. I banged hard on the windowpane with my fist, and the driver hit the brakes, flung his arms into the air and slammed the back of his head against the headrest and sat staring up at the roof. Then he leaned over and rolled down the window and said, yes, what is it now, in a rather irritated tone of voice. I'm not taking the train, I said. You're not, he said, and I said, no, I'm not. So what do you want, then, he said. I need a taxi, I said. He sighed, he said, this is a taxi. I know, I said. I opened the back door and tossed the rucksack in and practically threw myself in after it and sat down heavily on the seat. I didn't feel all that well.

He turned around, his elbow over the back of his seat, and looked at me. Suddenly he wasn't irritated any more, on the contrary he looked friendly. So, where are we going, he said. I thought for a moment, but I couldn't come up with anywhere. I don't know, I said. He ran his hand through his hair a couple of times. I could swear his eyes were moist. He turned away and looked out the windscreen. Then he turned back again. His eyes were still moist. Maybe we could just drive around a little, he said. Yes, I said, maybe we'll just drive around a little, that's fine, I said. Let's do that. He started the car again and drove out of the station area, across the bridge and down the gentle slope towards Lillestrøm. I leaned back in the seat and closed my eyes. We'll just drive around a little, I thought, then something will come to mind.

But nothing came to mind. We drove along the countless minor roads of Nedre Romerike, and after a while the driver became frustrated, it was so obvious he wanted to help me and had believed that after a few kilometres on the road I would see the light. But I didn't see the light. Finally I asked him to drive back up the hills again.

We parked at the bus stop right by the high-rise. He switched the engine off, we sat there, and suddenly he didn't want to take any payment. You must, I said, no, he said, I don't want your money. He had clearly been driving me on the principle of *no cure, no pay*. But I insisted, and in the end he took the money, without enthusiasm. Then

I got out of the car and said, thanks for the drive. I hesitated, and then I added, and thanks for your concern.

And then it passed. I did everything that was on the list. After a few days I started to long for her. It might have been something else, something other than longing, but I didn't really think so. It was longing.

Right, Audun said, so that's what you wanted to tell me. I don't know, I said. I couldn't think of anything else just now. That's fine, he said, in fact it was pretty interesting, you never told me about that incident. No, I said, actually I haven't thought about it much since then myself. I suppose I found it difficult. I can understand that, Audun said, though you could have told me. I would have liked that. I heard him take a sip from his glass. Whatever it was he had in it, the glass was not empty. Mine was. But is it really true, he said, all that detail, it's quite a while ago, is that how you felt back then. The part with the taxi driver may not have been one hundred per cent accurate, I said, but I thought it was rather nice, so I put it in. I'm glad you did, Audun said, it was very nice. And then he said, you know Arvid, it's already late, I really must get some sleep, I have to go to work early, there aren't that many hours left. But you've been drinking, I said, that's not so good, is it, if there are only a few hours left. It was a soft drink, he said, Pepsi. Oh, I see, I said. But it's a good place to stop. And it was true, my head was drooping over the desk. The last part of the story I had told with my eyes closed. We can talk more tomorrow, if you like, Audun said. I'd like that, I said. Great, he said, goodnight, then Arvid. Goodnight Audun, and thanks for calling. You're welcome, he said, and then we hung up, and I rose heavily from the desk and thought maybe I should have another glass of wine, there was more in the bottle, but then I let it be.

PART SIX

CHAPTER TWENTY-NINE

Four years later.

I finished the novel about the factory. It took me five years, and it was 234 pages long. Tolstoy spent less time on *War and Peace*. It was published in October. It did better than I had feared. Now it was the middle of March. I was standing by the bank of snow along Uelands gate, not far from Lovisenberg hospital. The snow was black with exhaust fumes. Behind me, on the pavement, stood Vigdis, my oldest daughter. She was sixteen. I was forty-three. I have two more daughters, they were twelve and thirteen then. They are all grown up now.

I stood in the snow because I was trying to hail a taxi that was on its way down from Nordre cemetery, but the taxi would not stop. I could have sworn it was empty, that the roof light was lit, that the driver turned his head and saw me standing there, waving, and I waved again, but he did not stop.

I was distraught. We had just been to the hospital where I had tried to get Vigdis admitted to the psychiatric ward. Not because I wanted to, but because it's what she wanted, we had spoken about it briefly, Turid and I, we were almost certain, or she was certain, I was not so sure. That in itself was nothing new. In any case, it hadn't worked. I turned around and looked at her and searched for something that could carry me onward, but she had closed her face. Vigdis, I said, come on. Let's walk a bit further down. She didn't reply, she gave me no sign, she looked the way she had looked most of that day, and she hadn't spoken a proper sentence for several hours. It was quite a feat.

I retreated from the snowbank onto the sand-strewn pavement and stamped the dirty snow off my shoes and began walking down towards Alexander Kiellands plass, where I thought it would be easier to get a taxi to stop. She followed slowly, not unwillingly, but rather with the pull of gravity on her body which this day had allotted her, or she had allotted herself, and what this day had allotted me, was the task of interpreting her state of mind, so that she didn't have to ask me for anything, that it was I was who was responsible for the choices we made before this day was done. The roles had already been assigned as we left home. She her home, I mine. It'd been a long time since hers and mine were one and the same.

The Mazda was at the garage, so a few hours earlier I had travelled by bus from Bjølsen where I still lived and down to the centre of Oslo and had taken the train as agreed from Oslo Central station to Lillestrøm, which was still a new and stylish station that year, and had walked down the stairs from the platform and now stood by the big glass doors on the side of the station where the river runs into the lake and the parking places spread out in the mud. And standing there I saw the car of the woman who was once my wife cross the bridge from the hill beyond, and there was a wind happening, for the banners snapped against their poles along the road, and the river ran in reverse, it was a swirling morning. And here came the metallic-blue Toyota, glittering in the low sun, heading straight towards me in the razor-sharp spring air, into the roundabout past the river and out again on the other side, which was my side, and parked not far from me, by the kerbstones.

They got out of the car, mother and daughter, Turid and Vigdis, and walked together across the flagstones, down to where I stood by the doors, and we greeted each other, not coldly, but formally, that's what it had come to, but then the transaction was accomplished, and I turned around and was about to go back into the station with my hand on Vigdis's shoulder, when Turid, my old flame, my irreplaceable all, came after me and laid her hand on *my* shoulder. I looked at her hand, it was brown and pretty, I knew it well, its narrowness, lightness, she was wearing a coat as blue as the car she'd arrived in, it was casually slung on, almost arrogantly open over the pretty dress in the crackling weather, and she looked better than the last time I saw her, not a single line had been added to her face, no circle under her eyes, she didn't look like that before, I thought, when she was mine, she has a new lover, that's why, I thought, and she touches him the way she once touched me, or even worse, she touches him in ways she had never touched me, and suddenly I felt severely cheated. It was that old feeling, for a brief moment it flooded through me, and then it was gone, and I thought, she deserves better. She deserves better than what I could give her. I have no one else but you, she had said once, although we were no longer married, but she was desperate then, she wouldn't have said that now, that she had no one else but me. Why would she. She had someone else.

She said, it's easier for you, Arvid, who is not so close to her. She withdrew her hand, and I thought, not so close to her. Hadn't Vigdis and I had long conversations almost every other evening on the phone. Hadn't she been close to me every day, every week, in the sixteen years since she was born more or less in the back seat of a taxi, on the way to a hospital too far away on the other side of town, on the west side, and who had held her in his arms then, in his hands, so tiny and light as she was, if not me. Didn't she tell me about her life, as I told her about mine. Wasn't I informed about her person as no one else could be. What the hell, not close to her.

And why did Turid think that I was able to do what no one else could do. It was true that most ideas we had come up with had been exhausted, and this, the very last, it was left to me alone to carry out. I didn't understand how it had come to this, other than that the burden now lay on my shoulders and I was not close to Vigdis. Turid had insisted, she had given me no choice, and everyone she knew who also knew Vigdis, pointed to me. I felt trapped.

So I didn't answer. I walked into the station building with Vigdis in tow and up to the platform where the train was already pulling in from the north, from Eidsvoll, Hamar, places like that, and then we had to get out again only four stations closer to the city, at Hanaborg, and down a footpath where she could cry, and suddenly she was sobbing. I had seen it coming on the way from the previous station, Fjellhamar, and understood that what mattered now was getting out at the very next station. I hadn't seen her like this for a very long time. I thought she had put it behind her, as she had put her fainting fits behind her too.

Now she stood doubled over by a bush, hitting her chest and crying, while I stood stiff-backed like a sentinel keeping watch in case someone walked past us on the footpath and asked questions I would find embarassing. But no one came, and she struck her chest harder, and suddenly she shouted, Daddy, Daddy, I can't breathe, Daddy, I can't breathe, and there was more panic now than despair in her voice, and she sank to her knees with her hands pressed hard against her chest, and then she hit herself again and whispered, Daddy, Daddy, I can't breathe, and I ran over and sank down next to her and held her hard around the shoulders and felt how thin she had got and thought, my God, where have I been. Was there a distance between us after all, a film, a veil before the eyes, in that case, my eyes, so I hadn't seen her for who she was, while she perhaps had seen me, for who *I* was, but I didn't want to think about that now, and I said, just breathe in Vigdis, just draw your breath in as far down as you can and hold it until you start feeling funny. Do as I say, I said, and she did, and I heard a long gasp, and then she went quiet. She didn't breathe, she stared straight ahead of her although her eyes were shut, and not a sound could be heard, not a wisp of air seeped out, and then it all came back up again, Vigdis came up again as from a deep lake slamming against the surface, and I thought she would fall from the impact, but I held her even harder and thought, when was the last time I held her like this.

From the city centre we took the bus down Storgata, past the Opera Passage, and the bus turned there, by the Gasworks plot, as we used to call it, then up past Jakob church, which strictly speaking was not a church any more, but still was when I grew up, and then onward on Maridalsveien, Uelands gate up the long hill, and we got off at the bus stop at the intersection where the road divides, to the left towards Ullevål, Majorstua, to the right towards Sagene, Bjølsen, close to where I lived.

Hand in hand we crossed Uelands gate up towards Lovisenberg hospital.

The psychiatric ward was two flights up and in to the left. It turned out to be a good deal smaller than I had imagined. I didn't know what I had imagined, probably something from a film I had seen, maybe *One Flew Over the Cuckoo's Nest*, or *12 Monkeys*, which had just been taken off in Oslo, and the images from those films were not pleasant to carry around, but honestly, I didn't think conditions were like that any longer, not here, not now, not in Norway, if they ever had been, and if they were, I would definitely not have been where I was on this day in March.

All the same, we went in, and I asked the first person in a white coat if there was a head nurse here, a superintendent, someone in charge I could speak to, and there was. The person in the white coat pointed up the corridor towards an open door. She's over there, behind that door. All right, I thought. Behind that door. And I said, many thanks, like my father always said, not thank you very much, but many thanks, he was born in 1911, that was probably why.

Vigdis and I walked down towards the open door, and there was a desk right outside, in the corridor, a little like the ones we had in primary school more than thirty years ago, and it may well have been one of those, for nothing I could see around me looked new in any way. Vigdis, I said, you just wait here a little, and I'll go in and talk to her, and Vigdis didn't say anything and didn't do anything, but stopped and stood there with her arms hanging straight down.

I knocked on the door frame and was about to enter, but it turned out there was just a closet behind the door and barely room for one person at a time, and when she turned around abruptly, we stood hardly a metre apart. I looked straight into her face, nothing else was possible. She was my age, and maybe she had been crying, and if she had, it was for reasons of her own, and she'd come over here to this closet to wash her face and dry it, there was a sink on the wall right behind her, and a tap. It seemed that way. As if she'd been crying. But still she looked me straight in the eyes the way I looked into hers, and she didn't even flinch, she didn't look down, in the end it was I who had to, and for a moment I stared at my shoes, which could have done with a shine after the muddy streets outside, before I lifted my gaze towards her face again and took my chances. I would like to have my daughter admitted to this ward. I see, she said. Just like that. No, not just like that, I said, there is a reason.

I don't know who she thought she had in front of her, if it was someone familiar to her, someone she had experience of, and that was exactly what I needed now, that someone experienced saw me for who I was, a man in my situation, who didn't reject me, but could carry me, and what she did was shut the door to the closet, fetch two chairs from a bit further down the corridor and set them in front of the desk. Then she sat down on the opposite side and said, sit down. Vigdis, I said, let's sit down, and Vigdis sat down, and I sat down. For some reason I placed my hands on the edge of the desk in front of me, where she could see them. I wasn't wearing a ring, but still bore the marks of one, a thin white groove on the ring finger of my left hand, a mark I could never get rid of, a stigma. Neither was she wearing a ring, nor the trace of one, and it probably wasn't what I wanted to show her, that I did not have a ring. Or maybe that's exactly what it was I wanted her to see, a single father in trouble. It wasn't true, I was not a single father. But I was in trouble.

She took out two forms from a drawer and placed them on the table with a professional look on her face and put a pen on top of those forms and folded her hands and laid them too on the table, but not in a Christian way. What reason, she said.

What reason. I tried to collect my thoughts, what reason, what reason. I looked around, for the first time really. Down the corridor a man was standing with his face close to the wall. Not very hard, not very fast, but very clearly he struck his forehead against the thick wall, thump, then a short pause, thump, then a short pause and another thump, and it looked painful, I wished he would stop. From the depths of the corridor a woman came almost running towards us, her knees high with each step and her forearms straight down, her fingers straight down, and she looked odd, her face blank and turned in on itself, the only living thing about her was her legs. Actually she was moving very slowly, seen from the side while she ran, but not once did she look in our direction, she didn't take any notice of us at all, like the Masai in *Out of Africa*, but Vigdis couldn't take her eyes off the woman, her face opened up a little, and she bit her lip slightly. I turned to look at her, we looked at each other, and a veil of despair spread over her face. I turned slowly back towards the lady in white, I ran my hand through my hair, maybe I'm not so sure after all, I said, if this is the right thing to do. I thought it was, but now I'm not sure. Maybe we should wait. I looked at Vigdis again and saw a faint *yes* in her eyes. Maybe we should not admit her, I said. There was a pause. The lady in white looked at me, for quite a while, I thought. I wouldn't have, she said, not now, and she didn't say it to put me in my place, no, on the contrary, she said it with empathy, she was on my side. It's not easy to know what to do, she said, I have grown children myself, it's not easy. No, I said. I was close to crying. The two forms were still on the table, but now they were unpleasant to look at, like receipts for thirty silver coins waiting for my signature, and she saw my gaze and pulled out the drawer and put the forms back and pushed the drawer shut. I took a deep breath. But I have to do something, I said. Yes, I think you do, she said.

CHAPTER THIRTY

Try Oslo hospital, she had said, and talk to them there, I can call and let them know you're coming, maybe they can help. Many thanks, I said, in the old manner. We stood up. Vigdis, I said, let's move on then. I took the hand of the woman in white, squeezed it, a little too hard, probably, and let go and started walking towards the exit. Good luck, she said. I turned around. I hope you'll manage, she said. I could have kissed her. Not because she had no ring on her finger, but for the way she smiled at me.

We came down to Alexander Kiellands plass, but no taxi would stop there either, regardless of the roof light, whether it was on or off, whether the seats in the back were empty or not, and I took it personally, why didn't a single taxi stop, what was it about me they objected to so much, did I look desperate, too desperate, yes, I was desperate, and only a taxi would do, everything else was too slow, I wanted it over with so I didn't have to think about what lay ahead of me at the end of this day, if there was anything there other than disintegration. I felt so tired. But finally I said, all right, then, we'll take the bus. We were standing not far from the bus stop by Tranen restaurant, I'd been there before, back when things were as they had been, those giddy, muddled evenings. They lay behind me now. Vigdis stood gazing towards Waldemar Thranes gate and the bridge over Akerselva river and the Solomon shoe factory, which didn't exist any more, but the building did. I remembered Christmas parties there, in the black-and-white photographs I wore a striking sailor suit with a whistle on a shiny white cord, but not like the one Alexander wore in Ingmar Bergman's film. The suit in the film was just plain sailor, light blue, short trousers, all hands on deck, whereas mine was bordering on elegant, black, long pressed trousers, more like first mate, more captain-like. No one uses a sailor suit today, I thought, it's a shame, it looks much better than our national costume, at least for boys it does, and should be mandatory for all boys at all Christmas parties, summer parties, why not birthday parties, jubilees, to suspend class distinctions even for a short while. Which was sheer nonsense, it would never happen, and why should it. Besides, sailor suits were expensive. We had bought ours second-hand, and mine had been passed down to me from my brother. And who wanted to go up there anyway, to the big house in Bergman's film, when there was a Christmas party at Salomon's shoe factory.

The red bus arrived, and not long after we were down by the almost brand new shopping centre called Oslo City, where we had to wait for the tram to come and carry us clanking slowly on towards the Old Town and Oslo hospital.

We got off at the junction between Oslo gate and Schweigaards gate, I thought it was a suitable distance to the hospital, so we could walk along the pavement like normal pedestrians and not as if there was something urgent going on. The sense of urgency was rapidly becoming unbearable.

We stepped down on to the pavement and began to walk. But Vigdis moved stiffly, arthritically, I wished she would walk like other people, for someone might pass us and stop and watch us and draw their own conclusions about why we were headed that way, towards the hospital, when everyone around here knew perfectly well what kind of a hospital it was. But I didn't know if thinking like this was for Vigdis's sake or for myself. I suspected the latter, and in any case Vigdis wasn't able to walk in any other way.

And then it struck me, right out of the blue. I was being tested. That's what this day was all about, suddenly it was obvious, maybe this was the time for the final exams, would I fail, would I pass, would I meet not only Vigdis's expectations but also Turid's, even the women at the children's psychiatric clinic, even their expectations I had to meet. I had been there with the girls only a few weeks ago, and it had frightened me, I was unable to say anything sensible, and the glances they sent me were withering. Turid was present too, but there was not much to be gained from that quarter, she was unusually silent and let me do the talking, but I barely understood why I was there. Who had asked us to come, and why. I was guilty, clearly, everyone in the room thought so, I could feel it, and they were probably right, for my guilt hung like a veil over the room, but precisely what I was guilty of I couldn't make out, my head was too hot, it was burning, I couldn't hear what I was thinking in the rush of blood, I just wanted to get out of that place.

But then it passed, right there. Something changed. It felt so delightful. Jondal, can you hear me, it just feels so delightful. And I said, Vigdis, what do you think, should we call it a day. I was relieved, but also exhausted, I said, we can do this another day, after the weekend, maybe, I don't mind at all. I was facing the door to the hospital. I waited, I didn't turn around. If I had to, I had to. Then I would ring the bell. Okay Daddy, Vigdis said suddenly, and I nearly jumped, it was the first thing she had said since Hanaborg station. I turned around, she was smiling faintly, and I smiled back, I said, fine, then we'll do it that way. I stepped down from the low stoop, and together we walked across the flagstones, and by the pavement on the other side of the road someone got out of a taxi, I waved and the driver saw me and left the roof light off and the engine running, and I said, Vigdis, what the hell, we'll take a taxi to Skjetten. I'm a writer after all, I've got plenty of money. But Daddy, she said, you don't. Maybe not, I admitted, but I can afford a taxi. That's fine Daddy, she said. Let's do it.

*

We crossed the road, hand in hand, that's what we did that day, up on the pavement towards the taxi, and the driver rolled down the window and put his elbow on the door frame, lifted his hand to greet us, he smiled and said, whither, in a funny archaic way, and I thought, I passed, just now, I could feel it, as we climbed into the taxi. Skjetten, I said. And take all the time you need. We're in no hurry.

PER PETTERSON is the author of eight novels, including *Men in My Situation* and *Out Stealing Horses*, which has been translated into more than fifty languages. Petterson has received the International IMPAC Dublin Literary Award, the Independent Foreign Fiction Prize, the Nordic Council Literature Prize, and the Norwegian Critics Prize. He lives in Norway.

INGVILD BURKEY is a Norwegian author and translator. Her published works include two volumes of poetry, a novel, a collection of short prose and, most recently, a book of stories, *Et underlig redskap*. Her second poetry collection, *The Most Imaginable of All Worlds,* was nominated for the Brage Prize. She was educated at Yale University and now lives with her family in Oslo.

The text of *Men in My Situation* is set in StonePrint
by Integra Software Services, Pondicherry.
Manufactured by McNaughton & Gunn on acid-free,
100 percent postconsumer wastepaper.